GOVERNMENT GAY

GOVERNMENT GAY

Fred Hunter

ST. MARTIN'S PRESS
NEW YORK

Design by Nancy Resnick

Library of Congress Cataloging-in-Publication Data

Hunter, Fred.
    Government gay / by Fred Hunter. — 1st ed.
        p.   cm.
    ISBN 0-312-15536-0
    I. Title
PS3558.U476G6   1997
813'.54—dc21   96-40472
                                                        CIP

First Edition: May 1997

10 9 8 7 6 5 4 3 2 1

For Joan Edwards,
who told me so

GOVERNMENT GAY

I don't do bars. It was only by a fluke that I happened to be there at all. My mother had some British Film Institute thing to attend: my mother is a Brit twice removed, once by geography and once by time. She came to America before I was born and stayed after she divorced my father because . . . well . . . the weather's better here. Anyway, she was seeing the latest in British film, and Peter was working. Peter is my husband. He refers to me as his husband, too.

Like I said, as a rule I don't do bars, but like everybody else I get bored when left alone on a Friday night and I don't mind *looking* at the well-groomed masses when I get a chance. Which is what brought me to Charlene's. I always cringe at the decor. Black walls, which I assume make it easier to keep clean, or keep dark, which those kind of places seem to insist on, and a huge pair of pink neon lips on one wall. Why, I don't know.

I was on my third bottle of Bud Light before anyone besides the bartender spoke to me for any length of time, which I suppose means I've let myself go. A voice just below my left ear actually said, "Is this your first time here?"

I looked to my left—and a little down—and saw a brown-haired man, younger than myself (thank God I haven't let myself go as much as I thought), who fell just short of handsome: his nose was a little long and his lips a little thin. There was one other problem that I hazard to mention: he seemed inordinately interested in my shoes, which would have made me nervous even if I'd been available.

"No," I said, "I used to come here before I got married."

So it's not sanctioned by the church or by law. As my mother says, "It's all the same to God." He got the point. He smiled in that way that said there was no longer any need for anxiety and we could be friends, and then went on to somebody else. I could have added that I used to come here before Charlie became Charlene, which would have opened a potentially interesting conversation, but there hardly seemed any point. Within seconds he looked like he'd found somebody who might be able to hold his kind of conversation.

Speakers were bolted up at opposing corners of the ceiling and were blasting, at a level one decibel short of ear shattering, a string of hits from the seventies. There were couples of every shape and size dancing, but Charlene's is thankfully free of the ever-popular swimming lights that seem to be such a staple of this kind of bar.

I was more than halfway through my current beer when the front door swung open and this big doughy guy walked in who looked like he'd just witnessed a mob hit. ("Mob hit" is the kind of thing that just springs to mind when you're from Chicago.) He made his way through the dancing throng and pushed up to the empty space beside me at the bar. I had long since grown used to the endless supply of arms that jutted past me, tight fists brandishing money and barking orders at the bartender, but it was still a relief to have one opening stopped. It slowed the traffic a bit.

He sat down without looking at me. I could see him reflected in the mirror behind the bar: he had dark, stringy hair and large pockets of flesh under his big, startled brown eyes and he smelled of the type of cologne you'd expect to find at Woolworth's. When he ordered a beer, above the din I could hear a thick accent that was Polish, or Russian, or German, or from one of those other places I'm not interested in. I was beginning to think that the startled look was because he'd come in here not realizing what kind of bar it was, and was too embarrassed to just turn around and walk out. It happens. And although, if my brothers and sisters will forgive me for saying it, he didn't look gay, he did look like he badly needed a drink. The bartender put a bottle in front of him, and he took a long pull at it, which when he was finished left only the sludge at the bottom.

The door opened again, and two men walked in, stopping just inside. They looked like they were used to disappearing into the wallpaper and climbing out of it when they wanted to kill someone, like the clay people in *Flash Gordon*. I didn't pay them any attention, and neither did anybody else that I could see, but the guy next to me was sweating, and I hadn't noticed that before. He looked like the sweaty kind, though. It wasn't attractive.

I pulled a cigarette out of the pack in my breast pocket and almost jumped out of my skin when the doughy man struck a match and held it out to me.

"Here," he said, his accent and his breath growing thicker.

"Thanks."

I drew in the smoke, and he tossed the glossy red matchbook in front of me. Being a gentleman, of course, I pulled the pack from my pocket and offered him one, hoping against hope that he would not take the action as a sign that I was welcoming any unwelcome advances. He took the pack, shook out a cigarette, and handed the pack back to me, and I stuck it back in my pocket. Then he lit his cigarette and tossed the matchbook back in front of me. I felt like I was in the middle of a smoker's mating ritual.

The tune playing overhead—I think it was "Disco Inferno"— seemed to pulse for a few minutes on its own and then changed to "That's the Way I Like It." If I remembered correctly, that was playing the last time I was in a bar, only then it was a current hit.

"Is it always this noisy and crowded in here?" said the doughy man.

I had that sinking feeling you get when you suddenly think

3

that someone is going to start hitting on you and is going to be embarrassing about it. I said a simple "um-hmm" and looked the other way, hoping that that would make it clear I wasn't interested.

I watched the teeming masses yearning to be laid pump to the beat, then turned back to my beer. A glance at the mirror showed that the two men by the door weren't there any more. I couldn't see them anywhere else. I listened to the music, drank my beer, and pretty much minded my own business—which wasn't any too easy at the rate I was being jostled. I smoked the cigarette down to a stub, then pulled another one out, and glanced down at the bar. The matches had vanished, and so had my sweaty neighbor. I looked at the cigarette for one of those moments of decision, and the not yet completely extinguished one in my other hand, and decided that at my age a monkey-fuck was unseemly, and made you look like a die-hard chain smoker.

I scanned the room and didn't see any sign of my former neighbor. Dorothy's words to Toto came to mind: "People come and go so quickly here."

I was reluctantly feeling the need to give up my own place at the bar. I had to pee. I hate public bathrooms. I just hate the idea of going into some public place and exposing my most tender asset while other people meander in and out. In order for me to work up the nerve to use a public bathroom, I have to go real bad. Especially in a place like this because, again with apologies to my brothers and sisters, you never know what you're going to find going on in the crapper in a gay bar.

Thank God there was nobody else in the bathroom, especially since it was about the size of a walk-in closet, with two urinals and one stall. Fortunately I was finished and all zipped up when I heard the door. I turned, and there were the two clay people I'd seen come in earlier. They advanced on me before I knew what was happening and grabbed my shoulders and slammed me against the wall.

I was saying something really effectual, like "What the fuck?" when the taller clay person barked at me, "Where is it?"

4

Since I thought they were after the usual and, well, they had to *know* where it was, I said, "I'm not interested."

That's when I learned that this was not your usual bathroom encounter. The shorter clay person balled up his fist and gave it to me full force in the jaw. My head snapped back and slammed into the tile wall. My brain felt uncomfortably like the clapper in a bell.

"What?" I sputtered.

The tall one, who had used my disorientation to take a pincer-hold on my throat, said, "We saw him talking to you!"

"I don't know what you're talking about," I said. The worst part about this was I really didn't know what he was talking about—I mean, I'd talked to half a dozen guys since I came in. I could taste the blood from my split lip.

The tall one took the palm of his hand and slapped it hard against the side of my face. I could feel my sinuses clearing and actually felt a moment's embarrassment that my nose was going to run and might drip down on the guy's wrist.

"Really! I don't know what you're talking about!" I said, and though I would like you to think I'm brave, I could actually feel panic rising in my throat.

"We saw him give it to you!"

I thought maybe if I looked as confused as I felt, it might get through to them that I didn't know what the hell was going on, but I'll never know. Before I could say anything else, the short one pulled out a switchblade, and there was a look in his eye that told me he'd been sharpening it on his grandmother's back. Now I really panicked.

"Help! I don't know what you want!" I shouted, while disco music pumped my words away.

It was at that point that the door opened. I've never done anything like this before, but adrenaline does crazy things to you: there was just a split second when their heads turned to see who was coming in, and I used it to grab their shoulders and push them hard back out of my way like a human saloon door. And I ran. And so did the guy who was coming in to use the john.

Sure, they took off after me, but they weren't as adept at plowing through a dance floor full of gyrating faggots as I am.

I ran about two blocks up Wells Street before I realized that I was so panicked I didn't know which way I was going. So I flagged down the first cab I could find that would stop for me, jumped in, and babbled my address.

"What the hell happened?" said Peter as he pressed the washcloth that was serving as a cold compress to my lip.

I like to think I have a fairly healthy self-image, but when I look at Peter Livesay, I'm humbled. He's the kindest human being I've met in my thirty-odd years, and he's certainly a hell of a lot more handsome than I think I deserve. He's got a lot of dark hair, olive skin that doesn't burn (something I envy him), green eyes with black flecks that make them look more incisive, and a smile that could melt flesh. His teeth aren't perfect, but that's one of those things that keeps him from being something other than human.

I suppose some men are nervous about bringing their boyfriends home to Mother. Not only was that not necessary in our case, but my mother fell for him so badly that at one point I was afraid she'd adopt him and add incest to the rest of our social problems.

He pressed the washcloth to my lip again and said, "What happened?" Apparently he didn't know how difficult it is to talk while someone's wringing out a Fieldcrest towel in your mouth.

I pushed his hand away and took on the dabbing duties myself, and told him the story.

"Gay bashers," he said.

"Gay bashers don't usually frequent gay bars," I said. "The outside of bars, yes, but inside?"

"Maybe they're getting more aggressive."

"That's not what this was about. I don't know what it was about, but that's not it. Christ, that hurts."

"Are you going to call the police?"

"Are you kidding?" I said, my eyes opening wide. "Going to the police would be like getting bashed again."

"Come on."

"A gay rights ordinance does not change the way people think."

We'd had this argument before, and Peter made noises about not wanting to have it again. I had to feel for him there. It was hard to argue with my face at the moment.

"So you don't think it was a bashing?"

"No . . . ," I said, and I could feel my cracked face looking puzzled. I was at a loss to explain what I really *did* think happened. It's hard *not* to feel paranoid after you've been assaulted, but in a way I was reminded of Cary Grant in *North by Northwest,* where he was mistaken for somebody else, then chased around the country while he tried to figure out who was who and what the hell was going on. I was seven years old when I first saw that movie, and it gave me nightmares.

"No, it wasn't that. They said, 'Where is it?' and things like that. I thought they were really stupid rapists."

I'd been lying back against a throw pillow on the couch, and at that moment a thought hit me and I sat up. The movement made my face throb.

"But you know," I said, "it felt like a drug thing."

"A drug thing?" said Peter, sitting back a little.

"Yeah, like they'd mistaken me for someone who was supposed to be getting drugs to them or something."

I was really offended by the expression on Peter's face. He was looking at me the way I would look at someone who'd just said to me what I'd said to him.

"I don't know a lot about drugs," he said, his voice dripping with doubt, "but I'd be willing to bet they'd know who their supplier was."

"Yeah, but—"

"And besides, it doesn't fit with the rest of it. Didn't they say they saw you talking to him?"

"If you want to be totally accurate, they said they saw *him* talking to *me*."

Peter got up and went into the kitchen to rewet the washcloth, and came back saying, "Who did you talk to, anyway?"

"Well, nobody, really," I said. "Just the usual. A few guys said hello to me, but other than that, nothing."

"Nothing at all out of the ordinary?"

"Uh-uh."

"Hmm," he said, pressing the cloth to my lip, which was beginning to feel a little less like I'd hit it with a brick. "I was probably wrong. It probably wasn't a bashing. It was probably all just some kind of weird mistake. But I wouldn't go near any more bars for a while."

He said that last part like it was a suggestion, not just for my safety, but like a gentle way of letting me know that I don't belong in any gay bar without him. That's one of the things I love about Peter. He's not the kind that'd throw a fit about my going out alone like that, even if it really upset him. Because, truth to tell, I'm crazy about him and he knows it. I looked in his eyes and it was one of those moments when you realize how much a person means to you—like you want to cry and you want to scream at the same time. Something in the middle of my stomach turned to jelly. He must've been feeling the same thing, because he smiled and started to lower his face toward mine, but I put out a hand to stop him and pointed to my split lip. He hesitated for a moment, said, "All right," and gently kissed the opposite corner of my mouth. It was at this moment that a key rattled in the front door, the door swung open, and my mother came breezing in.

My mother is the kind of woman who in an earlier day and age would have been described as a handsome woman. She's in her mid-fifties, has shoulder-length, brownish-blackish hair, and a face that is neither too angular nor too round, with gleaming blue eyes and an aquiline nose. She's one of those women who can wear absolutely anything and get away with it. At the moment she was wearing something that looked not unlike a sarong made out of the British flag. When I say she came breezing in, I mean it. She seems to possess some kind of internal gust of wind on which she rides through life.

She stopped when she saw the two of us and looked as if she'd just discovered the remains of Jimmy Hoffa.

"Bloody hell, what've the two of you been up to?" she said. Mother has one of those lilting English accents that are completely unplaceable.

I smiled, and that made my lip throb. Peter told her my story, and she didn't look any too pleased to hear it.

"This is absolutely disgusting!" she said in that voice that always put me in mind of the angry crowds setting a torch to Newgate Prison. "That this sort of thing can go on! Did you call the police?"

We explained the various reasons for not doing that, and for a while I was afraid that she might do it herself, but eventually she calmed down. She sat on the side of the couch and rested her right hand on my stomach. Her eyes were filled with the concern of a lioness who fears her cub might be just a little too thick to live.

"Listen, luv, are you sure you don't know what this attack was all about?"

"No, I told you," I said. And even though I really didn't know, I felt compelled to try extra hard to *look* like I didn't know. It made her laugh.

"Well, darling, I want you to promise me you'll be careful."

I sighed in a mock attempt to sound like this was a hardship I couldn't bear and said, "Mother, I promise, I'll be as careful as I can be."

She looked at me sideways, grabbed the tip of my nose and gave it a little tug, and said, "Bugger!" as she got up and headed for the kitchen.

"It's nothing to worry about," I called to her retreating figure.

Peter helped me off the couch and we headed for our bedroom, which is located on the second floor in the front of the house. Mother has the back bedroom, which is smaller. I originally thought she chose it because it was off the street and quieter, but in reality she likes it because it looks out over the back garden, which she spends the majority of the summer months tending.

When we got to our room, Peter closed the door behind us and actually started to help me off with my clothes. I told him I didn't need help, a little petulantly, and he just shrugged. We both stripped and threw our clothes in the matching wicker hampers we keep by the closet and climbed into bed. I have to admit the bed had never felt better to me. I sank into it like I was descending into a cloud, and would have dropped off right then were it not for Peter. He propped himself up on one elbow and looked at my face.

"That boxer look is good on you," he said with a broad smile. "It gives you a sort of action-adventure aura."

"Shut up," I said.

He leaned over and kissed my forehead, and I was beginning to wonder where this was going to lead—because, after all, this is the nineties and what can you do with a faggot with a split lip—when he rolled over on his back and sighed.

"Your mother's right. You've got to be more careful," he said.

"It was just some kind of stupid mistake," I replied, and closed my eyes.

That just goes to prove how wrong you can be. It was not just some sort of stupid mistake: it was a huge, incredibly bad mistake that would snowball into something we'd never forget.

TWO

My name is Alex Reynolds, and I'm a commercial artist—freelance. I work out of our home. I went into commercial art because I'm pretty good, but I'm not up to painting the Great American Landscape. The biggest campaign I've worked on was for Skedaddles. It was one of those restaurants where you can take your kids, so nobody in their right mind eats there. Peter and I ate there once so I could get a feel for the place while I was working on the ad, and I've never been in a restaurant where the staff ran so much or smiled so horrifically. Every single one of the wait-staff had pasted on their faces the type of smile that looks like it's held in place with a heavy coat of varnish. At first I thought the restaurant's name referred to the speed of service, but I came to realize Skedaddles actually means "Eat and get out." But I drew a great ad for them. I drew the best curly fries you've ever seen. They actually looked like they were smiling. And as a few of my friends pointed out, any resemblance to bed springs was purely subliminal.

Peter Livesay, my husband, is a salesman at Farrahut's, a rather exclusive clothing store for rather exclusive men. There is no Farrahut, and nobody knows where the name came from. The store is owned by Arthur Dingle, which serves as both his name and his description. Peter has been really successful as a salesman there, which he attributes to his expertise, but I attribute to the fact that the clientele is all on the fey side and really like having him help them into and out of their clothing.

My mother, whose name is Jean, does nothing for a living at the moment due to the fact that my ex-father neglected to change the beneficiary on all his various insurance policies before he was run over. As my mother said at the time, "That bloody bastard was insured up his bloomin' arse!" That was the last time my father was referred to as a "bloody bastard" in our home.

My mother owns the townhouse in which we live on west Fullerton. It's a three-bedroom affair with a large living room, a dining area, and a kitchen just big enough for the three of us to get in each other's way.

Saturday morning—the morning after my escapade at Charlene's—we had breakfast in what is known in modern architecture as the "breakfast nook," which is actually an enclosed porch with windows on three sides, so the sun pours in. It juts out of the back of the building, just off the kitchen, and has gardens planted directly behind it.

Mother was clad in a white kimono with a jade dragon printed up the back. It is one of the collection of kimonos she acquired on the trip to Japan she took to celebrate the death of my father. Somehow when she makes breakfast in one of these flowing robes I always expect the sleeves to catch fire, and for her to go up like some sort of crossbred phoenix, but she always manages to get through breakfast without being bothered to rise again. Mother does most of the cooking, not by design but because she enjoys doing it.

Peter and I were just polishing off the last of the eggs when the front doorbell rang and Mother went to get it. Before opening the door, she peeked through the living room window for a moment (as is her habit). Then she went to the front door and opened it. I don't know if I was just wary because of the previous night or if I've developed a strip of paranoia as I've ploughed into my thirties, but I got up and went over to the kitchen doorway to watch.

At the door was a man I can only describe as swarthy. I don't know what that word means, but I'll bet you'd find his picture by it in the dictionary. He was overtly handsome, but carried himself as if he were unaware of it. He had dark hair and dark skin and dark eyes, and was wearing a dark blue suit.

"What is it?" said Peter from the porch.

"I think it's a Mormon traveling alone," I replied. Peter made a face at me and went back to his eggs.

"Mrs. Reynolds?" said the man.

"Yes?"

"I'm here about an incident that took place last night in a bar called Charlene's."

My heart dropped into my stomach. I don't think I'd ever been involved in anything before that could be called an "incident."

"Yes?" said my mother patiently.

The man smiled and said, "My name is James Martin, I'm with the federal government."

He reached into the inner pocket of his suit coat and pulled out a small leather folder. He flipped it open in an attempt to flash his badge at my mother, but she refuses to be flashed in any form. She grabbed his little folder in mid-flip and examined his badge with the scrutiny of a dermatologist searching for melanoma, then handed it back to him.

"It doesn't say on there what branch of the government you're with."

"We don't usually give out that information," he said as he slipped the folder back into his inner pocket.

"Well, there you have me," said Mother, "I don't usually allow uninvited federal agents into my home."

He smiled in a way that said "Touché" and "You'll pay for that" in one slick gesture.

"I'm with the CIA."

"The CIA?" Mother repeated slowly, her brow furrowing.

I knew I would have to buy a pack of Tums before the day was out.

"We have information that someone from this house was involved in an altercation in that bar last night, and I'd like to speak to him."

"How do you know that?" said my mother, and I noticed her stiffen—probably a reflex from having been in England during the war—or at least, having seen movies of having been in England during the war.

Mr. Martin smiled and said, "The young man took a cab home from the bar." As if that explained everything. Then he added, "May I come in?"

"All right," said Mother, but her reluctance was implicit.

It was at this point I thought I'd better join the proceedings, so I came into the room and said, "What's this all about?" in the most befuddled tone of voice I could muster.

"This is my son, Alex," said my mother, then she turned to me and said, "This is James Martin. He's with the government."

Martin extended his hand and I shook it. His hand didn't tighten or go limp. It just stayed in mine for a moment as if it were there on sufferance, then he pulled it away.

"I understand you had a little unpleasantness last night," he said.

"Yeah?" I said. "How do you know that? Did someone complain?"

"No."

"I didn't file any complaint, either, so I don't see why you're here."

"You didn't file a complaint?" he said. "I'm pleased to hear that."

That completely stumped me. "Why?"

At this point Peter wandered into the room and said, "What's up?"

Martin looked to my mother and said, "Is this your other son?"

"Hardly."

14

There was a little pause, then Martin said, "I see." I didn't like the way he said it.

"I need to talk to you about last night," said Martin. "And it would probably be better if we were alone."

"They know all about last night, so they might as well stay."

"I see," he said again.

Mother motioned him to the couch and he sat. There is a coffee table in front of the couch, and we all pulled up chairs on the other side of it, so we looked sort of like a panel about to grill a student.

"Why are you glad I didn't report it?" I asked, not about to let the interrupted part of the discussion drop.

"Because it's not the type of thing we'd like any sort of . . . interference in," he said smoothly.

"Interference? I wasn't interfering in anything. I was just having a beer!"

Peter turned his head toward me and gave me a look so pained you would've thought I'd just broken wind at a high tea. "I think he means interference from the police," he said, and turned to Martin and added, "Is that right?"

"Correct," said Martin. "First I need to ascertain if you were a willing participant, or if you just . . . stumbled into it."

"I was just having a beer!" I said. "Minding my own business. And then I went to the john and these guys pulled a knife on me!"

Martin looked at me doubtfully for a moment, then said, "That's not the incident I was talking about."

"Mr. Martin," my mother cut in in her severest tone, "I'm afraid none of us knows what you're talking about. My son was roughed up in that bar last night." "Roughed up" sounds very quaint with an English accent: it came out something like "roofed up."

"We're aware of that," countered Martin. "But I was talking about his contact with our man."

"What man?" I said.

"You spoke with him."

"I spoke to a hundred men last night!" I said.

"A hundred? Really?" said Peter in a playful tone that was meant to get me to calm down.

I ignored him. "Which one are you talking about?"

"A big man. Very pale. Dark, limp hair. Bags under the eyes. Brown eyes."

"Sweaty?" I asked.

"Um-hmm."

What went on between the dough-man and me had been so slight and innocuous that half of me wanted to believe that this whole thing—the attack, my flight, and this man sitting here in our living room—was just some sort of elaborate joke. On the other hand, this man *was* sitting here and had identification, so I knew it couldn't be a joke. *North by Northwest* shot back into my head, and I had that same sick feeling I'd had last night, only worse: this guy looked a hell of a lot more threatening than Leo G. Carroll.

"We'd like to know what passed between you."

"We?" said Peter.

"My department," Martin replied without looking at him.

"Nothing passed between us," I said.

"He was seen speaking to you."

My wariness hit the wall there. I took a deep breath and said, "Look, Mr. Martin, my family and I aren't used to being questioned by a total stranger. I think if you want to know anything else, we need to know what the hell this is all about."

Martin sighed and looked down at the floor for a minute, then addressed the three of us with the utmost seriousness that we've come to expect of the feds through years of bad movies: "Before I tell you anything, I need your assurance that it will go no farther than this room. We are dealing with highly classified information, and I wouldn't tell you anything about it at all . . . if there were a choice." Here he looked at us as if we were being very bad little children. "But be that as it may, I need your assurance as good American citizens that what I'm going to tell you will go no farther." He looked at my mother and added, "Yours, too."

16

Mother bristled and said in her most offended upper-crust British accent, "I believe we are still allies."

"And she's a damn sight more acceptable in this country than *we* are," Peter grumbled under his breath.

Martin looked at us as if we were alien in more ways than one, took a deep breath, and then went into a formal recitation: "I can't tell you everything about this matter, it deals with national security. What I can tell you is that the man you spoke with at the bar is named Victor Hacheck. He contacted my department some time ago and said that he had some very sensitive information he would like to share with us."

"In exchange for what?" said Peter.

"Naturalization," said Martin simply. "We instructed him to take a flight to O'Hare. We thought that Chicago would be an unlikely place for foreign agents to be looking for someone who was planning to pass inside information to the government, so he was instructed to come to Chicago, and we set up a time and place for him to pass the information to me."

"At Charlene's?" I said incredulously. A lot of very weird things have happened at Charlene's, but probably the last thing I'd expect is for state secrets to be passed there. But then again, that was probably the point.

"No," said Martin with a tinge of disgust that I begrudged him. "At a bar on Rush Street."

"Did he get the directions wrong?" said Mother. It was impossible to tell whether or not she was joking.

"No, but somebody else got them right."

"What do you mean?"

"I mean," said Martin patiently, "that we weren't the only ones there. I was waiting for Hacheck on the east side of Rush Street, across from the bar. I wanted to see him first and size him up."

"Admirable," said Peter wryly.

Martin glanced at him and continued, "He arrived just before the appointed time, stood around outside the bar looking up and down the street. I was just about to cross to him when he looked south and a startled look came over his face. He bolted. He was pretty fast for his weight. He ran north, up North State Parkway, and then I saw what he had seen—two men."

"The clay people!" I said excitedly, and felt stupid almost the minute the words were out of my mouth.

"The what?" said Martin.

"I'm sorry, the guys that roughed me up."

"Yes. They were about a block away when Hacheck took off, and they took off after him. I followed."

"You followed?"

"Yes. They went north to Goethe, west to Wells, and north up Wells until Hacheck ducked into the bar."

"And you followed," I said.

"Yes."

"I didn't see you in the bar."

"Maybe you weren't being as . . . observant as you might have been."

I said, "Hmmph."

"The government has spent a lot of money to bring Hacheck over here and set up a safe house for him with a new identity and all that goes with it, only to have him bolt."

"Not of his own volition," I pointed out.

"Perhaps," he said, sitting back on the couch and folding his arms.

"What do you mean?" Mother asked. "Why else would he disappear?"

"Stranger things have happened, Mrs. Reynolds. Maybe he just didn't have the money for the flight, and wanted to get out of Russia very badly. Maybe the whole thing was a scam for free airfare."

"You can't believe that," Mother replied.

"As I said, stranger things have happened. He may not have had anything to sell, and instead of trying to bluff his way out with me and the government, he disappeared. It's easy enough to do in a country this size."

"But what about the two men who were chasing him?" asked Peter. "Surely you don't think they were a scam."

Martin shrugged. "That could've been something completely different. Maybe they thought he had money."

"Not if they'd seen him," I said. "Besides, you said he ran when he saw them, not the other way around."

"What do you mean?"

"He must have recognized them."

"Who knows?" said Martin with another shrug. "Maybe they reminded him of the Nazis of his youth. We can never tell with *those people.*"

I bristled at his use of the phrase. It's been used on my own minority so many times.

"But what information was he going to give you?" asked Peter.

"I don't know the whole of it, and what I do know I can't discuss." He turned his searchlight-like eyes on me. "And that is why I need to know what passed between you."

I looked at him for a minute. In a way, after that story, I wished I had more to give him. And in a way I was glad I didn't.

"Nothing."

"Nothing?"

"No, nothing. Nothing passed between us."

"Mr. Reynolds," he said with an evenness that sent chills up my spine, "he was seen talking to you. Can you tell me what he said?"

"All he said was, 'Is this place always this noisy?' or something like that. I thought he was trying to pick me up."

"And what did you say?"

"Um-hmm."

"That's *all* that passed between you?" said Martin in an extremely doubtful tone.

"That's all."

"Could it be that he passed something to you?"

I gave him a look that I hoped was as withering as I wanted

it to be, and said, "We hardly got close enough for that sort of thing."

His patience became even more measured. This guy didn't have any sense of humor. "What I'm asking you is did he give you anything?"

I shrugged and replied, "He gave me a light."

Martin didn't so much as twitch, but I could sense his interest. "He lit your cigarette?"

"Are you smoking again?" Mother demanded. The look on her face told me I'd better not be.

"No," I stammered. "Well, yes, but just that once. I only do it when I'm . . ."

She cut me off with "Honestly, Alex, we've had this talk over and over again. I won't have you smoking. You know how dreadful and stupid it is, and besides—"

I was almost glad when Martin cut her off.

"Could you save that for another time?" He turned to me. "This is important: what did he do when he lit your cigarette?"

"He lit the damn thing," I said with enough irritation to let him know that I didn't like him talking to my mother or me that way. "He just lit the thing. He didn't say, 'Permit me,' or anything like that. Of course, he probably didn't know that we were supposed to be in some kind of Sherlock Holmes movie or something."

Martin closed his eyes, just for a second, then he said, "What did he do then?"

"I don't know. I didn't watch him."

"He didn't say anything else?"

"I didn't want him to," I said. I was getting really hot under the collar now. "I wasn't inviting any more conversation. I didn't want to talk to him."

Martin sighed and said, "If you had, we might know what happened to him."

That really got me, because I was not having this guy's fate put on me just because I treated him the way I'd treat anyone I wasn't interested in. I said, "Look, I was just there for a beer, not to scout for the feds."

"Calm down, Alex," said Mother.

"No, really!" I turned to Martin and said, "It's not my fault you lost your man, and it's not my fault that I didn't make small talk with him about Soviet-American relations."

A silence fell among us. Martin looked at me for a moment and then said, "Did he give you the matches?"

"No," I answered after a pause, unable to hide my incredulousness.

"What did he do with them?"

"I don't know. The next time I looked, he and his matches were gone."

Martin drummed his fingers on his knees for a moment and looked steeped in thought. "The men who attacked you, what did they say?"

"They said something like they saw him give it to me, or they saw him talking to me, and I didn't know what they were talking about. I talked to a lot of people at the bar, and nobody gave me anything."

He scrutinized my face in a way that made me want to sink into the carpeting and disappear before he said, "Are you sure you're telling me all you know?"

At this my mother drew herself up to her full height, rested her hands on the sides of her kimono like a Japanese empress in a musical comedy, and said, "My son does not lie, Mr. Martin. Now, will that be all?"

"I'm sorry," he said to her so self-effacingly that it made me wonder if it was possible to blush on cue. "I really didn't mean to imply that he would."

My mother showed him to the door, and Peter and I followed close behind. Once there, Martin turned and handed me a slip of paper on which he'd written his phone number.

"If you should remember anything else, will you call me?"

"Um-hmm," I said as I looked at the paper.

With this he turned on his heel and strode down the front steps and the walk.

Mother closed the door after him and turned to me, her index finger pointing accusingly at my chest.

"Don't you ever go to a bar again!"

THREE

After Martin left, we went about our normal business. For us Saturday is a school day, meaning that Peter has to work. Since I freelance, my time is more or less my own, so I usually try to arrange my schedule around his. Sundays and Wednesdays are our days off. He donned his gray silk suit and maroon tie. There was something comforting about spending that time with him after the excitement of the past twenty-four hours.

Like most people who work out of their homes, I try very hard to stay to a strict schedule so that I don't get slothful and spend all my time wandering around Marshall Field's, scanning everything I would buy if I had money. But I was too anxious to work, so I let Mother talk me into going to the zoo with her. I always feel guilty when I blow off work, but I didn't have any pressing deadlines, other than a brochure I was designing for one of the smaller local professional associations, and that wasn't going to take up a lot of my time. It wasn't due for a couple of weeks, and they had such strict corporate standards that creativity didn't enter into the picture. Any residual guilt was dealt with by reminding myself that my lip still hurt. Who could work with that?

We headed out about ten. The Lincoln Park Zoo is a short

walk from our townhouse, and one of the things I like to think of as a true Chicago anomaly: a fully stocked zoo in the most humanly congested area of the city. The people who live in high-rise apartment buildings for several blocks around will suddenly, in the still of the night, be woken by elephants trumpeting or lions roaring.

We started at the north end of the zoo and made our way to the center, where all the concessions are located. It is also the site of the seal pool. The front of the pool has a large brass railing along which you can stand to watch the seals at play; the back has several tiers of seats where you can rest while you watch. We decided to stand by the rail. As we watched the seals, I ate a cup of something called "frozen lemonade." We'd been there several minutes when I spotted him. He was wearing a low-class corduroy version of what they used to call a driving cap, and a short coat that was much too heavy for the warm summer day. He looked like an overaged Bowery Boy. I almost dropped the cup and I was glad I didn't because I didn't want to draw attention to myself, although I figured that he had to have followed us: I couldn't believe that he'd just by chance decided to take a day off from spying and spend it at the zoo. It then occurred to me that if he'd followed us here, he knew where we lived.

Without turning my head, my eyes still on the seals, I said to Mother, "My God, don't look!"

Her head immediately swiveled around to me, and she said, "What *are* you talking about?"

"He's here!"

"Who?" she said, looking this way and that.

"Stop that!" I said to her, more sharply than I would usually talk to my mother because . . . well, she's my mother. "I don't want him to know we've seen him!"

"*We* haven't seen him," she said evenly. "Who on earth are you talking about?"

"One of the clay people is here!"

Mother did what they call in the movies a "slow take," and said, "Hmm?"

24

"One of the thugs that attacked me last night!"

I was still spooning the lemonade stuff into my mouth, at intervals so regular I must have looked like an autistic with an eating disorder. Mother's hands clenched the railing, and the muscles in her arms tightened. I knew if I wasn't careful, she would bolt up to where he was and confront him.

"Where?" she demanded.

"You're not going to do anything," I said with carefully measured calm. "I don't want him to know we've spotted him."

"Where?" she said again.

"In the bleachers. Far right side. Last row. Corduroy cap."

Mother lowered her head and rolled her eyes upward, so that she would appear to be looking down when in reality she was looking up. The short clay person was perched on the bench I'd indicated. He appeared to be staring down at nothing in particular in the pool. Mother let out a "hmmph."

"I wonder where the other one is," I whispered.

Mother said, "I don't like the idea of someone with a knife following us around."

She has a natural gift for understatement.

"Well," I said slowly, in order to give her the impression that I was actually giving my next idea some serious consideration, "I know this will sound nuts, but maybe it's just a coincidence. Maybe we just decided to come to the zoo on the same day."

Mother looked down her fine English nose at me and said, "Pah!"

"It could be," I protested.

Mother gave the man in the bleachers a brief, cunning glance, then quickly surveyed the area.

"Well, there's one way to find out," she said.

I had that sudden sinking feeling that Ethel Mertz used to exhibit whenever Lucy uttered those fateful words, "I've got an idea."

"You know," I said, "his partner has to be somewhere. I wonder if he's watching us from somewhere else."

"Let's go," she said, a cunning smile on her face.

I tried to use my almost nonexistent peripheral vision to see whether or not the man was noticing our departure, but I couldn't tell. We rounded the left side of the seal enclosure, passing around the back. The area behind the bleachers was a short sloping hill, which, under the present circumstances, reminded me of the now infamous grassy knoll in Dallas. I could just see the top of the clay person's head over the crest of the hill. He hadn't turned to watch us.

We made a leisurely beeline for the lion house, which has an entrance just across from the seals. Once inside, Mother said, "Let's go," again, this time in a more purposeful voice. We swept through the lion house, which was almost devoid of visitors since most of the cats were enjoying the hot weather in their outside cages. We got to the other entrance, and Mother stopped just inside the doorway, hiding by a post. I stood barely concealed behind another post on the opposite side. We watched the other doors across the wide expanse of the room. The footsteps of the few visitors who ventured in to visit the gift shop echoed loudly off the white-tiled floor. We watched for so long that we were beginning to think we'd been wrong.

Mother cocked her head toward the outer door, indicating it was time to leave. At that moment a figure appeared in the doorway on the other side of the lion house. From that distance, backlit by the bright summer sunlight, it was difficult at first to even discern if the figure was a man or a woman. It came slowly into the room, and as it passed through the doorway, there was that strange effect of sunlight passing from around it, like the parting of a celestial Red Sea, and the man emerged in full view. His eyes swept the room, and he looked a little unsure. Then he seemed to hear voices from the gift shop, and slowly made his way to a cage opposite the shop, where he stopped. I knew what he was doing: he thought perhaps we'd gone into the shop, and he was pretending to watch the contents of the cage until the people emerged, to make sure he hadn't lost us.

But that was all it took to convince my mother and me that we were, indeed, being followed: he was staring into an empty cage. Mother glanced at me, I nodded, and we left through the back entrance. We paused for a moment just outside the door to adjust to the bright light, and I heard footsteps, walking with a determined step toward the exit through which we'd just passed. Mother motioned for us to head south.

We veered through the masses of weekend zoo-goers, all in floral shirts and shorts, various kinds of sunglasses, and many dragging children behind them or pushing children ahead of them in strollers and carriages. This was my idea of what hell would be like: doomed for eternity to try to fight my way through an endless strollerthon of squalling brats and screaming parents.

"My God, he *is* after us," I said without looking back.

"Don't worry, I know what to do," said Mother.

I'm sure that, for most people, hearing those words from one's mother would be comforting and reassuring. Now I felt like Ethel Mertz on drugs.

We continued south, not bothering to make it look leisurely anymore, and Mother headed straight for the primate house. We hurried inside and found the exhibit, as usual, very hot, crammed with people and fetid animal smells. Mother quickly led me up the ramp to the second level, stopping just at the space where the second level is cut off from the first. A few of the other visitors were a bit more curious about my mother than the apes: she stayed crouched, peeking around the corner at the top of the ramp, watching the front door. After a few moments the clay man came in, his eyes darting around. He hesitated in the doorway as if unsure which way to go, or whether to go at all. Fortunately for us, he started into the crowd on the first floor, his progress impeded by the masses and strollers. We waited a few moments for him to get far enough around the curve to be out of sight, then hurried back down the ramp to the muffled protestations of the people trying to get up it.

When I said that it was fortunate for us that he went into the exhibit, I didn't mean because he chose the first floor: I mean because apparently he didn't know that the exhibit was circular and that the only exit came back around to the front. If he had simply stayed by the doors, we would have been trapped.

We hurried out through the door with Mother in the lead, much to the consternation of an overweight, spandex-clad woman who was toting a baby in the crook of her arm. The baby's legs were resting on the woman's protruding stomach, and she looked as if she found her position precarious enough without being jostled by a fugitive mother and son.

We kept up a brisk pace to the south entrance of the zoo: a small gate that stands sideways, facing west, so it's not entirely visible as you walk south. If you didn't know the zoo well, you could easily miss this entrance until you were right on top of it. We hurried across the park and grabbed a cab heading north on Stockton, the curvy street that winds through Lincoln Park, lunged in, and gave the driver our address.

I knew I was going to have to reassess my vision of Mother and me as Lucy and Ethel: her plan had worked.

FOUR

Getting a cab was a mistake. Threading through the cramped Saturday afternoon traffic around the park and then on Fullerton toward our house took much longer than it would have on foot. I had visions of our pursuer just strolling up alongside the cab and accompanying us home. But it didn't happen. Either we had really lost him due to my mother's well-honed ingenuity, or his partner was also keeping an eye on us and was still on our tail, or he simply didn't think it was worth his while to bother following us, since he obviously already knew where we lived. None of these explanations thrilled me.

In the cab my heart was pounding, my purple gauze shirt was soaked with sweat, and I was finding it hard not to pant. Mother, on the other hand, was positively luminous: her face glowed and her smile was broad and clear.

"Lord, I'm hungry!" she said.

I turned my most incredulous look on her and said, "How can you think of eating at a time like this? For heaven's sake, what are we going to do?"

"Well, I've been thinking about that," she said, and I could once again feel my heart sinking. "We are going to have to sit down and go over step by step everything that happened when you were at the bar."

I heaved a sigh. "I've been over and over that. I told the story to Peter, and you, and Martin, and I'm sick of it!"

Mother curled her lips at me. "I think if we're going to be followed about like the centerpiece in an old spy movie, we'd damn well better have another look at the circumstances."

"But—"

"No buts, darling. I'll have you remember you're the one that got us into this."

The cab driver was squinting at me from his pudding face in the rearview mirror, as if he thought he might be called upon to testify about our conversation in a court of law and wanted to make sure he could identify me. I blew a kiss at him in the mirror, and his eyes snapped back to the road.

"We don't even know what we're involved in," I said.

"Exactly. And as it seems to have gotten a tad dangerous, I think it's time we found out."

The cab pulled up in front of our townhouse. I paid the driver, giving him an extra-large tip, which I thought would make him feel like a sex object, and climbed out. Mother and I headed up the stairs, I pulled out my keys and unlocked the door, and swung it open.

We stopped cold in the doorway. Everything in the living room and dining room was thrown about: the chairs overturned, cushions tossed this way and that, drawers pulled out of the antique sideboard in the dining area and an antique secretary in the living room, the contents dumped haphazardly on the floor. We have a large entertainment center, one of those fake wood things that holds all your electronic equipment, up against one wall of the room, and I was relieved to find that the television, VCR, and stereo equipment had not been smashed or thrown to the floor. However, our videotape library of close to three hundred movies was scattered on the floor.

We stepped slowly into the room, in silent agreement that we should be as quiet as possible, straining to hear whether or not the perpetrator was still on the premises. We made our way through the living room and dining room and into the kitchen, where we saw that the back door, which opens into the breakfast nook had been clumsily broken open. I thought, "So that's how he got in," dredging up dialogue from the cop shows on television. We found something else interesting in the kitchen: the room had only been half ransacked. In the row of drawers stretching across the kitchen under the counter, the first few had been pulled out and dumped on the floor, but the rest were apparently untouched, as were the drawers in the china cabinet on the opposite side of the room.

"Oh, my God, Alex, we've been so stupid!"

"What do you mean?" I asked, really perplexed. I didn't see how the hell we could have anticipated a break-in like this.

"Don't you see? Your friend—the 'clay person' at the zoo—wasn't there to harm us, he was there to keep us under surveillance. I'll wager the minute he lost track of us, he called his accomplice here and told him to get out!"

It took a minute, but what she was saying actually did get through to me, and I went into the breakfast nook and sank into one of the chairs.

"God," I said. I don't think it was until that moment that the seriousness of our situation really hit me.

"I wonder . . . ," said my mother, her lips pursed and her brow furrowed as she surveyed the room.

"What?"

"I wonder if they know what they're looking for."

"What do you mean?"

She warmed to her idea. "Well, it seems to me that the easiest thing in the world would be for them to kill us."

"I really don't need to hear this."

"Yes, you do. You see, they could kill us quietly and get us out of the way, and then take all the time they needed to go through the house with a fine-tooth comb and find what they're looking for while we rot."

"Oh, thank you," I said, wrinkling my nose, "for that lovely visual image."

"Well, think of it, with me not holding a job and you freelancing, it might be a couple of weeks for anyone to notice that we're not up and about."

"You're really cheering me up no end, you know? And you're forgetting about Peter. He's off tomorrow but he works on Monday, so it would only be a day before somebody noticed we were missing." It suddenly dawned on me what I was saying. "Oh, please, I can't believe we're discussing this."

"It would still give them a fair amount of time to search the house without fear of discovery, without resorting to this ridiculous skulduggery of watching for us to leave and then going through the place."

"Then why not just kill us?"

"There's only one thing I can think of."

She paused for effect, but the only effect she achieved was to irritate me.

"What!"

"Perhaps they not only don't know what they're looking for, they don't know if it's a 'thing' at all."

"What's that supposed to mean?"

"Well, you said they asked you what that man in the bar said to you, and so did Mr. Martin. Maybe they can't kill us, or at least not you, because they think that man—Hacheck—may have passed the information to you verbally."

I looked at her and noted the earnestness of her expression. And frankly, I had to admit her reasoning was plausible.

"That's really great," I said. "I feel safer already. Don't you think we should call somebody?"

This was an idea that managed to bring both of us up short. It would always have been my first instinct to call the police if anything like this happened, but now I wasn't sure.

"Who should we call?" said Mother haltingly.

"I don't know!"

"Should we call the police or call that Mr. Martin fellow?"

"I don't know. Martin said to call him."

"He said to call if you remembered anything, not if we were ransacked. And I don't like the idea of him anyway. I don't trust him. That whole story of his sounds like a lot of rot. I don't like the idea of turning to him just yet."

We fell silent for a moment.

"Well," I said cautiously, knowing how much she was going to love this idea, "I know one way we can call the police in . . . unofficially."

"What do you mean?" said Mother in a tone that clearly showed me she knew what I meant but didn't want to.

"I mean we could call Frank."

For a moment that idea simply lay there like a broken egg while Mother looked at me as if I'd sprouted horns.

"No, we couldn't."

"Of course we could," I said smoothly. "He's a . . . commander now, isn't he?"

"Alex . . ." She thought for a moment, then said, "No we couldn't."

"He was sweet on you, wasn't he?" I gave that my best "Earl Holliman in *The Rainmaker*" delivery. Mother wasn't amused.

"I cannot call an old boyfriend and ask him to inspect my burgled home."

"For God's sake, it's not like asking him to give you a Pap smear! I'm sure he'd understand."

"He might understand too much."

"What does that mean?"

"He might think it's an excuse to start up with him again."

"Mother, I doubt if Frank is vain enough to believe that you would trash our entire house just to rekindle your romance with him!"

She took my face in her hands, which always smelled lightly of Oil of Olay, and smiled as she shook her head. "I do not need to further complicate my life, darling: you and Peter are complication enough."

I took her wrists, gently pulled her hands away from my face, and led her back into the living room, hoping that the sight of our splayed belongings would help her come to her senses.

"So what's it going to be?" I said. "You don't want to call Martin—and I can tell you I agree with that one—and we don't know how much more trouble we might cause if we call in the police. What are we going to do? Sit here amidst the rubble and cry?"

Mother surveyed the room with an expression on her face that I can only describe as disgusted, and seemed to come to some sort of decision within herself.

"No," she said, heaving a sigh that almost leveled the furniture that had been left standing. "You're right. I'll call Frank."

Frank O'Neil was not on duty, but he was at home and available. He arrived less than twenty minutes after Mother called, which should have shown me there was some credence to my mother's fears that he was still carrying some kind of torch for her.

The two of them had met when they took a night course in "The Greats of English Literature" at DePaul. Frank is the type of guy I'd like to think I'd go for if I were my mother's age: he's what I would call weathered handsome: his hair is gray with very little brown left in it, his forehead is permanently lined from frowning too often, his eyes look like they were once blue but have faded from seeing too much of the world. However, rather than making him seem old, this all lent him an air of sensual, world-weary knowledge.

Mother opened the door and let him in, and when he bent to give her a kiss, she jutted a cheekbone in his direction so pointedly I thought she might puncture his lip. But he was too slick for her. He shifted his head slightly and kissed her on the lips. She took it graciously, but I noticed a certain sadness in her eyes. I think Frank noticed it, too, because he suddenly broke away from her and came into the living room.

"Jeez! You weren't kidding, you were broken into! Hi, Alex."

"Hi, Frank," I said, shaking his hand and hoping that my eyes didn't look sad, too.

"When did you discover this?"

Mother followed him into the room and said, "A little over half an hour ago."

"So you haven't had time to find out if anything's missing?"

"Not really. I checked on what little of value we have, and I didn't find anything missing."

Frank was silent for a minute or so, picking his way carefully around the room and releasing an occasional "hmm." Then he said, "Yeah, your silver is thrown around but not stolen—and then there's all this stuff still here." He waved a hand at the entertainment center.

"Yes?" said Mother.

"Well . . . you know what this looks like to me?"

I suddenly felt that both Mother and I were afraid of what he was about to say. I blurted out, "What?"

"It looks to me as if whoever did this was looking for something specific."

Neither of us responded, and after a tense little pause, Frank turned to me and said, "What happened to your lip?"

"Nothing," I said, looking down at the carpet: I'm not a good liar to begin with, so I can't believe I'm any better at in front of a policeman, whether or not he's boinked my mother. "I ran into the bathroom door."

"Uh-huh," he said, making it clear that he didn't believe me. He turned to my mother and said, "What's the second floor look like?"

"Oh, I went up there after we called you. Whoever it was didn't get to the second floor. It hasn't been touched."

"Huh," said Frank, ruminating. "You know, you may have surprised him."

"Oh, no," said my mother, with a guilty glance at me, "I'm sure we didn't surprise him."

"She means we didn't hear anyone when we got here."

The glance had been mistake enough. Frank had been a policeman too long not to notice the kind of look that passed between my mother and me. He dropped his hands to his sides and said, "Jean, you want to tell me what's going on here?"

"What do you mean?" She fluttered when she said it. English women do not make good Southern belles.

"I get the feeling that the two of you know something—like who did this."

"Honestly, Frank, you know me better than to think I'd know the type of person who goes around breaking into houses."

I swear to God, I thought that any minute she would say, "The calla lilies are in bloom."

Frank let out an ostentatious sigh and said, "I know you well enough to know when you're not being straight with me. Sorry, Alex."

Mother glanced at me, not so much for approval but to let me know that she was going to go ahead anyway, and with an exasperated sigh launched into the story of the past twenty-four hours. Frankly, my gay toilet escapade had been repeated so many times by now, it was beginning to feel like an urban legend. However, Frank showed undue interest in the story, even though Mother was careful not to make any mention of James Martin's visit. Frank looked as if he sincerely doubted that his former flame was giving him the entire story.

"It sounds like you somehow got in the middle of a drug buy."

I was astounded. He had come up with the same idea I'd originally had. It was something of a relief . . . but of course, he didn't have all the facts.

"Do you really think so?" I said.

"Yeah, it's a possibility. Especially this business of following you and going through the house. They might have thought you got their drugs." Then he turned to Mother and said, "You know, I don't like the idea of this. You could be in danger."

"Oh . . . ," said Mother, surveying the room, "oh, I don't think so. Surely by now they realize that they've made a mistake and they won't be back."

She glanced at me again when she said this, and I could see that she was trying to convince herself more than Frank. Then she added halfheartedly, "Besides, it could just be a coincidence, our being burgled now. Just a coincidence."

Frank narrowed his eyes and stared at her, taking one of those long pauses that let you know that you're not fooling anybody, when you already know you're not. "Well, that might be possible, but I think the drug story is better."

His head swiveled in my direction and then back to my mother, and I suddenly found his choice of words unsettling.

"Unless," Frank added slowly, "maybe you haven't told me everything."

Mother gave a little laugh that would have been an embarrassment in a bad road company of *Mame*.

"Why no, of course not! We've told you everything, haven't we, dear?"

She nodded eagerly in my direction, and I piped in with "Oh, yeah, of course."

Frank pursed his lips and made a little smacking noise, then said, "Then why did you call me?"

Mother answered slowly, "Well, I thought perhaps you might tell us what we should do about it?"

"Put new locks on the doors. Get a dog. But first you should report it."

Mother and I both yelled "*No!*" in unison, and we couldn't have made ourselves look more culpable if we'd tried. I immediately started an in-depth inspection of my shoes, but I have to give Mother credit: her eyes sparkled in their most playful way, and she smiled Frank right in the face when she said, "We're a little nervy after this."

"You know," said Frank, looking more concerned and suspicious by the minute, "I *really* don't like this. You seem to have gotten yourself involved in something one way or the other, and I think I'd better see what I can do."

"That's not necessary, Frank," said Mother, her smile remaining in place, but her sparkle getting a bit tarnished.

He lowered his voice and said, "I'm worried about you. You know, my feelings haven't exactly changed since I last saw you."

"Do you think you could excuse us for a moment, Alex?" said Mother.

I went into the kitchen and stayed by the door, not in an attempt to eavesdrop but to be as close at hand as possible lest Mother's honor needed defending. Really. But I couldn't hear anything they said. I didn't reenter the living room until I heard the sounds of Frank being let out the front door.

"How much did you hear?" said Mother with a coy smile.

"How much did I hear? I didn't hear anything! What kind of person do you think I am?"

She crossed her arms, and her eyebrows arched in their centers, their inside ends almost dripping down into her eyes. "I don't know, Alex. Surely not the kind who would linger with his ear pressed against the kitchen door, the shadows of his big feet clearly evident beneath it."

"I don't have big feet!"

"How much did you hear?"

I shuffled a little, but it really was all lost. "I didn't hear anything. I was only trying to make sure that your honor survived the interview intact."

"My honor, my son, is my business."

"What did happen?"

"Just what I was afraid of," she said, sinking down into an easy chair. "He thinks we can still respark our relationship."

"You could do worse."

"Alex, darling, it's unseemly for you to involve yourself in your mother's love life." She sighed and added, "I think it was a mistake to call him, all the way around."

"What do you mean?"

"I told him I didn't want to report the break-in. I told him I didn't want him to do anything about it. But that doesn't mean he won't."

"Well, what can he do?"

"I don't know. But I don't want him stumbling around in something that you've stumbled into. It could be dangerous.

Worse yet, it could be dangerous for us if he makes these people think we've gone to the police."

It was my turn to sigh. "What do we do now? Call Mr. Martin?"

Mother stood, drawing herself up to her full height in her prison matron stance, looked me square in the eye, and said, "Not just yet. It's time you told me everything that happened last night. And I mean *everything*."

With her in this frame of mind, it was useless to protest. She grilled me for the next forty minutes. I would have had more of a chance with the feds, if I'd actually known anything.

She stopped me at every other juncture to ask a myriad of questions covering the small details of the larger information I offered: what the doughy man looked like; who was standing near us when we spoke; was I sure he hadn't given me anything; what were the exact words that the clay people used when they accosted me in the toilet (a scene that I had now repeated so many times it had taken on a surreal quality in my head, and I was no longer sure myself what had actually happened). She sank back into the easy chair and sighed.

"I don't see that that gets us any further along."

We sat there in silence for a moment. I felt like I had a tornado in my head. When I couldn't stand the silence from my mother any more, I said, "What to we do now?"

Mother surveyed the room dejectedly, glanced over her shoulder at me, and said, "Clean."

FIVE

We had made a fairly good-sized dent in the restoration of our happy home by the time Peter arrived home from work at four-thirty. He strolled in casually with the early editions of the Sunday papers, wrapped neatly in a plastic bag to protect his suit. He stopped in his tracks when he saw the remainder of the mess. To say the least, Peter didn't like the news. We decided to leave the rest of the mess for tomorrow and settled around the kitchen table with a pitcher of iced tea and the papers.

While Mother determinedly paged through section one of the *Tribune*, Peter absently thumbed through the arts section. I took a little longer than usual to become engrossed in the sales circulars, which to me are the only reason to buy the Sunday paper in the first place. When I was finished browsing, having found nothing of interest, I turned to the *Sun–Times* and started to flip through, half wondering if I'd find any mention of a Russian disappearing in Chicago. The only thing close was an item about an kidnapped American being returned in Russia.

I was halfway through the paper when an item arrested my attention. It was a notice of a murder: a man with no identification had been found stabbed to death behind Charlene's on Wells early that morning. The description of the body, though sparse, was enough to convince me that it was the dough-man. I let out a little shout.

"What on earth," said Mother, her attention drawn from the latest bleak economic forecast.

"Here, here," I said, wildly tapping my index finger against the item in the paper, "that's the man at the bar! The one everybody's interested in! He's dead!"

Both Mother and Peter looked at the article. Peter shook his head and said, "How can you be sure from that? They hardly say anything about him."

"It's him!"

"It says there was no identification on him. Come on, Alex!"

"It's him!" I said, noisily closing the paper and smacking it down on the table. "I'm going to go there."

"Where?" said Mother warily.

"To Charlene's. 'The scene of the crime!' I'm going to talk to them over there and see if they know anything."

"You most certainly are not!" said Mother in her most imperious tone. She motioned to the remainder of the mess in the living room and said, "Look what's happened already!"

"It's because of that that I'm going to get involved. I think it's time we asked some questions."

"We?" said Peter.

"Well, you and me," I said somewhat sheepishly. When I'd jumped up and decided to take the initiative, I'd automatically assumed that I wouldn't be taking it alone.

Peter looked at me for a moment with those soulful green eyes, scrutinizing me as if he hadn't already memorized the lot of me already. Then he said, "All right."

"Are you daft?" said Mother, finally realizing we were serious.

"I mean it, Mother. I'm tired of being in the dark. I want to find out what it is we've—I've—gotten us involved in."

Mother looked from me to Peter, then back again, her face a mask of stoicism that was impossible to read. After a moment she took a sip of tea, a wedge of lemon clinging precariously to the rim of her sweating glass, then set it down.

"All right, go ahead," she said simply.

I really didn't like the look in her eyes. It gave me pause, literally. I hesitated, then said, "We're just going to go and talk to Ernie, the bartender. He might have seen something."

"Um-hmm," said Mother, without any facial expression whatsoever.

"I can't see that it will get us in any more trouble."

"Um-hmm."

I hesitated again. "Really."

"Um-hmm."

"We should be back soon. We won't be gone long."

She turned back to the newspaper without another sound.

"What will you do while we're gone?" I asked warily.

"This and that," she replied without looking up.

Good God, we're in for it now, I thought.

We arrived at Charlene's before it had opened for the evening. I knocked on the door to no response, then I pounded on it. After a couple of minutes, when we had all but decided that "nobody was home" yet, Ernie the bartender's moon face appeared in the diamond-shaped window in the door, like a bouncer in a speakeasy. If I'd been in a better mood, I'd have said, "Joe sent me."

"We're not open yet, Alex," he bellowed through the door.

"We need to talk to you."

"We're not open yet," he said again, and he raised his wrist to the window and tapped on his watch as if that told me something.

"Ernie, we need to talk to you."

He grimaced and disappeared from view. I thought he'd just left us there, but suddenly we heard the locks snap and the door swung open.

Ernie has a very round head on which he sports a buzz cut, which may be fashionable on our kind but with his girth makes him look like Curly of the Three Stooges. I'm sure Ernie is not his real name, or at least not his original name. I think he changed it to Ernie because he thought it was more suitable for a bartender, no matter what kind of bar one might be serving in. But it couldn't have originally been Ernie because no self-respecting gay person who had been unfortunate enough to have been saddled with that moniker would have left it unchanged.

He stood to one side as we stepped through, and closed the door behind us with a bang, then resnapped the locks. There was something kind of discouraging about leaving the still-bright, early-evening sunlight for the relative darkness of the bar. To me an empty bar is sort of like an empty church, only not as ominous. They're equally quiet, equally hollow, and, depending on the layout, equally dark.

Instead of the eardrum-shattering seventies music of the night before, The Manhattan Transfer was purring coolly and quietly from the speakers. Ernie preceded us to the bar, crossing behind it as we took stools. On his left ear he wore a large gold loop that glinted in the harsh work lights. The lights made the room seem a sort of bright black. Behind the bar, Ernie plunged his hands into the murky water that filled one section of a large triple sink, apparently going back the chore that we'd interrupted: washing some bar glasses that for some unexplained reason had been left from the night before.

"What do you want?" he said, making no attempt to hide his displeasure at being interrupted.

"Well," I said, with a glance at Peter, "I wanted to ask you about that guy they found out back this morning."

He stopped and looked at me hard through his pudgy eyes.

"Oh, Jesus Christ! I spent the whole goddamn morning with the police, don't you know? Asking me about the same goddamn thing. As if just because the stupid fuck was found back there, I'd know something about it!"

"Well, do you?"

He slapped the glass he'd been rinsing down on the counter and started on another one; the clean glass slid about six inches on its ring of water before coming to a stop. "No! For Christ's sake, just because he was found out back doesn't mean he was in here!"

"But he was," I blurted out.

Ernie stopped again, his gold loop swinging for a moment after he'd ceased to move. "How do you know that?" he asked, his eyes getting even harder. I didn't like being looked at that way. I'd seen Ernie several times over the years, enough for him to know my name and me to know his, but I don't think I'd ever given him any consideration until then. I had heard that his taste ran to young men: not illegally young, mind you, but young enough not to have burned off their first layer of fuzz. I don't find him at all attractive, so I can't for the life of me imagine why a strapping youth would—but that wouldn't stop him from lusting after them. And looking at him now, his hard eyes boring into me, I could imagine that his taste might run toward someone over which he could wield power, even if that power was only age.

"How do you know that?" he asked again, since I hadn't replied.

"I was here, Ernie. You saw me."

He smiled. "No, I didn't."

My brows twitched and I said, "Of course you did, I sat right here. I had three beers."

"I didn't see you," he repeated as he went back to washing the glasses.

"But you talked to me. . . ."

Ernie didn't respond again.

Peter said, "I don't think Ernie sees anybody that comes in here, do you?" He addressed the last two words directly to Ernie.

Ernie smiled more broadly. "I don't know what it is. I have this really bad time remembering who's been here and who hasn't."

"Good for you," said Peter.

"Would someone fill me in?" I said. After all, I was the one who was taking up this investigation and it was definitely irritating to have everybody else but me seem to know what was going on.

"I think in a better world," Peter replied, "Ernie's memory would greatly improve."

"You got that right," said Ernie with a laugh that sounded like the bark of a German shepherd.

"Should I leave you two alone?" I said petulantly.

Ernie set the glass he was working on down in front of me, spread his hands apart and rested them on the bar, and leaned in toward me.

"People come here asking questions about anyone—or anything—people like the police, or anyone else for that matter, and I feel my memory just slipping away. It's really a pile of shit that what you are and what I am can still be used against us in this world, but that's the way it is. Hopefully—please God—not the way it'll always be. The police ask me who was in here at such and such a time, and I tell them, 'Sorry, officer, I was blind at the time.' And brother, you have no idea how bad it can be when somebody's found dead near your bar."

I glanced at Peter, who was still smiling but his expression had become one of admiration, and then I looked back at Ernie. After a momentary stare-down, he went back to wiping the glasses.

"But we need to know about that guy."

"Why?"

"Well . . ." I looked to Peter for some help, but didn't see any. "We just do."

"We all need a lotta shit we ain't gonna get," he said.

At last Peter spoke up. "Ernie, we need to know because the authorities were asking us about him. And they didn't believe that we didn't know anything."

"Ain't that a blip!" said Ernie with another barking laugh. "And I thought it was only me!"

"Look, you've known us for a long time, you know we're really in the fold. Can't you help us out?"

"I've known your names for a long time. Not the same thing as knowing."

For a moment I thought he was making an indecent proposition, but as the conversation continued, I realized that he had simply been saying that, under the circumstances, we couldn't necessarily expect his trust.

Peter cocked his head a little sideways and said, "So you can't tell us anything?"

Ernie just shrugged.

"And you couldn't tell the police anything?"

"What d'ya think would happen to me if I suddenly started seein' things? They'd be here all the time, asking questions. I'd never get any peace—and neither would any of my customers."

Here he looked at me, and it certainly helped my discomfiture. Then he looked back at Peter, and I sensed that there was something of a standoff going on between us all. At last Ernie smiled broadly and shrugged.

"But I think you guys are all right. I can tell you what the police don't know."

"You can?" I said, not quite sure what he meant or how he would know, but Peter seemed to be on top of things. He said, "Go on."

"Well, the cops don't know the guy's name or anything about him, really. I guess that's why they were so hot on my trail—like, *I* would know something about him—like we're in some kind of secret brotherhood and we all know each other. Jesus! I couldn't help them with any of that."

"Um-hmm."

He paused for effect, then said very pointedly to Peter, "They also don't know that he talked to your friend here."

"Why the hell does everybody in the goddamn world think that guy was talking to me?" I said at the height of exasperation.

Ernie leaned toward me over the bar again. "Probably because he was pointed in your direction and his lips were moving!"

I had a flash then about how I'd gotten involved: my mind went back to last night and I suddenly realized that anyone looking on from a distance, or even close up, would've thought I was talking to Hacheck, but would have had no way of knowing what we were talking about. It didn't seem quite as idiotic to me now that nobody seemed to believe that the conversation was innocuous.

Peter got confirmation for this when he looked at Ernie and said, "Did you hear what was said?"

Ernie screwed up his face as if he thought Peter was nuts. "Are you kidding? With all that noise?"

We decided to hang around for a while and see if anyone showed up who had been there last night and had a better memory than Ernie, even though his faulty memory was becoming very endearing.

I was beginning to think that if somebody hadn't killed Hacheck, I would have been tempted to do it myself. If he was indeed some sort of foreign agent, or even just some moderately savvy person who was willing to pass information to the American government for a price, then he must've known that if he spoke to me at all, his pursuers would probably assume he'd been passing information to me. I had a growing certainty that he'd purposely gotten me involved to take the heat off himself.

And it hadn't worked. He'd gotten killed anyway. And I was still involved. I was beginning to wish that he actually had told me something. At least then perhaps I could have told these idiot agents, or whatever they were, something and gotten them off my back. Then again, once they had the information, they probably wouldn't need me . . . alive.

Ernie provided us with a pair of beers on the house, then turned off the work lights, turned on the bar lights, and started the bar music, which once again consisted of hits from the seventies. ELO's "Don't Bring Me Down," which seemed entirely appropriate under the circumstances, cascaded off the walls.

It was half an hour before anyone else came into the bar. I didn't notice anyone I'd seen the night before. It made me wonder if everyone had gotten matched up Friday night and didn't need to return. It was a pleasant thought. By seven o'clock, though, the place was starting to get crowded.

A little after seven, Jo and Sheila showed up. They're a pair of self-described aging lesbians we've known for years, though we don't see them all that often. Sheila is a waitress at a restaurant whose name I can never remember, and Jo owns an "elegant casual" clothing boutique for men and women. She'd been very nervous about opening it, but as so often happens, the gay community sort of rallied around her, and over the past couple of years she'd built up a pretty healthy business that catered to both gay and straight clientele. The two women stood at the bar for a few minutes to soak up a little of the festive ambiance, then they noticed us and plunked themselves down at our table with a couple of beers.

"You look interesting," said Jo, pointing to my lip.

"I had a little run-in in the john," I replied.

Jo's blond eyebrows went up. "Really, I thought you gave up that sort of thing when you discovered your little Peter."

This was just like Jo. She'd always been able to double back on her own entendre.

"He just ran afoul of somebody," said Peter, "by accident."

"Uh-huh," said Sheila, taking a large swig of her beer.

We bantered on for a while, generally catching up on all that had passed over the months since we'd last seen them. At one point there was a lull in the throbbing bass line that had been playing almost continually, and "Take My Breath Away" breathed out of the loudspeakers. Peter and I glanced at each other, and he took my hand and we joined the crowd on the dance floor. I have to say this was one of those moments when I felt very close to him, and in the midst of all these attractive young men who so desperately wanted to find Mr. Right, I became acutely aware of how fortunate I was.

It was a little after eight, and I was feeling more than a little bilious after all the beer we'd had, when the door opened and I glanced up to see a face that I recognized. It belonged to the young man who had shown an inordinate interest in my shoes the night before. He was clad in a white shirt and white pants. Although I couldn't see his shoes, I was sure they were impeccable. He looked much more unsure of himself than he had when I last saw him. I glanced over at Peter and cocked my head toward the door.

I was deciding on how I would approach the young man when he spotted me and a look of panic came over his face. He bolted from the bar.

I was out of my seat in a flash, heading across the room and out the door after him. As I rushed away from the table, I could hear Jo saying, "Well, *that* was discreet!"

It was now dark outside but in his very white getup it was easy to see him tearing south on Wells Street.

I took off after him, and even though I had a few years on him, I found I was a better runner. Or maybe the situation was just starting to get to me, and adrenaline was providing the impetus I needed. I called to him to stop and that I just wanted to talk to him. He ignored these requests. Finally, I caught up with him, and as we ran, I was just barely able to reach out and catch hold of his shirt. It was enough to jerk him back so that I could get a stronger hold on him and bring him to something of a halt.

"Let me go!" he yelled.

"What's the matter?" I said.

"Let me go!"

"Why did you run when you saw me?"

"If you don't let me go, I'll start screaming!"

He was squirming in my grip enough to cause my wrist some pain and to twist his shirt into knots. As we struggled, I got a clear look at his face. Though his features were contorted with either fear or anger—I couldn't really tell which—it was evident that his face was badly bruised. It hadn't been that way last night.

"What happened to you?" I said, trying to infuse my bewilderment with a tone of compassion.

He stopped struggling, looked me straight in the eye, and said, "You! You happened to me. Now let me the fuck go!"

My hand slid from his shirt and fell to my side, and at the first sign of release he was off. He ran across the street, zigzagging through the heavy traffic, and disappeared.

It was at this point that Peter caught up with me.

"Well, that was a rather pathetic display!" he said with a smile.

"Huh?"

"You looked like an oversexed chicken hawk!"

"Oh, shut up!" I said irritably.

"What was that all about?"

"I don't know. I don't know. All I know is, he was in the bar last night. And Peter, he didn't have those bruises last night, either."

"Well . . ." Peter seemed to be turning this over in his mind before he spoke. "Just because he got roughed up doesn't necessarily mean that there's some relation. He could have just picked up the wrong guy."

"Yes, there is. I asked him what happened, and he said, 'You happened to me.'"

There was a pause during which Peter looked off in the direction in which the young man had fled, as if he'd left a trail of exhaust.

"Let's get home."

Before we left the area, Peter insisted on stopping back in the bar and saying good-bye to Jo and Sheila, and offering some kind of explanation for our actions.

"It was somebody Alex thought he knew. . . ."

"From high school," I chimed in.

"Uh-huh," said Jo, lifting the bottle of Heineken to her lips.

"He hadn't seen him in a long time, and wanted to catch him."

"So it seems," said Jo with a smirk. "It also seems his 'friend' didn't want to be caught."

Peter glanced at me, looking uncharacteristically unsure of himself, then said, "Well . . . yeah, as it turned out, it wasn't really his friend."

"Yeah," I said stupidly, "I don't know who that guy was."

"I do," said Jo, her smirk growing so wide as she took a drink that I would have gladly shoved the bottle down her throat if she hadn't been such a close friend.

"Who is he?" I said more anxiously than I should have.

"Really, Alex! Right in front of your lover!" said Sheila, laughing.

Peter had regained his composure, and took the reins. "It's all right. Actually, we both want to know. How do you know him?"

"I don't *know* him, really. But he shops at my store now and then. In fact," Jo continued, gesturing toward the door as if the young man could still be viewed there, "I think that shirt he was wearing was one of mine."

"Do you know his name?"

"Sure, it's Jerry . . . Lasker?" She scrunched her face up as if trying to remember something. "No, I think I have the last name wrong." She rested her chin in her hand, furrowed her brow, and looked at Sheila. "Was it Lasher?"

"You're thinking of your days in the leather bars."

Jo looked up at us and shook her head. "His first name is Jerry, I can't remember the last name. It's something like Lasher or Lasker."

"It's important," said Peter.

Jo thought for a minute, then brightened. "Well, he charges things, so I may still have one of his slips, if you really need to know that badly."

"It *is* important," said Peter again, nodding his head, "if it wouldn't be too much trouble."

"I'll check."

We said our good-byes to the girls, and Peter made a point of stopping to thank Ernie again, then we left the bar.

We arrived back home about ten. As we strolled up the front walk, I noticed that all the lights in the house seemed to be on, which didn't really strike me as odd: Mother didn't like being alone in a house with part of it darkened. But when we went in and I called out to her, my voice was met with dead silence. I tensed up immediately, and put my hand on Peter's arm and could feel that he had also tensed noticeably. I called to Mother again, but there was no answer. Peter and I nodded at each other, then he went upstairs and I went on through the first floor. I checked the hall closets (although I don't know why I would expect to find her there in any case), the living room and dining area (resisting the temptation to open the cupboards), then passed through the swinging door into the kitchen. She wasn't there, or in the pantry or breakfast nook: all of which you could take in from the center of the kitchen. I was in the process of screwing up my courage to look in the basement (in which I always expect to find a dead body, even when my mother's not missing) when Peter swung through the kitchen door.

I was so startled that I clasped a hand to my heart and gasped audibly. When I saw it was Peter, I thanked God for my fairly good bladder control.

"Christ! You scared me! I didn't hear you coming!"

"I was trying to be quiet," he said, knitting his eyebrows at me.

"Why the hell didn't you make any noise?" I said, my momentary panic switching to anger. I could feel my face get hot.

"I didn't want anybody to hear me."

"I'm your husband!" I said, with an irritating surety that I was becoming irrational. "I *get* to hear you!"

"I meant so nobody else could hear me," he replied calmly.

"I know what you meant. As soon as my heart stops pounding, we can go on."

"She wasn't upstairs. Nothing looked wrong."

"Obviously she's not down here, either."

"Did you check the basement?"

I hoped that little twinge of fear I felt didn't read on my face. "No, I was about to do that when you came in."

"I'll do it with you," he said, and we went over to the door, which was to the left of the stove.

Just as I was reaching to turn the knob, we heard the front door open and the sound of my mother's voice. We looked at each other in unison and almost burst out laughing with the relieved tension, but then we heard a male voice. I put my index finger to my lips and signaled to Peter. We both went to the kitchen door and cocked an ear to it. We could hear my mother happily chatting away.

Peter said quietly, "Well, she's all right," and reached up to push through the kitchen door, but I stayed his hand.

"She's brought a man home!" I said, my ear still to the door.

"Oh, don't be such a Puritan, Alex. Your mother's still young."

"Shhh!"

"Would you like something to drink?" said Mother rather jauntily.

We heard a slightly muffled male voice that both Peter and I seemed to recognize at once.

"It's Frank," said Peter, raising his hand as if to push through the kitchen door.

"Wait!" I said.

"Why? Frank's not going to care if we pass through the room, for Pete's sake."

"Mother may mind," I said.

There were more muffled sounds from the living room that sounded suspiciously like nuzzling to me.

"They're kissing," said Peter.

I glared at him and said, "This is the second time today I've listened to the two of them through the kitchen door. I'm beginning to feel like the underhouse parlormaid."

I would have found the situation perfectly embarrassing were it not for the gentle smirk on Peter's face, which let me know that whatever we were doing, it was not as serious as I might have thought it was.

"They're coming into the dining room," said Peter.

"Now Frank, I think we'll be better off in here."

"I was comfortable on the couch."

"I wasn't," she said playfully. "Now just sit at the table and I'll get you a drink."

"All right," said Frank.

"Look, dear," Mother continued to the sound of shuffling chairs and seats being taken, "I told you when I called that I wanted to get together . . . as friends. So you'd know I was sincere about what I said to you this afternoon."

"Uh-huh," said Frank.

"Honestly. As I said, just because we . . . just because our relationship has changed doesn't mean that we can't be friends."

"I'm going to vomit," I whispered.

"Do you think we can do that, Frank?"

The chair creaked in such a way that he must have leaned back on it, and he said, "Well, all right. Friends it is." He sounded as if he was trying to sound happy about it. He wasn't succeeding.

"What would you like to drink?"

"Scotch, neat," he replied, then added in a curiously forlorn tone, "as you well know."

We heard the sounds of Mother retrieving a bottle and glass from the sideboard, the clink of glass against glass. As she did this, she said with the kind of nonchalance that the British normally reserve for full-blown farce, "You know, I read something very interesting in the paper this afternoon about a body being found last night. . . ."

My mouth dropped open a few inches, and Peter's hand flew up to his mouth to stifle a laugh and nearly didn't make it. His eyes gleamed in my direction, and he said softly, "Only your mother . . ."

"Which body?" Frank asked.

"Oh," said Mother, slightly flustered, "the one found in an alley."

There was a pause, then Frank said, "Why are you interested?"

She gave genteel little cough. "Because it was in this area . . ."

There was another pause during which I could only imagine the look on Frank's face. "This wouldn't be the man found behind a bar . . . a certain kind of bar."

"Well . . ."

"Charlene's?"

"Well . . ."

Frank pressed into her like a prosecuting attorney. "When I

54

talked to you this afternoon, you said that Alex was attacked in a gay bar. Would that bar happened to have been Charlene's?"

"Well . . . as a matter of fact, it was. And that's why I'm so concerned. You know, Alex has been to that bar, and I'm very worried about him being at a place where they find dead bodies." She paused for a moment, then added, "It's a mother's concern."

At this point Peter was almost consumed with laughter, but my anxiety level was about to go through the roof. I could feel myself being led away in chains.

There was an even longer silence before Frank said with utmost seriousness, "Jean, do you think there's any relation between Alex having been at that bar last night and the body being found?"

"No, of course not! There's no question about Alex being involved!"

"I would hate to think he's somehow connected with that."

"No, no, no! My interest is purely motherly. I'm just worried about the type of places my son goes."

Frank continued in that serious tone, "Do you think . . . or know . . . that the dead man was one of the thugs that accosted Alex?"

"No, I'm sure he wasn't one of them."

"How can you be so sure?"

"I'm a mother."

"We're going to jail," I said to Peter. "I know it, we're all going to jail."

"Jean . . . we haven't been able to identify the man that was stabbed behind the bar. You wouldn't happen to know who he was?"

"No, of course not!" said Mother, her tone anything but confidence-inspiring. It didn't escape me that this was probably the first time in our lives that we knew something the police didn't. It also didn't escape me that this was the first time we'd ever lied to the police, even if it *was* Frank.

"And the two men . . . the ones that attacked Alex . . . neither of you know who they were or what they wanted?"

"No . . . ," said Mother more slowly. "Of course not. How can you think that?"

"You want me to believe that it's just a coincidence that Alex was attacked in a bar where someone was found killed and then your house was broken into?"

There was a shrug in Mother's voice when she said, "We really have had very bad luck lately."

"Maybe I should talk to Alex," he said abruptly.

I stifled a gasp that I'm sure could have been heard in the next county, let alone the next room. Mother didn't respond.

There was a brief silence, then Frank said warmly, "Jean, if you're in any trouble, you know you can come to me, don't you? No matter what it is? Even if we're just . . . friends."

"Of course," said Mother sweetly, "and don't think I don't appreciate it."

Peter put his finger to his lips and motioned to the back door. I furrowed my brow, not getting what he wanted, but he gently took my arm and we quietly made our way to the back door. Peter pulled his keys out of his pocket, grabbed the doorknob and rattled it, then pulled open the door, jangling his keys with the other hand. He nudged me with his elbow. I said "Oh," and then called out, "Mother, we're home!"

Mother and Frank had risen before we reached the dining area, and Frank was looking at her as if he thought that given enough time alone with her, he would have been able to get the truth out of her. He would've been disappointed.

He muttered something about how he'd been about to leave anyway, and Mother ushered him apologetically to the front door, where she gave him a peck on the cheek before closing the door after him. The scene had been befuddled and clumsy, and was rather painful to witness.

Mother paused by the door with her back to us for a moment, then turned to us and said, "How much did you hear?"

"What?" I said. Peter laughed.

"I told you if you wanted to be discreet you should keep your big feet from the bottom of the door. Now how much did you hear?"

"Enough to know you should be ashamed of yourself," I countered.

"I beg your pardon!"

"Acting like an overaged Mata Hari!"

Mother bristled. "Oversexed, perhaps—not overaged."

"How can you do that? You've said repeatedly that you're through with Frank—how can you go out with him just to get information? You're using him!"

Her eyes narrowed, "Oh, yes, 'eartless I am. I'm a vixen. I use men up, drain them dry, then spew them out like so much rubbish!"

I always know I'm in real trouble when she starts dropping her "aitches."

"I never thought I'd see the day when my own son would be accusing me of using a man!"

"Well, you *are* using him!" I blustered.

"I'm only using him a little," she said with finality. "And besides, what I said to him was true: I do want us to be friends. But I also wanted information. What I was really hoping was that they'd found out the government was involved, and then we could have told him everything."

"And instead, you have him thinking I'm mixed up in it somehow!"

Mother paused a moment, then said, "Yes, that was unfortunate, wasn't it?"

I sighed.

"Cheer up, darling," she said, waving it off. "I'm sure he doesn't think you're really involved in that man's death. It was just that you were at the bar last night. Speaking of which, did the two of you find out anything tonight?"

Peter answered, "Well, the one thing we found out is that the police don't know that Alex was seen talking to the dead man. In fact, they don't really know anything."

"That's all? There was nothing else?"

"No, but we had a brief encounter with a battered youth that Alex spoke with last night."

Mother turned her questioning glance at me.

"He wasn't battered when I saw him," I said, "but something happened to him last night. We have to find him and find out what it was."

"Why? What difference does it make?"

"Because . . ." I started, then stopped. I suddenly had one of those guilty rushes you sometimes have when you realize that you accidentally did something to hurt someone else. Although even as this feeling came to the surface, I knew it was irrational since all I'd really done to him was offer him a gentle rebuff. Then again, all I'd done to Victor Hacheck was offer a gentle rebuff, and he was now dead.

"Alex?" said Mother, her brow furrowing with concern.

"Because he said whatever it was that happened to him, I caused it."

Mother scrutinized my face for a moment, then said, "How is that possible?"

"I don't know. I don't know what the hell was going on in that bar last night, but somehow my presence there seemed to have affected people, and we've got to figure it out."

"Can we find him?" said Mother.

"Oh, yes," said Peter, "the dyke underground is working on identifying him."

"The what?" said Mother, her face amused and puzzled.

He explained, "Jo and Sheila—you remember them? They think they know him and they're trying to figure out who he is."

"I'd put my money on them," I said.

Mother thought for a moment, then sighed. "Maybe we really should just call this Mr. Martin fellow and let him handle it."

"I don't know," said Peter, shaking his head. "I don't like it that the police don't know he's involved. I feel like we're withholding information from everyone."

"There's one thing I don't understand," I said.

"Only the one?" said Mother wryly.

"Well, Hacheck was killed last night. Why didn't Martin know that? He only said Hacheck was missing."

Peter shrugged and said, "Maybe he didn't know."

"Oh, come on!"

"Maybe he didn't want you to know. Maybe he thought it would scare you."

"If that's what he was thinking, he was right!" Then another thought occurred to me. "But wait a minute, if Hacheck was killed behind the bar, it must've happened right when he left . . . and he left, at least I think he left, while I was there."

"So?" said Peter.

I took a deep breath and said, "Well, Martin was watching the front—that's how he got the number of the cab I caught—and those two guys took off after me."

"Yeah?" said Peter again, not following.

"Peter, that's the three people we know about. Martin and the two clay people. If they all went after me, then who killed Hacheck?"

"Oh, God!" said Mother.

SIX

I spent a mostly sleepless night mulling over whether or not to call Mr. Martin and fill him in on the happenings since his visit. I felt like one of those cartoon characters from the fifties that have a little angel appear on one shoulder and a little devil on the other, whispering opposing viewpoints in the poor idiot's ears. The little devil told me that not wanting to get enmeshed in an increasingly murky government problem was smart and nobody would blame me. On the other hand (so the little angel whispered), it is one's duty to do what's right, and it's right to get involved when you may have important information. However, whispered the devil innocently, I didn't have any pertinent information. The angel countered with the fact that we'd been followed and our house had been broken into, and if that didn't seem pertinent, it was at least significant. I couldn't help interjecting at this point that like it or not we were already involved—after all, it's my head and I do get to have my say.

I don't think I fell asleep until around five o'clock—at least, that is what the clock read the last time I looked at it. But I had made a decision.

To say that I awoke the next morning would be highly overstating the case. It was more like I slogged my way into the mire of semiconsciousness. When I finally realized that further sleep was hopeless, I pulled my tatty, baby blue bathrobe over my naked frame and trudged down the stairs, leaving Peter sleeping peacefully. I don't know how I looked, but I definitely felt like something the cat had coughed up.

I found my mother seated at the kitchen table, clad in a red kimono with gold dragons embroidered around the ends of the sleeves. She was eating toast and lime marmalade, and looking disgustingly luminous for seven o'clock on a Sunday morning.

"What are you doing up so early?" she said, swallowing a bite of toast and reaching for her teacup.

"I could ask you the same thing."

She cocked an eyebrow at me and said, "I don't mean to sound dire, darling, but you don't *look* like you should be up yet."

I poured myself a cup from the teapot and joined her at the table.

"I didn't sleep well."

"I heard. Was something on your mind?"

There is something dangerously deadpan about the way my mother says things at times. Even though we've been together all my life, I still don't always know when she's joking. I decided to let it slide.

"I was trying to decide whether or not to call Mr. Martin and tell him what's happened here. I can't see that it would get him any further along in finding what he's looking for, but I can't see that it'd hurt, either."

"Did you come to any conclusion?"

"Yeah. Like it or not, it's my duty."

Mother set her cup down and stared into it as if she expected an answer to float up through the tea, like answers used to float up in the "8 Ball" toy we had when I was a kid when you turned it upside down. I wish things were that simple now.

"I think you're right," said Mother at last. "We don't know

him, but he is with the government and he did ask us to keep him informed." Her tone of voice, coupled with the solemn look on her face, told me that this was one of those occasions when she agreed but wished she didn't. "But won't you have to wait till tomorrow?"

"I don't know—I somehow think that somebody will answer at the CIA, don't you?"

She shrugged and took another bite of toast. Nothing affects Mother's appetite.

"But at least I'll wait till after breakfast." I thought maybe a little food would reaffirm my decision. I had a bowl of cereal, two pieces of toast, a hard-boiled egg, a banana, and a can of Coke while scanning what was left of the Sunday paper we'd bought the day before, all the while mentally trying to avoid the matter at hand. When nine o'clock rolled around, I retrieved the piece of paper on which Martin had written his number, dialed it, and waited. While the phone rang, I fleetingly wondered whether the CIA had an answering machine, and if anyone in their right mind would leave a recorded message there. Then it crossed my mind that they recorded all their calls anyway. That wasn't a comforting thought, either. The phone was answered with one word: "Yes?"

"Mr. Martin?"

"Yes?"

"This is Alex Reynolds."

"Yes."

"Some things have happened since you were here yesterday, and I thought you should know about them."

"Go on."

I went through the whole story, from our being followed by the clay person, and how we eluded him, to our coming home and finding the house ransacked.

When I told him about the house, he interrupted with "Did you report it to the police?"

"No," I said, and I hoped that I didn't sound guilty. After all, we didn't actually report it to the *police,* we reported it to Frank, which isn't the same thing. And I didn't want to get this guy on Frank's case, because in movies and books there's always tension between the feds and the locals.

I went on to tell Martin that I'd gone back to Charlene's last night (though I didn't tell him that we were sleuthing), and that I'd run into the young man, Jerry something, who seemed to have been beaten up for some reason, though why or by whom I didn't know. Martin made noises that seemed to indicate that he thought what had happened to Jerry was superfluous, which I found annoying because it gave me the sneaking suspicion that Martin thought people of our kind were often beaten up as a matter of course.

When I got to the end of my story and what we thought of everything that had happened, there was a long pause during which I thought I could feel Martin being irritated with me—though why he should be, I couldn't say. At last he said, "Mr. Reynolds, in light of recent events I need to ask you once again if you are *sure* that Victor Hacheck didn't give you anything or say anything to you that would indicate what information he was carrying?"

"No!" I said with exasperation. I was getting really tired of answering that question. "But I do know one thing."

"Which is?"

"Victor Hacheck is dead. It was in the paper yesterday."

There was a silence of the kind that inspires paranoia in the hearts of many Americans before he said, "Yes, I know."

I wanted to ask when he'd found out, or why he hadn't told me, but I knew he wouldn't answer so I didn't bother. There was another pause, then Martin said in a voice that sounded ominously pleasant, "Well, if you're sure that Martin said nothing and gave you nothing, then it would appear that the matter died with him."

"He didn't," I replied, then added, "What about the people who ransacked our house? Are we in any danger here?"

There was a slight hesitation, which made my heart beat faster, before he said matter-of-factly, "I don't think so. They probably realize by now that they've made a mistake. They probably won't bother you again, but please contact me if they do."

"Now wait a minute—" I said hotly. I was certainly in no position to accept his assurances as lightly as he seemed to give them.

"And," he said, cutting me off, "I can let it be generally known that you have nothing to offer."

There was something about the way he'd said it that made me feel certain he could do this, and that realization gave me a sort of sick feeling in the pit of my stomach.

"Won't you guys ever know what it was all about?"

There was the briefest silence, then the sound of a deep breath, and he said, "Mr. Reynolds, we appreciate all of the assistance you've given us in this matter."

And with that, the phone went dead.

I have to admit that I felt let down. As scary as the past day or so had been, it was exhilarating. One doesn't often find oneself doing Hitchcock on location without a script. But it was over, and our respective lives would now go on. And I found myself fighting a wave of disappointment. I mean, sure we'd been in danger, I'd fled for my life, along with Mother I'd eluded a foreign agent, and we'd found our home invaded: but as Mother would say, it made for a change. And within another moment I found myself not only fighting disappointment, but resisting an increasing concern that I was becoming seriously unhinged. After all, how in the hell do you form an emotional attachment to having your life in jeopardy? I suspected that that was not normal.

I turned the television on and stared at it, oblivious to what was being shown. Well, not totally oblivious, since they were showing an old Sherlock Holmes movie with Basil Rathbone, but after an hour of it, I suddenly realized that I didn't know which one they were showing. But I knew we had it on tape. You know you're in bad shape when you spend an hour in a semicomatose state in front of your television set watching a movie that's interrupted every ten minutes with five minutes of commercials, even though you have an unedited, uninterrupted copy of it in your entertainment center. I had a sudden nostalgic pang when I thought of our movies having been tossed all over the floor the day before, as if I already longed for the days when we were chased by thugs.

Sunday is one of Peter's days off, and when he's off, he has a habit of sleeping in. It's another one of those talents he has that I begrudge him, since I simply cannot sleep if the sun is out. I can't even sleep if the sun is *supposed* to be out. The movie ended at eleven o'clock, and I went up to our room and found him lolling in bed. I would have been really irritated with his failure to get up to console me were it not for the fact that he looks so cute when he lolls. It didn't matter that he didn't know yet that the case was over—though I have to admit I had that fleeting, irrational thought that if he really loved me, he would know.

Anyway, he was rousing when I came in. He somehow saw my furrowed brow through his half-closed, sleepy eyes, and I sat on the side of the bed and related the details of my conversation with Martin. When I finished, he ran his hand along my forearm and said softly, "Oh, I'm sorry."

That is why we have been together for so long. He understands.

The positive effects of Peter's condolences didn't last me very long. I was in a blue funk most of the day. To quell my disappointment, Peter suggested that we have lunch at an outdoor café. An outdoor café in Chicago consists of a normal restaurant throwing some tables and chairs out on the sidewalk, in the way of pedestrians and the exhaust fumes of buses. But it's romantic. After lunch we whiled away the afternoon pursuing what appeared to be the most popular pastime for gays on a hot Sunday: browsing through Marshall Field's. Nobody followed us. Nobody chased us. Nobody so much as looked at us furtively over the top of a newspaper.

We got home just before six, and as we approached the front door, I had the slight hope that we'd find the house ransacked again, and so find that our part in the little drama was not over. But my hopes were dashed the minute we opened the door: everything was anticlimactically in place.

I think that despite my protestations to the contrary, I'd liked being involved and would have enjoyed unraveling a foreign plot that had eluded the usual government agencies. It's not as if I was entertaining a vision of suddenly becoming America's first special agent in light loafers, but then neither was Cary Grant when he was mistaken for an agent in *North by Northwest*. It occurred to me for the first time how Grant must have felt when the movie was over—I mean, what his character felt. After all the excitement of chasing agents across the United States and winning the affections of Eva Marie Saint, what kind of life would they be going back to? Would she give up the life of a seductive secret agent to make him oatmeal in the morning? And what about Cary? Wouldn't returning to the life of an advertising executive seem rather futile after foiling a foreign plot? I didn't think I could ever look at that movie the same way after this.

As I lay in bed that night with Peter softly and rhythmically whistling through his nose, I realized that this was the kind of irritating trend of thought that succeeds in keeping one awake all night.

I suppose I must have dozed off at some time during the night, because I found myself waking at quarter to seven the next morning. Peter had stopped his whistling, and his breathing was so low I actually leaned over and put my ear close to his face to make sure he really was breathing. He smacked his lips a couple of times and rolled over on his side.

I lay on my back and stared at the ceiling for a few more minutes, and then decided that trying to sleep anymore would hardly do me any good: after all, the sun was up. So for the second morning in a row, I crawled out of bed, more dead than alive, to face the day. Only today the only interesting prospect I had was to go back to work on that damn fucking boring corporate flier.

I quietly moved to the closet and removed my wicker hamper, which I brought downstairs and set next to the kitchen table.

We keep the washer and drier in the small utility room off the kitchen. Monday morning is when I do my laundry. It makes me feel like I'm starting the week off fresh.

Mother wasn't up yet, but I knew she would be soon. Monday morning is also the time when she usually cleans house. She could afford a cleaning woman, but like most of the British she's not afraid of hard work, and I don't think anyone else could get the house up to her code anyway. Doing it herself saves her aggravation.

I grabbed a can of Coke from the refrigerator, popped it open, and took a long drink. Then I sat by the table, flipped open the hamper, and started sorting clothes. I threw pants in one pile, shirts, underwear, and socks in another. I shy away from white underwear and white socks, which do nothing more for me than create an extra load. I sighed wearily at the amount of clothes I had to wash.

I took the pile of pants into the utility room and dropped them on the floor, then I opened the washer, poured a scoop of detergent from the box we kept handy, and set the dial to NORMAL. I then started to arrange the pants tastefully around the agitator. When I got to the black denim pants I'd worn to the bar on Friday night, I pushed them into the washer, which was filling with water, and in doing so happened to touch the left pocket. To my surprise, it felt like something was in there.

I was puzzled because being right-handed I almost never stick anything in my left pocket. I pulled the pants out of the washer, their legs, which had already gotten wet, slapping against my bare calves, and stuck my hand in the pocket. What was there felt like cardboard of some sort. I pulled the object out, and when I saw what it was, I let the pants slip to the floor, and I almost followed them. All the strength seemed to have gone out of my legs.

There in my hand was a matchbook. A matchbook with a glossy red cover. The matches with which Victor Hacheck had lit my cigarette.

SEVEN

Victor Hacheck did not give me his matches, I didn't take them, and therefore I could not have them. And yet there they were. Looking down at the little red object in my hand I had a sudden, overwhelming sense of dread: I finally realized a little too late that I had been targeted for the right reasons, and it had somehow been more comforting to think it had been a mistake. I suddenly felt like a sitting duck—as if all the foreign agents in the country were about to converge on our utility room with machine guns drawn. I tore through the kitchen and living room, up the stairs, and ran into our bedroom. Peter had rolled over on top of the covers but was still asleep. In my panicked state I barely noticed how cute he looked in his khaki boxers. I leapt on the bed and shook him.

"Wake up!" I said in an intense whisper.

"Whaaaa?" he said by way of reply, his eyes opening to slits.

"Wake up!"

"Whaaa?"

I knew I would get nowhere with him until he was able to put the "t" on the end of the word, so I shook his shoulders harder, bouncing him on the bed, and whispered even more loudly, "Wake up!"

"What?" he said.

Success.

"I've got to show you something! Wake up!"

"What is it? What time is it?" he said, turning over and pulling himself up to a half-sitting position with some effort.

"It's almost seven-thirty. That's not important. Look!" I shoved the matchbook at him.

Through his tired eyes, he managed to look at me as if I were completely out of my mind.

"Yeah?"

"This was in my pocket. The pocket of the pants I wore to the bar the other night."

"Um-hmm?"

"It's the matchbook. The one that guy—that Victor Hacheck guy in the bar—used to light my cigarette."

Peter took the matchbook in his hand, turned it over, then said, "I thought you said he didn't give you anything."

"He didn't! I don't know how it got there."

"You mean he stuck that in your pocket and you didn't notice?" he said, curling his lip.

"For God's sake, there were a zillion people in that bar! I was bumped and jostled every two seconds! I could've had sex with somebody without knowing it."

"Yeah, right," said Peter, curling his lip a little more.

"Oh, God!" I said, sinking onto the bed. "What a horrible thought."

"What?"

"I'd just like to think that if somebody was tooling around in my pants, I'd notice it. Now I know how people get their pockets picked."

"Except something wasn't taken out of your pocket, something was put in," said Peter pointedly as he handed the matchbook back to me. "Did you open it?"

"No."

We both looked at the matchbook as if we were sure it was booby trapped, and we hadn't a clue how to disarm it. Finally Peter said, with a decided lack of confidence, "Go ahead and open it, it isn't gonna bite."

I let the matchbook lie flat in my left hand and stared at it. After a moment's contemplation, having decided that Peter was most likely right and there wouldn't be a bomb inside something that was supposed to be carrying information, I reached down with my right thumb and flipped it open. I continued to stare down at the open matchbook, and Peter craned his neck over to see what we had found: absolutely nothing. Half of the matches had been used, and the remaining ones looked perfectly normal. The cardboard casing was completely clear and unmarked.

I don't know what I'd expected to find there, but I can admit with some embarrassment that after a lifetime of watching movies from the forties, I really expected some code, or a series of indecipherable numbers, or names, or *something* on the inside of the cover, even if it was just the phone number of a trick the guy had met at the goddamn bar. But nothing! That was a blow. But one thing was now clear: I hadn't noticed the matchbook being slipped into my pocket, but the clay people could have seen him do it, so they weren't simply being insane when they said they saw him give it to me. I don't know why I found that comforting, since I was holding in my hand something that at least one man had been killed for.

There was a knock on our bedroom door, and Mother called softly, "Boys, is everything all right?" You would have thought we were having a sleep over.

Peter called, "Come in," and in she came, this time in a blue satin kimono with a silver dragon on each side of the chest, so they looked like demonic geckos clinging to her breasts.

"I heard a lot of noise. Is everything all right?"

I hopped off the bed and showed her what I'd found. She took it in her hand, stared at it, and turned it over with her thumb.

"A matchbook?"

"Not *a* matchbook," I said with exasperation. "*The* match-book!"

Mother looked back down at the bright red object, her expression changing from perplexity to scorn.

"I must say this isn't very impressive."

"Oh, for God's sake!" I snapped, snatching it back from her. "I don't give a damn how impressive it looks, this is what this cloak-and-dagger nonsense is all about! This is what Victor Hacheck was killed for!"

"Well, what do you intend to do about it?"

"We were just getting to that when you came in," said Peter as he climbed out of bed. He retrieved a rumpled T-shirt from the floor and pulled it on.

"I don't think it really wants discussion," said Mother pointedly. "I think we need to get it out of the house."

"Now that we know we've got the damn thing, we can just call that Martin guy from the CIA and hand it over," said Peter.

"Right," Mother added, looking at me as if she were just daring me to disagree.

"No," I said.

"What?" She looked aghast.

"No, I'm not calling anyone. I agree we need to get this thing out of the house, but I mean straight out. I'm not going to call Mr. Martin, I'm going to take the damn thing down to him."

"You don't know where he is," said Peter.

"He's in the CIA. He has to be in the Federal Building. Where the hell else would the CIA be?"

Mother screwed her face up into a question, her eyebrows arching to little points in their middles, and she said, "Why not just call the man and have him come and get the thing?"

"Because I don't want to take the chance . . . ," I replied. I looked down at the matchbook in my hand, and thought for a moment, trying to get my ideas in order so I could put them clearly, then continued: "Look, from what Martin said when I called him yesterday, it looked like everybody concerned was satisfied . . . at least, would be satisfied . . . that Hacheck hadn't

71

passed anything to me and we aren't involved. But who knows if our phone is tapped—I realize how paranoid this sounds—but what if our phone is tapped, or somebody's still watching the house or something? I don't want to take the chance. I don't want anybody outside the three of us—not even Martin—to know that I have this thing until I hand it over to him myself at his office, not here."

"Well," said Mother, a gleam in her eye that I could've sworn had some pride in it, "if you're going unto the breach again, I'll be going with you."

"The hell you will!" I said.

She just smiled.

In the end I had to capitulate, because there is no arguing with Mother once her mind is made up. Peter had really wanted to call in sick or take the day off to come with us, but I nixed that idea, because no matter what we'd been through in the past couple of days, it seemed excessive for three of us to carry a matchbook to the Federal Building. However, he wouldn't let us go without first extracting our promise that we would call him the minute we got home. So Peter got dressed and headed off to work, and Mother and I headed for the Loop in a cab.

The Federal Building is a tall, dark, steel-and-glass structure located way at the south end of the Loop on Dearborn. It's another one of Chicago's famous Mies van der Rohe buildings, and is supposed to express simplicity of design, but to me it looks exactly like what it is: a big, ugly office building.

We slipped through one of the revolving doors and went to a huge building directory. I was surprised to find that the CIA was not listed, but then, when I gave it a little thought, it seemed to make sense given how secretive they are. On the other hand, I couldn't imagine why you'd have an office if you didn't want anyone to find it.

Mother stopped a blue-uniformed guard and asked where the office of the CIA was. The guard blinked her large eyes at Mother and turned her head sideways for a glance at me, as if she'd like to get a good eyeful of anyone who'd be looking for the CIA. She pointed us to the second bank of elevators, and gave us the number of an office on the 17th floor.

We rode in silence up to the appointed floor in an elevator full of people who I thought should look a hell of a lot more shifty than they did. I don't know why I thought the Federal Building should be filled with anything other than run-of-the-mill office workers, but somehow, that's what I expected.

The doors slid open with a slight rattle on the seventeenth floor, and Mother and I stepped out and followed an endless, sterile hallway around the interior of the building until we found the office number the guard had given us. We entered to find a middle-aged secretary seated behind an industrial-gray metal desk, pouring over a report of some sort. Her unnaturally blond hair was piled up on her head in a way that I'm sure required a lethal dose of Aqua Net. There were deep crow's feet sloping from the corners of her eyes across her cheeks, and even deeper creases across her forehead. As we crossed the threshold, her head snapped up from the report and her eyes fastened on us. Her eyes were large, brown, and sunken, as if the years of taking in secrets had pushed them farther back into her head. She stared at us as if she were logging our faces for future reference.

"Yes?" she said in a phlegmy voice.

"We're here to see Mr. Martin. James Martin," I said.

She paused and ran her eyes up and down the length of me in a way that made me feel as if my fly was open and Little Alex had flopped out unawares.

"You don't have an appointment."

"No," I said, trying to sound cagey, "but all you have to do is tell him my name, and he'll see us."

The woman sucked in the right corner of her mouth. "And your name would be?"

"Alex Reynolds." Despite my attempt to sound forceful, my name sounded incredibly foolish to me at that particular point.

The secretary stared me in the face for a few more moments, then without removing her eyes from mine, she picked up the receiver of the phone on her desk and pressed a button. I could hear a buzz from behind the door to the left of her desk. A man's voice clacked in her ear.

"Yes. Sorry, sir. There is someone here to see you."

More clacking.

"I know. He says you'll want to see him. He says his name is Alex Reynolds."

There was no more clacking. That little moment of silence did my heart proud, because for that slight pause I thought, well, for once someone's one-upped a CIA man—he's probably really surprised that we came here.

The little silence was broken by a few words hastily babbled through the receiver into the secretary's ear. She smiled, and I half expected her to display fangs. As she rose from her chair, she looked at Mother and said, "And your name would be?"

"Jean Reynolds." She tried to sound sure of herself, but her widened eyes showed that she felt out of her element.

The secretary swung open the door to the inner office, called in "Jean and Alex Reynolds," and motioned for us to go in.

As we passed into the inner office, the secretary closed the door behind us with a thud that put me in mind of prison bars closing in James Cagney movies.

Both Mother and I stopped in our tracks, our mouths dropping open, as the man rose to greet us, without moving from behind his desk.

"I'm sorry, Mr. Reynolds," he said pleasantly, "but I don't believe I know you."

It was not James Martin.

EIGHT

On the desk there was a nameplate that looked heavy enough to be used as a weapon if need be. It had a textured black background with raised brass letters that spelled out JAMES MARTIN. But the man who stood before us was not the man who'd come to our house. This guy looked like a senator from one of the southern states: his hair was mostly gray and mostly out of place, though he had apparently used some sort of grease in an attempt to keep it combed back. His eyes were blue and bulgy, and he had a paunch that his belt was straining to hold in. He looked like he'd be inclined to bluster. He wore a white shirt with light gray suit pants, and the jacket was draped over the back of his chair. His tie was loosened and askew, and he didn't bother to even attempt to put it back in order. It was evident that our interruption was not important.

"Mr. Martin?" I said incredulously.

"Yes?"

"Mr. James Martin?"

"Yes," he said, eyeing me with a smile, as if he suspected I was the village idiot.

"Excuse me, but this is the CIA office, isn't it?"

"Yes, it is."

I looked at him for a moment, then said, "Now this is going to sound like a *really* stupid question, but there couldn't be another James Martin working in this office, could there?"

"Now look, young man—"

"Forgive me," said Mother, heading him off, "but you're not exactly what my son and I were expecting to find here."

This was one of those moments when he looked as if he might bluster. He eyes bugged farther out at my mother, and he started to say something, stopped, then apparently decided to say something else: "Who were you expecting?"

Mother narrowed her eyes suspiciously, as if she wasn't quite sure who was trying to fool whom, and replied, "I was expecting to find the man who came to our house Saturday, calling himself James Martin and saying he was from the CIA."

"Is it possible," I said, cutting in, "that you have another agent here in Chicago—I mean someone not working in this office—who has the same name as you?"

"An agent? Young man, there isn't a CIA office in Chicago."

I stared at him blankly for a moment, then waving my hands at the surroundings, said, "What's *this?*"

"This isn't an actual CIA office, this is a recruitment office."

"A what?"

"A recruitment office. We're here to screen possible recruits from this area for the CIA. And as far as staff goes, you've seen it all: me and my secretary out there are all there is."

"Then where is the CIA?"

"In Washington," he said, his tone implying that I did not have sufficient brain power to be talking to him.

"So you're telling us that no agents from the CIA are working here in Chicago?"

"No, I'm telling you that if there was, I wouldn't know anything about it. They'd be working out of Washington."

Mother stiffened her spine, crossed her arms, and gave the man her sternest look. "Mr. Martin, someone came to our house and said he was James Martin from the CIA. Now, don't you think that's a little odd?"

He clucked his tongue disgustedly, dropped into the swivel chair behind the desk so roughly that it let out a couple of loud, protesting cracks, and waved a hand ungraciously at the two slightly padded seats facing him. Mother and I sat.

Martin's desk was of the same industrial design as the secretary's, but slightly larger, which I assume was some sort of status symbol. It was covered with a mass of papers, and on the left-hand corner was perched an antiquated computer that looked like it had never been given the most cursory swipe with a dust cloth: there was hardly an inch of it that didn't have some sort of dark smudge or fingerprint.

"I like to think my name's unique," he said with a smarmy senatorial smile as he typed something on the keyboard, "but it's not. It's pretty common. It's not beyond possibility that there's another James Martin out there."

He typed something else and hit the "enter" key, then sat back in his chair.

"This may take a few minutes."

He entwined his fingers behind his head, revealing large and very unlovely damp stains under his arms. He didn't seem to be the least self-conscious about them. He rocked in his chair and smiled at us, as if waiting for an answer from the computer were some form of torture that he thought surely would make us crack. After a couple of minutes there was a beep. He glanced at the green letters on the computer screen, and his smile immediately became a frown through which he emitted a sound that was something like "hmmph."

He sat up quickly and hit the "enter" key again, his bushy gray eyebrows knitting.

"Well, that's kinda . . . I wouldn't have expected that."

"What?" said Mother flatly.

"It looks like I'm it."

"You're what?" said Mother with marked patience.

He looked her square in the eye and said, "The only James Martin in the CIA. Well, that's a puzzle, ain't it?"

Mother and I glanced at each other. It crossed my mind that *this* James Martin seemed less the CIA type than the fake one had. But then again, for all we knew, a recruitment officer might be nothing more than a regular personnel employee.

Mother turned back to him and said, "There really is something very odd going on here."

"Well, maybe you could tell me what this man who said he was me wanted."

I looked at Mother and said, "Well?"

"Go ahead, darling," she said. "After all, this *is* the Federal Building so I suppose we can assume that this man is who he says he is"—she cast a doubtful glance in his direction—"at least we can *assume* that this one actually works for the CIA."

I took a deep breath and launched into the story from the beginning, which Martin punctuated with an occasional "hmmph." I stopped just short of telling him about the matchbook, which was in the left pocket of my jeans. Mother gave me a glance that told me she approved, and we both turned back to Martin, our eyebrows arching question marks in our familial way.

"That's it?" said Martin gruffly.

"Pardon me, but isn't that enough?" said Mother.

Martin pushed himself back from his desk with a little squeak of his chair's wheels, but he didn't rise: he simply folded his hands in his lap, pressing his thumbs together.

"It's not quite enough," he said, watching the actions of his thumbs as if they belonged to someone else. "It doesn't explain why you felt the need to see this man who called himself Martin today."

Well, I thought, if he was smart enough to get that, then I supposed it was all right to go on to the discovery of the matchbook.

"Where is it?" he said when I'd finished.

I pulled it out of my pocket and handed it to him. He took it in his right hand, stared down at it, then reached over with his left and turned it over. He let out another "hmmph" and flipped it open. He didn't seem very impressed.

"This doesn't look like too much to me," he said at last, tossing the matchbook onto his desk.

"Well, there must be something to it," said Mother, who apparently was no longer able to hide her exasperation, "or we wouldn't have been followed and everything."

He glanced up at her and said, "You were followed here?"

"Oh . . . no, no, I don't think so. But I mean, we were followed at the zoo and all, and our house was turned upside down."

He made a little sucking sound through his lips, then said, "Frankly, Ms. Reynolds, your whole story sounds kind of . . . kind of . . ."

"I might hazard to say," she said evenly, "that it is no more bizarre than the rest of what goes on in the CIA on a daily basis. Perhaps your actual agents are more accustomed to these kinds of goings on."

That one really hit home: you could see it on Martin's face. It occurred to me at that point that perhaps being a personnel person at the CIA was a pretty lowly position, no matter how important doing background checks on potential agents might be. After a moment, he recovered himself. He scratched the back of his head and clucked his tongue.

"I suppose you're right, ma'am," he said with every indication of having been properly put in his place. "I suppose I should get on to one of our people in Washington and have them check it out."

"I should think so," said Mother firmly, not yet willing to let him off the hook, "If nothing else, I should think you'd want to find out who this person is who is claiming to be you!"

"Yeah, there's that, too," said Martin slowly. "Then again, that's the part of your story that makes the least sense to me. Now how could this fella know that you wouldn't come here and find out he was lying about who he was?"

"Oh, that's easy!" I said, and a glance from my mother let me know that I sounded a little too willing to give out information.

"He gave us his phone number. You see, we came down here without calling because we didn't want anybody to know that we'd found this damned matchbook until we got rid of it. I'm sure he never expected us to do that."

"Well, that's the one thing I *can* do right away," he said, scooping the matchbook off the desk and shoving it in a drawer. "I can take custody of this thing while I check this whole thing out."

I don't know, but the offhand way he did it really did not inspire confidence.

"Now you say he gave you his phone number?"

"Uh huh."

"You got it?"

I reached into my pocket, pulled out the crumpled and now soggy slip of paper on which the bogus Martin had scribbled his phone number, and handed it to the real Mr. Martin.

"Good! Maybe we can track him down through this," he said, pushing back his chair and rising. He pulled open the top left-hand drawer of his desk, withdrew a business card, and handed it to me. "Now, I'll see what I can do to sort this whole matter out, and I'll look into whoever this fella is. If he *is* one of ours, I'll see to it that you're not bothered again. And if he isn't one of ours . . . well, we'll see what we can do to make sure you're not bothered again, anyway. Now don't you worry."

"It's rather difficult not to worry," said Mother pointedly, "after all that's happened."

Martin gave a patronizing laugh and put his sweaty palm on my mother's shoulder. Mother gave a little shudder which Martin apparently didn't notice.

"It'll all be sorted out soon. You leave your address and phone number with my secretary, just in case we need to get in touch with you. I promise you we'll get it taken care of."

"When?" said Mother, still not letting him off.

"Why, as soon as possible, ma'am."

"Well, that was rather flat," said Mother with typical British understatement as we climbed into a cab.

"What were you expecting? That we'd be suddenly inducted into the CIA hall of fame?"

"No," said Mother down her nose, "but I thought at least he'd know what we were talking about. You can't imagine how safe it makes me feel to know that the CIA doesn't know what the CIA is doing."

The words to an old hymn went through my mind when she said that, "As it was in the beginning, is now and ever shall be, world without end, amen, amen."

"Oh, Jesus! I just thought of something."

"I hate it when you swear like that," said Mother, puckering her face at me. "What is it?"

"Well, it's just that if that bogus Martin is truly a fake, then he might be working with the clay people. And if that's true, then *he* might have been the one who killed Hacheck."

"But he traced you through the number of the cab you caught—how could he have done that if he was busy killing this fellow?"

"I *know* that the clay people followed me—they could've given it to him."

"Oh, Lor'," said Mother plaintively, "it inspires even less confidence in our judgment to know we've entertained a murderer unawares."

I couldn't disagree with her on that one.

When we arrived home, I fulfilled our promise to Peter and called him at the store and filled him in on what had happened. Peter is not a very responsive person on the phone, and the lack of feedback from him was kind of unnerving after the way the morning had gone. When I finished relating our meeting with the real Mr. Martin to him, there was a dead silence on the line, which was finally broken by the sound of my husband clucking his tongue.

"I don't like it, Alex."

"Who does?" I said irritably.

"None of it sounds right."

"I realize that, but what can we do? It's been taken out of our hands, and to tell you the truth, I'm relieved. . . ."

I could almost hear Peter smile over the phone. There was a pregnant pause, and then he said with purposefully infused skepticism, "Really?"

"Yes. I'm . . . relieved. I just wish . . ."

"Yes?" his voice came through the receiver, still smiling.

"I just wish I didn't feel like such a goddamn loose end. I feel like I left a movie in the middle."

"I know," he said softly.

I was silent for a moment, then added halfheartedly, "But I feel safe."

"I'm hip."

The afternoon proved to be pretty much what you'd expect. Mother set about with her usual housecleaning, which had been shunted aside by necessity with my finding the matchbook and our subsequent trip downtown. I had a sandwich and watched her through the propped-open kitchen door. There was a definite lack of enthusiasm in the way she moved around the living room dusting, humming to herself in the most dispirited way. I was surprised to realize that her spirits had been dampened by our visit to the CIA, and it really made me wonder about the two of us. I mean, I think we like a little bit of excitement in our lives, just like any normal human beings, but the way we were feeling now, you would think we were getting rather vulgar in the thrill-seeking department.

I tossed the remainder of my sandwich in the garbage can, and felt thoroughly disgusted with myself. I passed through the living room on my way upstairs, and was glad to note that Mother's humming was becoming peppier. She's naturally resilient.

I went to my little studio on the second floor, where some of my rough sketches of ideas for that idiot association's flier were lying on the table next to a large booklet outlining the corporate standards to which I had to adhere on this little project. I had not yet been able to make it through the booklet since it was about as exciting as eating sand, but I thought this was as good a time as any to try to apply myself to my work. I flipped it open and began reading from where I'd left off: an odious chapter on the corporate colors and the corporate logo and the corporate typeface and how they could be used and couldn't be used and should be used on all corporate publications. All a bit too *Mein Kampf* for comfort.

Fortunately, my reading was interrupted by the phone. After a brief pause, Mother called up the stairs in a tone that had almost regained its normal musical qualities, "Alex, it's for you. It's someone named Jo."

I called down, "I'll pick it up," and trotted into my bedroom to get the phone on the nightstand by the bed.

"Hello?" I said over the click of Mother hanging up the downstairs receiver.

"Alex! That you?"

"Yeah, how are you doing?"

"*I'm* doing fine," she said flatly. "What the hell's wrong with you?"

"What do you mean?"

"You sound like your cat just died or something."

I really hate it when someone you don't know all that well seems to be able to read your mood.

"No, I'm all right. Everything's fine. I was just working. . . ."

"Sorry, I didn't mean to interrupt," she said with a sharp note in her voice.

"It's all right. I think it was putting me to sleep. That's why I sound . . ."

"Never mind," she said. "Did you ever catch up with your little friend?"

"Huh?"

"Your little friend. The one you chased out of the bar the other night."

"Oh! Oh, no. But it's not important any more. I don't really need to talk to him."

"You're shittin' me! After all the trouble I went through to find him?"

"Huh?"

There was a brief pause, then Jo exhaled sharply and said, "Alex, are you sure you're awake?"

"Yeah, yeah, I'm sorry."

"I hope you still want to know where he is, because I've been going through my goddamn receipts all morning, you know?"

"Oh, yeah, thanks." God, I really did sound like I'd just woken up. I shook my head briskly to clear it.

"Well, I was right, his name is Jerry Lasker, and here's the info. . . ," she said, her tone of voice clearly implying that she felt she'd wasted her time helping us out.

I grabbed the stub of a pencil on the nightstand and scribbled the address and phone number on a little pad as she read them to me. When she was through, I said, "Thanks. This'll really help us out. Thanks."

"Yeah, right," she said. "You owe me a beer. No, you owe me two beers. And you owe Sheila one, too."

"Sheila? What did she do?"

Jo heaved a very heavy sigh into the receiver, obviously exasperated that I would miss something that was supposed to be a joke, and said, "She sat by and listened to me bitch you out while I went through these goddamn piles of receipts!"

When Peter arrived home at about five, I was starving—more from the letdown than from actual hunger. Peter was upstairs changing and Mother had just started dinner when the doorbell rang. I performed Mother's usual routine of peeking through the living room window at the caller before opening the door, and let out an audible gasp when I saw that the person on our doorstep was none other than the real James Martin, the one from the CIA recruitment office.

Mother came into the room when she heard me, and I opened the door and let him in.

"Mr. Martin . . . ," I started to say, but he walked by me brusquely, at full tilt both physically and orally.

"I'm afraid we got a problem here," he said, stopping in the center of the room and looking from my mother to me.

"What is it?" said Mother.

"You think we could sit down?" he said, then looking about the room, he added, "And you think we could have those curtains closed?"

"Now, really Mr. Martin . . . ," said Mother, her expression clearly saying that she was a bit tired of the cloak-and-dagger attitude these people had a habit of adopting.

"It is important, ma'am," he said, with a little tilt of his head as if he would have liked to defer to a woman if it had been a less important occasion. "I know this may all sound pretty silly to you, but it is important."

Mother crossed to the front windows with a reluctance in her step that I knew was meant to convey that she felt she was humoring an overaged adolescent. I ushered Martin onto the couch, where his bogus counterpart had been seated just two days earlier.

Peter came down the stairs at that point, dressed in jeans and a blue denim shirt, and I introduced him to the real Mr. Martin. Peter shook his hand in the most desultory fashion and took a chair by the coffee table.

When Mother had drawn the long tan curtains, she joined us.

"What is the problem, Mr. Martin?"

He took a deep breath and rolled his eyes, as if he knew we weren't going to like what we were about to hear and wanted us to know that he wasn't responsible for it.

"Well, I've talked to our boys out there in Washington, and they wanted me to come and talk to you."

"What about?" I interjected. "I mean, I thought our part in this was over."

"I'd like to say it is, but it isn't really," he replied.

"Oh, come on," I said, "you've got the damn matchbook. What the fuck do you want now?"

Mother looked like she would have corrected me under normal circumstances, and the fact that she didn't told me that she must be really fed up with the feds.

Martin sighed heavily and said, "I can understand . . . I can understand how you feel that way, I surely can. But you see, the thing is . . . it kind of goes deeper than you thought—or that I knew about."

"So what?" I said, though I was interested. "I don't see how that affects us."

He sighed again, and his manner became very apologetic. "The fact of the matter is, it doesn't affect you, directly. But the thing is, you can really help us out."

"How?" said Mother, her brow furrowing.

"Well . . . it seems that we do have some boys here working on something."

"Then maybe this other Martin is the real thing," said Mother.

Martin shook his head, "No, no—that's just it. There isn't any James Martin involved. I was right about that—I'm the only one with that name in the CIA. The Washington boys contacted the boys that are working here, and they came in to see me this afternoon. Seems they don't know who this guy is who's saying he's me, and they want to find out."

"What about the phone number?"

"It's a cellular phone. It gave them a name—probably false—and they have no way of knowing where he's hiding. Or staying."

"So what does this have to do with us?" said Peter, who was obviously liking this less and less by the minute.

"Well, they all had a good long talk about the situation in my office, and they came to a decision."

Martin stopped at this point, apparently more for effect than anything else. He had, however, chosen the wrong audience: none of us was impressed and the pause only served to irritate us further.

"What?" Peter finally snapped.

Martin's head swiveled around to face me. "They decided that it would be best if you contacted him for us."

"What!" said Mother, jumping to her feet. "The bloody hell he will! I'll not hear of it!"

"Mrs. Reynolds. . . ," said Martin, palms up, placating.

"I'll have none of it!" She moved toward him, towering over his plumpish, seated figure. "You people are supposed to be trained . . . prepared for this sort of thing! You're the professionals! You can't expect my son to place himself in jeopardy on your behalf. You take care of this yourself!"

"Ma'am," he said, in a tone that I can only describe as Southern-condescending, "one man has already been killed, probably by this impostor. We need to get a line on him."

"Then do it!" Mother snapped. "That's your business."

"Mother, please. . . ," I said calmly, "let's at least hear what he wants me to do."

She looked at me a moment and I thought she was going to let me have it, but instead, to my surprise, she smiled.

"Very well," she said, tilting her nose toward the ceiling as she lowered herself primly back into her chair. She nodded benevolently at Martin and said, "Go ahead."

Martin looked at her doubtfully, then turned to me. "What the boys would like you to do is to call this impostor, this Martin fella. He gave you his number and everything, so he probably won't take it amiss that you call him. We need you to call him and tell him you want to meet him—"

Peter interrupted, "Now wait a minute—"

"Peter," I said, cutting him off. I was really getting tired of people speaking for me. "He didn't say I have to meet this guy, just that I'd have to make the call." I turned back to Martin and said, "Right?"

Martin hesitated a minute, took a stained handkerchief from his back pocket, and wiped his forehead. "Well, I'll come to that in a minute."

I must say that took me aback. All three of us stared at Martin as if he were someone who was bound to make an ass of himself at a party. He stuck the handkerchief back in his pocket and looked at me.

"We want you to tell him you'll meet him at ten o'clock tonight, but not here. Tell him you want to meet him on Kingsbury Street, under the expressway. You know, the Ontario Street overpass."

"Now wait a minute," I said, stopping Peter in the very act of saying the same thing. "Why would I want him to do that? And why would he do that if I wanted him to?"

"Our agents have that all worked out. Just tell him that you've found what he was looking for. Tell him you found it and you want to turn it over to him, but you don't want him to come to the house."

"That's just what I mean—he's already been to the house. Why wouldn't I want him to come here?"

Martin sighed heavily again, this time apparently to convey that I was being a little too slow for his liking. "For the same reason you came down to my office—because you don't want any trouble at your house, because you don't want the CIA there again. If you do it right, he'll buy it." He smiled in a way that was meant to be self-effacing. "I did."

"Why don't *you* want him to come here? Wouldn't it be easier to take him—or capture him or whatever you want to call it—here?"

"No, we want to do this outside of a residential area . . . just in case there's any trouble."

"Any trouble?" said Mother in a tone of impending doom.

Martin retrieved his handkerchief again and wiped the back of his neck. As damp as the little piece of cloth was already, it did little more than smear the sweat around.

"This is why I'm in personnel. I'm not cut out for this type of work!" He put his handkerchief back again and smiled sheepishly at Mother. "Yes, ma'am, in case there's any trouble. And that means just what you'd expect it to mean."

"I daresay," said Mother.

I said, "So what you're saying is you want me to call him and send him over there to be captured by the CIA."

"That's exactly right," he said, eagerly nodding. I knew we

would soon be seeing his handkerchief again, as a line of large droplets of sweat had reappeared on his forehead to replace the ones he'd wiped away earlier.

"And nothing else?" said Peter skeptically.

"Well. . . ," he said slowly, "I'm afraid this is where it gets a little stickier."

"It couldn't possibly," said Mother.

Martin hesitated for a moment, looking at each of them in turn and then finally settling his eyes on my mother. "We'd like your son to go there to meet him."

"Absolutely out of the question!" said Mother with finality.

"Mother . . ."

"Don't mother me," she said, then turned to Martin and said rapidly, "You say yourself that it's potentially dangerous. That's why you want this 'meeting' to be away from the house, isn't it? In case . . . some sort of gunfire breaks out, or worse? Do you think for one minute that I'd let my son go into a situation like that?"

Martin was watching her with what I took to be a mixture of understanding and helplessness. I felt that it was time for me to rescue whatever might be left of my manhood. There was something about having my mother face up to the feds for me that made me feel as if my balls had dropped off and rolled under the table.

"Mother, it's really not your decision to make," I said as gently as I knew how.

"I mean," said Martin, the handkerchief reappearing as I feared it would, "we could just have your son call and set up the meeting, then try to nab him when he came there, but what would we have? No proof of anything. With your son there, we'd have more ammo. . . ."

Mother visibly cringed at this and said under her breath, "Oh, rather!"

"I mean, in convicting this guy once we have him. If he was actually seen receiving information, we could get him on more than just impersonating me . . . I mean, somebody in the CIA. But like I said, it would even help if he would just make the call."

I looked at Mother and hoped that I didn't look as childishly excited as I felt. "Besides, you and I and Peter are the only ones who know what this bogus Martin guy looks like. If I don't go, there's no telling whether they'll get the right man or not."

"There's that, too," said Martin, agreeing readily.

Mother raised an elegant eyebrow and said, "Who else would be under the Ontario Street overpass at ten o'clock at night?"

The four of us fell silent for a moment, then Peter turned to me and said, "I'm inclined to agree with your mother."

"I can assure you that he'll be as safe as if he were at home in his own bed!" said Martin, and Peter and I could not help exchanging a quick, amused glance.

Martin noticed this and added, "What I mean to say is, we'll have the area under surveillance at every moment. All you need to do is make the contact and we'll move in."

"With guns drawn," said Mother wryly.

I could tell Martin was losing patience with the lot of us when he looked at Mother and said, "It usually works best that way."

"It's all right," I said to Mother, then turned to Martin. "I'll do it."

Martin smiled broadly, wiped his brow with his now soaked and sodden handkerchief, and said, "You'll be doing your country a great service."

"You have no idea how happy I am to hear that," I intoned.

A few minutes later I was at the phone, with the now withered piece of paper that had just been returned to me. Mother, Peter, and Martin hovered so close by that I thought I was in imminent danger of developing a chafed neck.

I dialed the number and the phone was almost immediately answered by the bogus Mr. Martin.

"Yes?"

"This is Alex Reynolds."

"Yes?"

"I . . . I've found something. I think it's what you've been looking for."

"What is it?"

I don't know why, but this was not the response I was expecting. I said, "A matchbook."

There was a noticeable hesitation before he replied, "A matchbook?"

"Yes," I said, for some reason feeling the need to impress upon him that this was important. "It's the matchbook that Victor Hacheck used to light my cigarette at the bar. He must've slipped it in my pocket somehow without my knowing it."

"You're sure it's the same one?"

"It's very distinctive."

Through the receiver, I heard the bogus Martin take a deep breath, then as he exhaled he said, "I'll come right over and get it."

"No!" I said too loudly.

There was another slight hesitation, then he said, "No?"

"No. I . . . I don't want anyone to come here. I don't want anybody else—the CIA or anything to come here. We've had too much trouble already. I'll bring it to you . . . I mean I'll meet you."

I knew I was doing this badly, and I looked at the real Mr. Martin, standing there in our living room, and grimaced. He simply motioned for me to go on; Peter shrugged at me, the elegant movement of his shoulders and the twinkle in his eye reminded me that I had something to live for; Mother just looked worried.

"I'll meet you somewhere."

After a pause, the voice on the phone said, "Why?"

I thought perhaps that sounding angry would make the scenario sound more plausible. So I attempted that as I said, "Because after everything that's happened to us I don't want anybody else connected with this to come near our house again. I have to think of the safety of my family. . . ."

Mother rolled her eyes.

"So I don't want you near here. I'll bring it to you. Somewhere out in the open."

I explained to him that I would meet him on Kingsbury Street under the Ontario Street overpass. There was a lengthy pause, during which I assumed that the bogus Martin was coming to some sort of conclusion. When he responded, I was shocked at his tone of voice: he sounded amused.

"All right," he said, "and when would you like to meet?"

"When would I like to meet you?" I repeated loudly, looking at the real Mr. Martin. He silently mouthed "ten o'clock" at me.

"Ten o'clock," I said into the receiver, mentally kicking myself for not having remembered this.

"Fine," said the bogus Martin as calmly as if he were making a date for dinner. "Till then." And he hung up.

I turned to the three anxiously waiting faces and said, "It's all set. I'm meeting him there at ten o'clock."

"Good . . . great!" said Martin, stuffing his handkerchief into his back pocket and heading for the door, much to the amazement of our little family.

"Where are you going?" said Mother.

Martin looked at us in what should have been confusion but looked a little more like fear to me. "Home."

"Surely you're going to go with Alex to this . . . this meeting he's just set up."

Martin looked both startled and afraid. It didn't inspire confidence in someone who had just set up a clandestine meeting with a spy in what amounts to a dark alley.

"Oh, no, no," said Martin rapidly. "You remember, I'm not any sort of agent—I'm just personnel. I was just asked by the agent boys to set this up with you because I'd already met you. But I'm not supposed to be involved in any way, shape, or form— that was the word from on high."

From the look on his face, it was plainly evident that he was relieved to be excluded from this particular party. My confidence was rapidly seeping out of my body through every pore. And just when I thought I'd retrieved my testicles.

"Well, that's just too bloody marvelous, in't it?" said Mother sharply.

Martin shrugged sheepishly. "All he has to do is go down there, meet that impostor, and our boys will be down on him like flies on a cheap suit—or something like that!" He was shuffling closer and closer to the front door, and I had begun to worry that if someone didn't open it for him pretty soon, he might go through it.

"I couldn't be any help there. Our boys made that clear."

Peter slipped around Martin and opened the door for him. Martin was very abject and profuse in his apologies, going on at interminable length (while still giving the impression of trying to get the hell out of our house) about how sorry he was that he would not be "in on" the sting tonight, and how all his life he'd longed to move up the CIA food chain and be where the action really was, and how he always felt cheated that the younger fellas always had all the luck and always got to have the excitement, and how he was always overlooked. He managed to pass through the door just before I thought his protestations would give him a coronary. It was a relief to be done with him.

Peter closed the door, then turned and faced me. I couldn't read his expression, which was probably because he didn't know what to think. Mother looked like she knew exactly what to think: that the setup stank.

I looked at the two of them in turn and said, "Why do I feel like I'm being led to the slaughter?"

NINE

An argument ensued in which Mother and Peter expressed their opinions of the situation. Mother was positively indignant. She believed that the CIA should be able to take care of its own problems without putting young idiots in jeopardy. She did not even have the good grace to realize what she'd just said.

Peter, on the other hand, was of the opinion that since the CIA did not recruit homosexuals, I should not have allowed myself to be drafted into their ranks. In the course of expressing his feelings on the matter, he pointed out that it was perfectly natural for the CIA to press me into play since they'd see me as "just another expendable faggot." I was able to deflect that argument by reminding him that this could be the first step in the gay integration of the CIA. He wasn't amused. His response was a withering stare as he sneered, "Oh, yes, one small step for gays, one giant flounce for the CIA!"

There was one thing on which they agreed: they were going with me. Now, this set me off, because I didn't see why they should be put in jeopardy along with me.

"Look," I said, "if we are all agreed that I'm an idiot for doing this, fine. But if I'm going to be an idiot, I'm going to do it alone.

There's no sense in putting the two of you in danger."

"Darling," said Mother, folding her arms across her chest, "you are not doing *High Noon* on location—this is not a movie—so, if I may be perfectly frank, cut the crap!"

"You're not going alone," said Peter crossly. He is awfully handsome when he's cross. The green of his eyes deepens and shines, and you feel like you could run naked through them.

I let out a laugh and said, "I don't think the CIA could bear the brunt of drafting two faggots on the same day."

"Alex . . . ," he replied, his tone warning.

I held up a hand to stop him. "Look, I agreed to do this. And if you insist on going along with me, all I'm going to do is regret my decision."

"Alex . . . ," said Mother.

"And besides, it would ruin everything. This bogus Martin is just expecting me. If he sees three people waiting for him, he really won't come."

"Huh?" said Peter.

"You know what I mean. He may think something's wrong . . . if he doesn't already."

"What do you mean?" said Mother, her brow furrowing. I suddenly realized I'd seen her forehead crease more in the past two days than I had in the past two years. It made me wonder if our foray into the secret-agenting business would line her face.

"Well, he sounded kind of . . . suspicious over the phone. I think. I'm not sure. He sounded funny. But he said he'd come. And there's going to be all those agents there, watching us. So I'll be all right. I'll be fine. Really."

The three of us stood there looking at each other for a few moments, the disagreement seeming to crackle in the air between us. Finally a smile played about Mother's lips, and I knew I'd lost.

At twenty to ten the three of us crossed the little patch of land known as our backyard, and went into the garage. Mother climbed behind the wheel of our robin's-egg-blue Honda Civic—which she said she had chosen because it brought out her eyes—

while I flipped open the garage door. She pulled the car out into the alley, and I closed the door while Peter climbed in beside her. I took the backseat. Before we left the house I had retrieved a half-used matchbook from one of our kitchen drawers, just in case I had to show the bogus Martin something before the feds closed in on him. I thought that I was showing some admirable brain-power for having thought to do that.

We went south on Halsted to Chicago Avenue, then turned left and headed for Kingsbury. There was a dead silence in the car as we proceeded on our way. The absurdity of being driven to a government sting by my mother did not escape me. Had we discussed the matter with the real Mr. Martin before he'd so unceremoniously fled as if we were some sort of pariah, I'm sure that he would have at least attempted to veto the idea of my being accompanied to the site. Then again, it is better all the way around that we didn't get to discuss it with him, since the outcome would have been the same, with the additional wasted breath.

Mother hung a right at Kingsbury, the street which runs through old and new warehouses alongside the north leg of the Chicago River. Though we were silent, I'm sure they noticed, as I did, that the lighting on this street wasn't exactly on a par with the city's major arteries: a fact that did nothing to help my flagging confidence. In the distance the Ontario Street overpass loomed, a broad expanse of darkness beneath it. We continued slowly down the diagonal street, until Mother pulled to the side of the road, beside one of the newer and better-lighted buildings, about a block and a half north of the overpass.

Mother and Peter looked as if each thought the other should say something. For the life of me, I couldn't think of any appropriate parting words for going to meet a secret agent, so I said, "Well, I'll be back," as hopefully as I could manage and pulled the door release.

"Wait," said Mother loudly.

I hesitated and she looked at me over her shoulder with an uncharacteristic expression of foreboding on her face. We held this pose for a second, then she blurted out, "You be careful!" and grabbed my face in her hands and kissed me.

When she released me, Peter said, "Yeah, buddy. Come back to me," and he reached around, cradling the back of my head with his right hand, and gave me a kiss.

Without meaning to, my two loved ones were determined to undermine the little that remained of my courage. To save what I had left, I resorted to a mild form of anger, rolled my eyes, and said, "For Christ's sake, I'll be right back." At least I sounded confident. And as any good psychologist will tell you, sounding confident is the first step on the road to . . . what escapes me at the moment.

I popped open the car door and stepped out onto the deserted street, closing the door behind me before I had a chance to have second thoughts. I started to walk south.

The streetlights on Kingsbury are a bit more far between than the ordinary Chicago city street, probably due to the fact that nobody in their right mind would be out there late at night. There really is nothing to see. But the sparseness of the lights added considerably to the relative darkness: I say relative because the city of Chicago is never exactly dark. Even not fully lighted sections are still privy to the sort of electrified haze that hovers around the city. You have to get pretty far outside Chicago to find the total darkness of unlighted county roads. But for the urban version of darkness, this street would do much better than I cared for at the moment. And when I was about half a block away from the overpass, it crossed my mind that things were bound to get darker.

A beat-up, sea-shit-green Pinto went by me with its brights on, half blinding me. Rap music was blaring from its open windows, along with some laughter I felt was being directed at me from the unsavory characters inside. Somehow I just knew they were unsavory. They didn't stop or even slow down: they just kept going, laughing all the way.

As I continued on, another hymn was called up from the depths of the church-going upbringing I'd left behind:

Jesus walked that lonesome valley.
He had to walk it by himself.
Nobody else could walk it for him.
He had to walk it by himself.

I found myself walking in time to my mental music.

I reached the overpass, and as I had feared, this area was even darker than the street. Warehouses in various stages of disrepair border the three open sides of the area, cutting off any hope of additional light and adding to the general gloom.

The Ontario Street overpass joins with the Ohio feeder ramp to form an exit and entrance to the Kennedy Expressway. The overpass spans a good city block, and the area underneath is bisected by a row of huge, sixty-foot-wide two-foot-thick concrete support columns supporting the roadway overhead. The area underneath, not to be wasted space, is used as a parking lot. This lot was almost empty because of the late hour. Lights were mounted on each side of the overpass and between each column, but they provided faint illumination at best, even when all of them were working—and on this particular night, very few of them were.

My heart was pounding so hard I thought blood might spurt from my ears as I entered the more feral darkness under the streets. Overhead I could hear the traffic speeding on its way both out of the city and into it, like a steady bloodstream reminding me that life, if not help, was not far away. I wandered between the towering columns, wondering for a moment whether I should call out to make my presence known: it was possible that the bogus Martin was waiting behind one of the other columns. But then, I thought calling out would be worthless since if Martin were here, he would no doubt see me eventually; there certainly didn't appear to be anyone else around. My lack of preparation for my newfound employment as special agent was brought home to me when I realized that I didn't know whether it was better for me to be plainly in sight or to be hidden.

I finally stopped by the middlemost column and leaned against it, further shielded in its shadow. There were only two cars in this section of the lot, both in such dark areas that I couldn't even make out their colors. I stood there trying to appear calm while my heart gave every indication that it was going to pop out of my chest. After a while I was gripped by what is probably the most common feeling of anyone who finds himself in the situation that I was in: I felt I was being watched. From the shadows I scanned what I could see of the area. One of the warehouses was in serious disrepair and looked as if it might be on its way to being torn down. It had several broken windows, with jagged glass slicking up like livid, sharpened teeth. The other two warehouses still had their windows, but some of them were open.

The feeling of being watched shouldn't really have bothered me as much as it did, since I knew I was surrounded by CIA agents, although I had neglected to ask how many there would be. But it was unsettling: all those empty windows staring down at me like great, black eyes in the darkness. It suddenly occurred to me how vulnerable my position was.

I checked my watch—actually, it wasn't my watch, it was Peter's. I have a cheap Timex that I wear only when I have appointment to keep, but I was wearing Peter's because it had a luminous dial and because it was comforting to have something of his with me. It was ten-fifteen. I was trying not to be even more anxious because the bogus Martin was late. I tried unsuccessfully to reason with myself that he hadn't actually sounded suspicious on the phone when I set up this meeting, but I didn't convince myself. Then again, I could explain away his being late by the fact that whatever he was, if he was smart, he would be checking out the situation before he came into it. He was probably one of the people I could feel watching. And that didn't help my mounting paranoia, either. In my mind's eye I could picture that swarthy face peering at me from an unknown vantage point. I realized that I was in grave danger of creating a revisionist picture of the man, where every move and gesture he'd made on his one visit to our home was infused with a sinister quality that I knew in my heart he hadn't displayed. But now his moves seemed all the more sinister as I imagined him out here in the darkness.

The sound of the traffic overhead was interrupted by the faint sound of gravel underfoot. My heart went from unrestrained speeding to grinding to almost a complete halt. I forced myself not to peek around the column. I pressed myself further into the darkness against the column as the steps grew closer. The person approaching was definitely proceeding at a slow pace, as if he were being extremely cautious.

The steps had almost reached the column behind which I was standing, and my fingers curled and pressed against it as if they would have liked to dig firm holds into the concrete. A silhouette came slowly into view on the sidewalk at the end of the column and seemed to waver there uncertainly for a moment. I couldn't see his features in the darkness, but he was definitely pausing for some unknown reason. After a moment he turned toward the column, unzipped his pants, pulled out his organ, and relieved himself against the concrete. When he was finished, he zipped himself up and stepped back out onto the sidewalk. He looked left, then right, but didn't move.

A minute passed, and I could stand it no longer. I inched away from the column and said, "Mr. Martin?"

The figure whirled around, staggered backwards, and fell painfully to a sitting position onto a fire hydrant by the curb. I came away from the column and looked at him. In the night haze of the city I could now make out that he was quite disheveled, quite scared, and quite drunk. He also wasn't Martin.

"What? Stay away from me!" he said, his thick voice slurring the words.

"I'm so sorry!" I said, and moved to help him up, thinking that little plug on the top of the hydrant must be very painful to someone who wasn't used to that sort of thing.

"Stay away from me!" he yelled, waving a hand drunkenly in my direction as if to fend off my advance.

"I'm . . . really, really sorry! I thought you were someone else."

"Jesus Christ, you nearly scared the piss out of me!" I thought that hardly likely since he couldn't really have any left. He shook his head briskly and tried to focus his eyes on me. I was sure from the smell of him that he was not going to be successful on that point. But he seemed to focus enough to realize that I wasn't a threat to him. It must have been the look of confusion and chagrin on my face. I reached out toward him again, and he waved both of his hands at me and said, "Get away, get away! I can do it!"

I wasn't at all sure that he *could* do it, but he somehow managed to struggle to his feet and made off as fast as he could, swaying from side to side and putting out a hand to brace himself as he passed each column.

I sighed with relief as he crossed Kingsbury and disappeared from view. Then I checked Peter's watch again and it was almost ten-thirty. I really was beginning to despair of Martin's showing up at all. It was proving that I was right in my hunch: he had recognized this whole deal as a setup, and he'd either checked out the area without my knowing it and decided against entering in, or he had simply blown me off and was sitting in his comfortable, air-conditioned room somewhere, having a good chuckle by himself or with his spy friends at the thought of my waiting out here under this hot, deserted overpass. I silently cursed him.

I decided to give it ten more minutes. I figured by that time not only would I have withstood this beyond my own natural endurance, but Mother and Peter would probably be frightened out of their wits on my behalf. While the minutes slowly ticked by, I mulled over in my mind whether I should try to locate one of the CIA agents and tell them that I was giving it up. Then it crossed my mind that it was a little surprising that one of them hadn't come down from their roosts in the warehouses (if that's where they were stationed) to tell me to go home.

The second hand of the watch finally clicked over to ten-forty. I sighed heavily, mostly from relief, and stepped out of the shadows. I walked along the cracked and broken sidewalk that bordered the parking lot, past one of the huge columns, past the broad, engulfing darkness of the next section of the parking lot. When I passed the second-to-last column, I was jolted to atten-

101

tion as I was grabbed and pulled back into the shadows behind the column. An arm was fastened like a vise around my neck, something cold and hard was jabbed against my right temple, and a heavily accented voice whispered in my ear, "Cry out and you're dead!"

With one hand he grabbed my shoulder, spun me around, and slammed me back against the column, my head hitting the concrete with a dull thud that reverberated inside my skull like the last echoes of a clap of thunder. I found myself face-to-face with the larger of the two clay people.

"Where's your friend?" he demanded in an accent that I won't even try to approximate.

I blanked for a minute. "Which one?"

"You know who I mean!"

I wasn't about to tell him that Peter was just around the corner. I stammered, "I don't know."

"Never mind," he growled impatiently. "Now, where is it? Where the fuck is it?"

"Look . . . ," I said, but I was cut off as he shoved my head against the concrete column again and took two steps back from me. If I spent much more time as a special agent, my brains would be permanently dislodged. This time it wasn't a knife, it was a gun, which he leveled at my heart.

"I want to know right now what you did with what Hacheck gave you."

My mind raced. I didn't know which would put me in a worse position: if he thought I had it or if he knew I didn't have it. My mind finally latched onto one thing: we were surrounded by heavily armed CIA agents, so I didn't really have anything to worry about. Emboldened by this fact, I said, "So where's your partner?"

The right side of his mouth jaggedly curled upward, and he said, "Why, he's taking care of the rest of your little family."

Oh, God, I thought, *they* aren't surrounded by the CIA. The CIA didn't even know that Mother and Peter had driven me here. Every muscle in my body jerked forward, as if I was involuntarily propelled in the direction of our car, but the sight of the gun held me back. My thoughts must have registered on my face because the clay person waved the gun as if it were an extra head that was nodding no at me. Of course, it was then that my quickly atrophying brain realized that my position was worse than I'd thought: if he fired, the bullet would reach me before the CIA reached him.

"You don't need to worry about them any more," he said, his accented words dripping from his mouth like hot tar; "they will, by now, already have been taken care of."

"You bastard," I spat.

"We did not ask you to interfere in this business."

"I'm *not* involved in this business."

He smiled. "You're here."

It was certainly hard to argue with that one. Part of my brain was trying to decide how to proceed with this man who could certainly kill me if those damn CIA agents didn't get off their asses and get him first, and the other part was wondering if it was too late to help Mother and Peter.

"How did you know I was here?" I said at last.

His smile widened, and for the first time I saw how crooked and rotten his teeth were. In one of the most alarmingly incongruous wanderings I'd yet experienced, I wondered if everyone in his country had bad teeth. He said, "I was sent to meet you."

Oh, Jesus, I thought, that bogus fuck Martin really had known something was wrong when I called. And why shouldn't he have, I thought, berating myself for my ungodly stupidity. Why on earth, if something hadn't been up, would I have told him I wanted to meet him in this godforsaken place? Mother would have cringed if she had known how many times I managed to take the Lord's name in vain in one brief stream of thought.

"Now," he said, waving the gun at me again, "we are tired of playing these silly games with you. We want what Hacheck passed to you. We want it now."

I looked at him. If this man was to be believed, Mother and Peter were already dead. I experienced one of those internal moments of truth that nobody should ever have to face in their lives: I realized that I had nothing to lose. I decided that whether or not the CIA thought it would strengthen their case against these spies or whatever they were, I wasn't going to give this motherfucker anything.

I straightened my back, much as my mother does when she's affronted, squared my shoulders, looked this son of a bitch of a foreign clay person in the eye, and said evenly, "I have already turned it over to the CIA."

To my utter shock, he didn't threaten me or even shoot me right then, as I'd expected. His smile grew even wider, and he said, "No, you didn't."

"What?" I said, unable to hide my confusion.

His smile faded and his grip tightened on his gun. "I told you we are tired of playing your games."

"But—"

He waved the gun again and said, "You will turn it over to me or you will die."

"I told you, I turned it over to the CIA," I said, looking down my nose at him. I was astounded to find that even when about to die, I didn't like being called a liar.

"Then we must say good-bye," he said.

His thumb twitched, then moved to the hammer of the gun. He was doing it slowly, apparently enjoying himself. I tried not to look at the gun and kept my eyes on his. I thought maybe, just maybe, it would be harder for him to kill me if I looked him in the eye. His right eyebrow raised slightly as if he was surprised by my stance, but for my part it was a wasted effort. His eyes were as cold and dead as the steel of the gun, as if they had looked into the souls of many who had gone before me, and none of us had been found worthy of life.

He pulled back the hammer of the gun, and I heard the shot. Several things happened simultaneously: almost before the sound of the shot, his head flew back and there was a burst of red, like a greasy, miniature firework bursting from the back of his skull. Then his head snapped forward. He wavered for a moment on legs that were behaving as if they'd become rubberized, then dropped to the ground. If I hadn't been so shocked, I'd have cheered. I stayed pressed against the column, for a moment unable to move.

In my shock I suddenly realized that something was wrong: I mean something besides having just seen somebody get shot. I thought I should hear footsteps rushing to the scene. I mean, he was dead so I thought the G-men should be running out of the goddamn warehouses to make sure everything (by that I mean me) was all right. But all there was was silence: a silence that scared me even more.

Not wanting to make any noise myself, I slowly lowered myself to my knees. I inched my way toward the dead man, trying to stay in the slanting, darker shadow of the column. I reached out, took the gun by the barrel, and shook it from his hand. The gun felt much heavier than I expected, as if by sheer weight the weapon would remind you of its lethal nature. As quickly and quietly as I could, I slid back up against the column. There I stood for what seemed like ages but in reality was less than a minute, pressed to the concrete wall: every professional association's nightmare, a gay commercial artist with a gun.

Many things went through my mind, the most disturbing of which was the possibility that the CIA agents were not the ones who had shot this man. If that were the case, they were lying low because they didn't know where the shot had come from, and couldn't come out in the open. Then I would have a *big* problem here: I didn't know if I'd ever be able to move. It also crossed my mind that if this guy had been shot by someone other than the CIA, that person was probably down here among the columns, and my life was, as my mother used to say, not worth an hour's purchase. I started to edge my way toward the far end of the column, away from the street, when another shot rang out and nicked the edge of the column, sending out a little burst of concrete dust. That sent a veritable flood of sweat pouring down over my eyebrows, stinging my eyes.

It was at that moment that I heard an approaching car. I

quickly decided that if I could get the driver to see me, perhaps I could get him to stop. I started to make my way along the column to the street end, and panicked when I realized that the car was approaching too quickly: I didn't think I'd make it to the street before the car passed. I tried to move as fast as I could and still remain quiet, scraping my back against the concrete. My heart was beating even faster than it had when I'd waited here alone in the dark because I was sure that I'd practically have to run in front of the car to get them to see me, and when I ran out into the open, I'd be vulnerable to the sniper.

The car careened around the corner off Kingsbury just as I reached the end of the column. I braced myself to spring out into the open, and was just about to do so when, to my amazement, the driver slammed on the brakes and skidded to a stop. The back door of the blue Civic popped open, and Peter yelled, "Get in!"

"What?" I said stupidly, which I think could be excused at that moment.

"Get in!" said Peter, more forcibly.

I glanced to the left and right to see if anyone was evident, but could see nothing but those damn staring warehouse eyes. I figured that running the few feet to the car couldn't be any more dangerous than staying where I was, so after a moment's panicked hesitation, I fled across the sidewalk and threw myself into the car, pulling the door shut behind me. My feet were barely off the sidewalk before Mother gunned the motor and screeched forward.

"I thought you were dead!" I said, tears of fright welling up in my eyes. I don't think I've ever been so close to hysteria in my life.

"We thought *you* were dead," said Peter as the car sped down the street. "We heard shots, and then nothing. We thought we'd see you, or the CIA, or somebody. But there was nobody! Nothing!"

"We couldn't wait any longer, we just rushed in!" said Mother in a voice like an exhilarated gust of wind. She steered the car onto LaSalle Street and headed north, not much minding about the speed limit.

"Wait! What about the CIA? They'll want to talk to us or something," I said, somehow feeling we were going to catch shit for leaving the scene, even if the scene belonged to the feds.

"They'll know where to find us," Peter intoned. He looked back over the front seat when he said this, and even in the darkness I could tell that his face was pale.

"We're bloody well not 'anging around where shooting's going on!" said Mother. "What the bloody hell do they mean getting you involved in something where you're likely to get shot! I never should have allowed you to do it!"

"It wasn't up to you," I said breathlessly.

"Then *I* shouldn't have allowed it!" said Peter, for the first time in his life sounding more stern than my mother.

I fell back against the seat. My clothes were sopping with sweat, and I had that feeling that you get every now and then that the world is spinning a little too fast.

"For God's sake, slow down!" I said to Mother. "We don't want to get stopped by the police!"

Mother eased up a little on the gas pedal, but her hands gripped the steering wheel so tightly that her knuckles were white.

"What in the hell happened back there?" said Peter. "Did someone get shot?"

"Oh, yeah, somebody got shot all right."

"But it wasn't you. Thank God for that. Who was it? Martin?"

I sighed, and found myself curiously unable to exhale the strain I was feeling. "It was one of the goddamn clay people!"

"What?" said Mother loudly, glancing back at me in the rearview mirror.

"Martin wasn't there! It was one of the goddamn clay people. The big one."

"How in the hell—what's that?" Peter's eyes widened as he pointed to the gun which dangled from my right hand.

I looked at it for a moment, and in my present daze it took me a while to remember where I'd gotten it.

"It's a gun," I said.

"A what?!" Mother exclaimed as she stamped on the brakes, flinging the three of us forward.

"A gun."

Peter turned his saucer eyes in my direction and looked as if he didn't recognize me.

"A gun? You didn't . . ."

"No, I didn't shoot anybody!"

"Where did you get that?" Mother demanded.

"I took it from the dead man."

"Oh, Lor'," said Mother, pressing the gas pedal again and speeding forward, "it's worse than I thought!"

"What was one of the clay people doing there?" asked Peter.

"I don't know! All I know is I waited forever, and nobody came. Then that foreign bastard came out of nowhere and had a gun on me!"

"Well who . . . who shot the guy?"

"I don't know. He was about to shoot me, and he was shot first. I guess it was one of the CIA guys, but . . ."

"But what?" said Peter with even less patience.

"But there was a second shot. Close to me. And the agents didn't come out of wherever they were hiding, and . . . and I don't know . . . I'm just so glad you're both alive!"

I reached over the back of Peter's seat and hugged him, hard. Tears were beginning to run down my cheeks.

Mother stopped at the light at Fullerton and looked over at us.

"What's all this, then?"

I released Peter and gave Mother a little wet kiss on the cheek.

"I thought you were dead."

"Dead?" she said, sounding absurdly like Mary Poppins.

I nodded my head and sat back in my seat as the light changed, and Mother made a left-hand turn onto Fullerton.

"Why on earth should *we* be dead?" said Mother when she'd completed the turn.

"While that foreign prick was holding me at gunpoint, he said his partner was taking care of the two of you."

Mother and Peter exchanged a glance as if each one thought the other might have some idea what I was talking about. Mother shook her head and said, "Well, nobody bothered us. We didn't see anyone."

"Nobody?"

"Not even a car," Peter added.

Mother said, "So we're all right and you have nothing to be upset about, 'ave you?"

My head dropped back onto the seat, and I closed my eyes. I don't think I've ever been so exhausted. And yet at the same time, I couldn't quiet my mind. That bastard with the gun had sounded so sure. And I couldn't think why he would tell me that Mother and Peter were dead when he was about to kill me. Unless it was out of pure spite. That might be it. But something was wrong. I could feel it.

Suddenly it hit me. My eyes popped open and I yelled, "Oh my God! Wait! Stop the car!"

"What?" said Mother.

"Stop the car! Stop the car! Pull over!"

We were only about two blocks from our townhouse when Mother pulled the car into an illegal spot in front of a fire hydrant.

"What in Heaven's name is it?" said Mother.

"That guy, the clay person. I asked him where his partner was, and he said he was seeing to my little family."

"Oh, Jesus, Alex," said Peter, "he must have been lying."

I shook my head rapidly. "No, no, I don't think he was. I think I just misunderstood him! Don't you see?"

"What?" said Peter.

"The house! He's at the house! They didn't have any way of knowing that the two of you would be coming with me . . . they must have thought you'd be waiting at home. So, the big one came to meet me and get rid of me, and the little one . . . he must have gone to the house to take care of you!"

Peter and Mother looked at each other. Mother's lips were parted slightly and Peter's jaw was firmly clenched. It was evident that they thought this idea made perfect sense, and neither of them liked it. I didn't like it, either. I put a hand on the back of my mother's headrest and said, "What are we going to do?"

Mother sighed again and scanned the four corners by which we'd stopped. She didn't appear to be looking for anything in particular, her eyes just seemed to be wandering while she thought. Suddenly she reached down and unhooked her seat belt.

"Wait here," she said as she popped open the door. "I'll be right back."

"Where in the hell are you going?" I demanded.

"Don't worry, I'll be right back."

She jumped out of the car, looked both ways, and then hurried across the street against the light. She headed straight for a pole on which were mounted back-to-back pay phones. One phone was free, the other was being used by a young black man having a rather vociferous conversation.

The man glanced at my mother as she approached, then turned his back on her as if she wouldn't be able to hear the conversation he was holding at the top of his lungs if he wasn't facing her. Mother reached in the pocket of her skirt, pulled out a handkerchief, picked up the receiver and wiped it off, then dialed. She had a hurried conversation of which we couldn't hear a word, though her face told us that she was speaking very excitedly. After a moment she hung up the phone and walked swiftly back to the car.

As she climbed back into the driver's seat, I said, "What did you do?"

She shrugged and said, "What could I do? I called the police and told them a man with a gun was trying to break into our house!"

Both Peter and I smiled.

TEN

We parked and waited down the street from our house until a patrol car showed up. Mother introduced herself and she did a credible job of producing a story that was long on drama and short on details about having been at home alone when she heard a noise, peeked through a curtain, and saw the man. She acted suitably befuddled when it came to explaining which window she'd looked through and how she knew he had a gun since, as the redheaded, befreckled officer pointed out, it would have been unusual for a perp to be prowling around with a gun in his hand, which he somehow managed to make sound obscene. Mother explained breathlessly that she just *knew* he had a gun, and she actually managed to elicit one of those "typical woman" smiles from the redhead, which made me angry because he made no attempt to disguise it. You would think that someone who is paid by our tax dollars would at least try to look like he didn't think you were an idiot.

"And where were you two during all this?" he said, turning to Peter and me.

"Out," Peter replied flatly. "We just got back."

The other officer, an extremely handsome Italian-looking

man, dark skin, dark mustache, dark hair, dark eyes—not that I was noticing—asked Mother for her keys, and then the two officers told us to wait by their car while they investigated. The redhead mumbled something to the Italian as they walked up the steps, and they both quietly laughed. But they didn't think the situation funny enough to take chances, and both drew their guns before the Italian slid the key in the door as quietly as possible and opened it. After listening for a moment, they disappeared inside the house.

Unless you have experienced it, the sensations you go through while waiting for the police to search for an armed man inside your house are something that you simply can't explain. On the one hand, I told myself this was just a clever precaution on Mother's part—to make sure that the coast was clear. On the other hand, it was perfectly logical to believe, given what the now-dead clay person had said to me, that his partner really was here and would undoubtedly be armed.

After what seemed ages, the Italian policeman appeared in the doorway and beckoned to us. From the stoic look on his face, it was impossible to tell if he'd found an empty house or a dead body.

"It's all clear," he said as we passed through the door, "but somebody's definitely been here."

He led us through to the kitchen, where his partner was squatting by the back door, which stood wide open.

"We found it like this," said the redhead as he continued his examination of the doorjamb.

"Oh, my God," said Mother, all color draining from her face, "he *was* here!"

The Italian turned his beautiful, quizzical brown eyes on my mother and said, "But you knew someone was here."

She mumbled and stuttered and finally managed to get out, "Oh, yes, of course."

There followed a rather lengthy bout of questions, during which Mother described the man she saw—well, actually, she described the man we'd seen at the zoo, since we were fairly certain that that was who'd broken in. The redheaded officer got a bit testy about Mother's fuzziness on the facts, such as which window she'd looked through when she saw him, but of course, it's rather difficult to come up with an accurate eyewitness account of what you thought happened when you hadn't actually been there to see it. But Mother did manage a credible story of having seen him through one of the back windows, heading for the back door, and how she'd fled in terror out the front door to the nearest pay phone.

"Locking the door behind you, ma'am?" said the redhead skeptically.

Mother looked startled, then shrugged and said sheepishly, "Force of habit."

When she'd finally managed to put together a clear enough story for them, the Italian officer took her hand and said very sincerely, "You did well. You were very brave."

And that's when Frank arrived. At first I thought it was an unexpected appearance, and that Mother's fears about calling him in lest he thought she was trying to rekindle their romance were justified. However, we were soon to learn that his visit was not at all unexpected.

"What are you doing here?" said Mother as he walked past her into the living room.

The officers greeted him, said they were just about finished there, and quickly left. Frank turned to my mother.

"I want to know what the hell is going on, Jean."

"What . . . prompted you to come here just now?" she replied, stalling.

"All of my people have orders to notify me of any calls they get pertaining to you or this address."

Mother's back stiffened noticeably and her features drew together. "I think that's going a bit far, don't you?"

Frank was not going to be put off on this occasion. He met her solid gaze with a steely one of his own. "No, I don't think it's going far enough! First, Alex here is present at a bar on an evening when one of its patrons is murdered. And he's beaten up. Then you call me over here because your house has been broken into and ransacked. Then you call the police and report someone with a gun is trying to break into your house. It would take a bigger jerk than I am not to recognize that something is going on here, and I want to know what it is."

Mother was stumped. It really had gotten to the point where it would be folly to deny that we were in the soup. I was just glad that he hadn't mentioned the murder of the big clay person on his list of our escapades.

Frank broke the silence with "Look, Jean, if you're in trouble, and you obviously are, then tell me about it. I'm the goddamn area commander, for Christ's sake—I can help!"

"Frank, I . . . I can't," said Mother at last.

He smoothed back his hair and wandered to the windows. He parted the heavy curtains slightly and glanced out. With his back to the three of us, he said, "You know, there's an interesting thing about Victor Hacheck. . . ."

"Who?" I blurted out too quickly.

Frank turned from the window and stared at me. He wasn't smiling but there was something about his expression that gave a sense of triumph. "The man who was killed at the gay bar. It turns out his name was Victor Hacheck. It seems he had something to do with the CIA."

"How do you know that?" said Peter.

Frank's gaze pivoted over to Peter. "Because someone from the CIA came to talk to me about him. Seems the feds don't want us lowly cops looking into that murder—they think we might blow something they're working on."

"Who did you talk to?" said Peter.

"Someone named Nelson. More than that I can't say."

Peter and I exchanged glances. Nobody named Nelson had been mentioned to us.

"So you're not investigating Hacheck's murder?" I said.

"Well, I agreed that we'd try to keep it quiet, but I told Nelson that there was no way I was going to just let a murder in my area go."

114

Frank looked at each one of us in turn, then continued, "Now what I want to know is, what do the three of you have to do with this? Are you mixed up in it somehow?"

Mother and Peter and I glanced at each other.

"Sit down, Frank."

Mother explained the whole lurid story to him while I listened and Peter made tea. It was by rights a rather involved story, what with the real and bogus Mr. Martins and all, but there are some things in which Mother excels, and one is in the relating of facts without embellishment. However, she did stretch it a bit when she explained that she hadn't told him about it sooner because she didn't want to get him involved in something dangerous. I think she did this merely to assuage the manly pride so common to straight men, because I was beginning to think the real reason she hadn't told him the whole story before was that she'd been enjoying our foray into espionage and hadn't wanted Frank to interfere.

She did leave out a few facts: mainly tonight's encounter and the man being shot. I'm not sure why she did this, other than the fact that Frank was, after all, a policeman and my presence at two homicides in one week might be too much to overlook, even for someone who loves her. She simply explained that we had "run into" one of the bad guys this evening, and had managed to put him off, but had been afraid the other would be waiting at our home, hence our call to the police.

By the time she had finished, our tea had been served and we were seated around the room and the atmosphere was a little more relaxed, as if we were sitting there discussing a movie we'd seen.

Frank turned to me and said, "You say you turned the matchbook over to the feds?"

"Yes," I replied with a nod.

"Then why did this agent or whatever he is think you were lying? Were you?"

I might have been offended under normal circumstances, but under these I simply looked baffled. "No. I really turned it over to

Martin—the real one—at the CIA office. Mother was there."

She nodded her assent.

"Then I don't get why this guy thought you still had it."

"Neither do I, but he did."

Frank stood up, shaking his head and clucking his tongue disgustedly. "I don't like the idea of you being involved in this at all."

"I told you," said Mother with a roll of her crystal-blue eyes, her tone becoming more exasperated, "we became involved by accident."

"Well, you didn't have to *stay* involved! You didn't have to go mixing around with these people!"

"We didn't go 'mixing around' with anyone! They came here and mixed with us! We didn't invite them!"

"That's not what I meant!" said Frank hotly. Frank's skin reddens when he becomes angry, as he was now. Unfortunately, on him it doesn't look like temper, it looks like the flush of chronic alcoholism.

"Blaming the victim . . . ," Peter muttered, "typical."

Frank shot him a glance and then said to Mother, "I only meant that if you were in danger, you should have called me."

"I *did* call you!"

"You didn't tell me what was wrong!"

"That's beside the point."

"I should have been told you were in danger!"

"Why," said Mother icily, "so you could protect me?"

Frank glanced down at the floor, the redness of his complexion deepening. He clenched and unclenched his hands. "No. You just should have reported the whole thing to the proper authorities."

"The proper authorities in this case," said Mother, affecting English primness, "were the CIA. And we didn't go to them, they came to us."

"An impostor came to you!"

"Well, we didn't know that at the time," said Mother, waving her hands as if she were brushing away a minor point. "And besides, when we found that blasted thing that was passed to Alex,

116

we took it to the CIA straightaway." Frank started to say something, but Mother cut him off quickly with "The *real* CIA!"

She folded her arms and squarely faced Frank. She fell about five inches short of his six-foot-two-inch frame, but for some reason whenever she faces up to him, she exudes height.

"Jean," he said sternly, "be reasonable. At least let me have somebody watch the house. The ways things are going, even *you* must understand that you need protection."

Peter burst into the conversation before my mother could answer. "No, no way!"

"Look . . ."

"There's no way I want the police watching this house!"

"What do you have to do with it?" said Frank. He may be fairly liberal, and he may love my mother, and he may accept me and my relationship with Peter in theory—but it's amazing how when your authority is challenged, all that can go out the window. I didn't like the look on his face or his tone of voice when he said that to Peter, because both implied that Peter didn't belong here at all.

"I won't live in a goddamn police state! No matter what the cause!" Peter was turning a bit red in the face himself, and I feared we were headed for real trouble. But I had to agree with him. I wouldn't want to live in a house being watched by the police for any reason: it would anticipate trouble in a way that I find more distressing than the trouble itself—as if the presence of the police would cause trouble instead of preventing it. That may seem illogical, but that's the way I was thinking.

"Well, it's not up to you, is it?" said Frank with a derisive twitch of his nose.

Peter turned to Mother, and she looked back at him, smiled, and said, "It's all right, dear, I agree with you."

"Jean, you're acting like—"

Mother held up one smooth, well-manicured hand, palm toward Frank, and said, "Franklin, do not under any circumstances finish that sentence!"

Frank looked down at the floor again and ran a hand through

his hair, his frustration palpable. When he raised his eyes to my mother, they had taken on a forlorn quality that hadn't been there before. He said quietly, "Jean, why won't you let me do anything?"

Mother's hand dropped to her side, and her face softened. In her eyes there was evidence that the love she'd had for Frank before their breakup had survived in a different form, something that was no longer romantic but still loyal and capable of being touched. Touched, but not ignited. After a moment she turned to Peter and me and said, "Boys?"

Peter and I glanced at each other, his face saying, "Let's get out of here."

He didn't know quite how far out of here I wanted to get. I said aloud, "Oh, yeah, well . . . we have something to do."

We crossed the room, passing Mother and Frank, who stood facing each other in a silence that was partially embarrassed and partially anxious. Peter had started up the stairs before he realized that I was halfway out the front door. We both stopped, and Peter shot me a questioning glance, which I answered with a nod toward the outside. He stepped back down the stairs and passed me, and I was about to close the door when Mother realized we were leaving the house and called, "Wait! Alex, where are you going?"

"We're just going to move the car," I called back, closing the door behind me before she could protest. All things considered, it would probably have been best for us to stay indoors the rest of the night, but I had no desire to hang around the house while Mother and Frank worked out whatever they needed to work out. And besides, we really did have things to do.

Peter was on me before we'd even hit the front walk.

"Where the hell are we going? It's almost midnight!"

"We've got to get to the bottom of this," I said, hurrying down the sidewalk. I was hurrying partly because I was anxious to start really trying to work this mess out on my own (with the help of Mother and Peter), and partly because the atmosphere on Fullerton Avenue in the middle of the night is conducive to hurry. It's so dark with the closely packed townhouses and other buildings and occasional foliage that you get the sense, justifiably or not, that people are watching you—probably because there are so many vantage points from which to do so. And hurrying has a practical side: a moving target is harder to hit.

"I agree, we have to get to the bottom of this mess," Peter said, "and we obviously can't rely on the CIA—Christ, we can't even tell who the real CIA men are—but in the middle of the night?"

"It's not far from here."

"What's not? What are you going to do?"

"Well, what I *want* to do is find out why Jerry Lasker is afraid of me."

It was during this short walk to the car that I realized something for the first time: I was really feeling exhilarated. Now that I had decided to take positive action in unraveling what was going on around us, acting instead of reacting, I could suddenly understand what I'd sensed in both my mother and myself earlier. I'd been wrong about the cause, though. I hadn't been indulging in a sordid thirst for cheap thrills when I'd been disappointed because I thought the business was ended. And Mother hadn't been exulting in luridness when I noticed the glow on her face as she pressed the gas pedal as we made our getaway from the rendezvous earlier this evening. It had been something deeper.

Though I had, over the years, built up a good freelancing business, and I like to think that I'm fairly well regarded in the field in which I work, I can't say that designing covers for corporate brochures was doing anything to enhance the world or enhance my own . . . self. As for Mother, she lives off my former father's former insurance and all, and fortunately doesn't have to work, and she's probably the kindest person I've ever known, but the look in her eyes as we sped up LaSalle showed me something that I should have noticed long ago, since I love her: something was missing from her life. Hell, not just her life, *my* life, too. We were both, along with Peter, living comfortably, and that was exactly the problem. I don't think either Mother or I realized it until this whole business began, but our lives had become comfortable and purposeless. And then one night in a bar a matchbook was slipped into my pocket, and suddenly our lives had some sort of direction.

So, as I led the way to the car, I suddenly felt like Olivia de Havilland in *Government Girl*—ready to bypass the system, take on the big boys, and fight for what was right. All right, so in my case it was "Government Gay," and I didn't have any idea what was going on or what I was getting myself into. At least I felt that I had something important to do: figure out why Victor Hacheck was killed, and what the significance of the matchbook was. I hesitated only a little when I remembered that two people had already been killed and there was no reason to believe that we wouldn't be next.

ELEVEN

Jerry Lasker lived just east of State Street in one of the brownstones that have been converted from large, luxurious apartments into small, dingy ones. I parked the car illegally at the end of the block, edging the bumper up against the bumper of a ancient green Ford Mustang that was already illegally parked. It was that old game of "if my bumper is touching his and his is touching the bumper of a car that *is* legally parked, then we're all safe." As if the police don't think it matters what you're touching as long as it's not yourself.

The address that Jo had given me was in the middle of the block. It was a dark gray building (not a brownstone, as I'd originally guessed) that was in desperate need of a good sandblasting, but the result of that would probably be to uncover a lighter shade of gray. The building was three stories tall, and sandwiched so tightly between two others that it looked as if they were trying to squeeze another story out of it. There were five steps leading down to the front door of the building, which made it look to me as if the entrance had been sunken into a moat. I wondered if the residents flooded it when unwanted visitors rang their bells.

Peter had worried that midnight was not a good time to go

calling on anyone, especially someone who might be involved in this case (he actually used the word "case"). I said it wasn't that late, but I was relieved when we reached the building and found that lights seemed to be on in most of the apartments. We went down the stairs into the moat and through the door into the vestibule. Although from the front there appeared to be perhaps three large apartments, the left wall of the vestibule sported no less than a dozen mail boxes, and under each box was a dirty white doorbell. Each and every button had a lightning bolt–shaped crack through the middle. I located the one for Jerry Lasker and pressed it. The crack apparently ran through the entire button, which made it feel squishy to the touch.

The inner door buzzed and clicked almost immediately, and Peter and I glanced at each other a little nervously, wondering who Lasker might be expecting, because we were pretty damn sure it wasn't us. I opened the door and passed through it, and Peter followed closely, letting the door close noisily behind us. We started up the staircase, which was so narrow there wasn't even enough room for a railing, but a railing would have been redundant anyway. If you were to trip and fall, the walls were close enough together to catch you. The stairs were covered with a rust paisley carpet with a pattern so busy I was sure it must have been chosen to help hide the dirt. It didn't work.

We continued up the stairs, trusting that like anyone else Lasker would open his door once having buzzed in whoever it was he was expecting. Of course, we got all the way to the top of the building before we found a door that had been opened a crack.

"You're late," Lasker called in a lilting voice, and as he swung into the doorway coquettishly, he added à la Bacall, "but I don't care!" The instant transformation when he saw us was amazing: his entire body jerked to attention, his eyes bulged, and the blood drained from his already pale face, making the purple bruises appear more virulent. He grabbed the door with both hands and attempted to swing it shut, but I was too quick for him. In anticipation of this move I had stuck my foot in the door.

I had seen this done in at least a thousand movies. However, not once did I get any indication from any of them that blocking a slamming door with your foot actually hurts! Especially when the suspect on the other side of the door hasn't seen the same movies you have, and doesn't know that after the initial effort, he is supposed to stop slamming the door and talk to you. When the door failed to close on the first attempt, Lasker glanced at it as if it had turned against him, oblivious to the fact that I was the one stopping it, and tried about six more times to slam the door, bouncing it off my foot each time. And he kept yelling, "Get out of here! Get away from me!"

With tears beginning to well up in my eyes, I finally managed to grab the door and hold it fast. Not wanting to scare Lasker any further, I didn't push the door open and walk in (the way they do in the aforementioned movies). I said as quietly and calmly as I could that we really only wanted talk to him. He continued to look skeptical and more than a little scared.

Finally, I said, "Jerry, I don't know what happened to you, but you've got to believe me, I didn't have anything to do with it. And I really need to know what happened, because . . . it might have some bearing on something that happened to me."

Lasker looked at me blankly for a moment, then blinked a couple of times. I had the uncomfortable feeling that he was trying not to cry. But at least he seemed to be calming down. He let out a shuddering sigh and said, "How did you know my name?"

"Oh," I smiled, "we have mutual friends. They recognized you at the bar."

"Who?" he said, a trace of skepticism in his voice.

"Jo and Sheila—you know, Jo owns On Our Own—the store?"

After a minute he brightened a little and said, "Oh, yeah! Jo and Sheila! Yeah, I know them."

He seemed to relax a bit, but continued to block the door. Finally, I said, "Jerry, we really do need to talk to you about last Friday night."

His face clouded over. "You mean about the bathroom?"

This took me by surprise. "Yes. Yeah. Can we come in?"

He thought for a moment more and then swung the door wide. Peter and I passed through, then Lasker closed it behind us. When I turned to face him, I realized for the first time what he was wearing. He was clad in a sheer black nylon robe (I guess you'd call it), and underneath was a matching pair of bikini briefs. Two layers of nylon did not exactly leave a lot to the imagination, and ordinarily I wouldn't be crass enough to remark upon anyone's endowment, but I have to say that if my house caught fire I would call him before I'd call the fire department. And I have to admit two other things: I was embarrassed to see a virtual stranger like this, and I was embarrassed that he didn't seem to be embarrassed at all. So Peter and I began the uncomfortable game of ignoring the proverbial pink elephant in the room.

"I'm expecting somebody," he said as if he'd read my mind.

"I see," I said, and then suddenly realized that that sounded as if I'd meant it literally, and amended, "I mean, I understand."

There was something else revealing about his outfit—well, there was more than one thing but only one that was pertinent to our investigation—and that was that it showed the rest of his body was as badly bruised as his face: there were several large bruises on his chest and side that looked as if they were transforming from purple to yellow, and a couple on his legs that I could only imagine were caused by some well-placed kicks. It made me cringe to see them.

I guess I'd been silent for too long, because Lasker finally said, a bit anxiously, "So, like this guy's coming over, so whatever you wanted to ask me, you should go ahead."

He pulled open two wooden folding chairs that had been propped up against the wall, and while we were settling ourselves in, I noticed the room for the first time. I call it a room because it was hardly an apartment. I guess this was what would qualify as an efficiency in a more modern building. This place looked as if it was half of what used to be the kitchen at a time when the whole floor was one dwelling. It had an extremely high ceiling, which gave you the feeling of being in the bottom of a pit. The ceiling was a mass of cracked and peeling paint that looked like it'd been tinted by years of chain-smoking. A narrow counter stuck out of one wall, and beneath it was the smallest refrigerator I've ever seen. The one major piece of furniture was the double bed that took up most of the room. It was unmade but partially covered by an elderly, badly preserved quilt. There was one floor lamp in the room, with an old tattered shade with gold fringe around the rim. If it carried a three-way bulb, the last two ways had already died, because the lamp barely gave off enough power to light the room. There were two large windows, one on the east wall and one on the south, that did nothing to help the overall gloom. Of course, it was the middle of the night, but the east window faced a wall that couldn't have been more than two feet away, and the south window faced the fire escape of another building, approximately two yards away. Even in broad daylight, there couldn't have been much light in this room.

Lasker sat on the bed and with a nod at Peter said, "Who's this guy?"

"Oh, I'm sorry—this is my husband, Peter Livesay."

"And who are you?"

I could feel my face turning red, "God, I'm sorry. My name is Alex. Alex Reynolds."

He smiled, and it occurred to me that this guy was a lot younger than I'd first thought when I'd seen him in the bar. There, when he was still intact, I'd assumed he was in his mid to late twenties. But now, with a few bruises, the dim light, and the sheepish smile he offered us, I realized he was probably barely twenty, if that. It somehow saddened me to think he'd been beaten like this while so young, though I don't know what that had to do with anything.

"Pleased to meet you," he said with youthful coyness.

I smiled and we fell silent for a minute.

"What do you want?" he said, breaking the silence.

I glanced at Peter, realizing for the first time that I didn't exactly know how to proceed, and all Peter's face told me was that he would rather be home in bed. I decided that the best thing to

125

do was just come right out and ask Lasker questions point-blank.

"Well, what I wanted to know is what happened to you." I waved my hand in the direction of the bruises on his chest and said, "I mean, about those. When we ran into you the other night, you said that I'd caused it. What did you mean?"

Lasker's eyes grew wide and Bambi-like. He sounded almost like a frightened child when he answered, "I was beat up. I was beat up by one of those guys."

"What guys?" I said, knowing of course that he was talking about the clay people. I still couldn't understand how in the hell Lasker had crossed them.

"One of them chased me and beat me."

I glanced at Peter, who repeated the question to him.

"What guys?"

Lasker turned his wide brown eyes toward me. "I had to take a piss, and I walked into the bathroom and walked in on some . . . private thing, I guess."

"So *you* were the one who walked into the bathroom!" I exclaimed. In my panic to escape, I hadn't noticed who it was that had come in on us, I was just glad for the interruption. "Well, it was a private thing, but not in the way you mean."

"I guess," he said, and his voice sounded sad, as if he were made unhappy by just the memory of his bad luck, "but when I realized something funny was going on, I got the hell out of there, and I ran out of the fucking club, and one of those guys chased me."

Lasker sounded totally unnatural when he swore, like a child who's trying out naughty words for size.

"But I don't understand," said Peter, taking the lead. "Why would he chase you if all you did was happen into the bathroom at the wrong time?"

Lasker let out a low laugh that for him I guess denoted irony. "I asked him . . . I said that when he . . . when he was beating me up. I kept saying, 'What did I do?' "

"Did he say anything?"

"Yeah. He accused me of following them." Lasker turned his

eyes back to me and added, "They thought I was with you for some reason. 'Cause I walked into the bathroom. He seemed to think I was going in there to help you."

I shook my head incredulously. "But I don't understand. Why would they think that? We spoke before they came in."

Lasker lowered his eyes and appeared to be contemplating his knees, but from the way his forehead wrinkled it was evident that he, too, was trying to figure this out. Peter and I watched him in silence, giving him the time to reach back into his memory. At last he looked up, though his expression was doubtful.

"Well . . . they did stand by me at the bar for a little while. I mean, they didn't pay any attention to me, but they were right by me."

"Did you pay any attention to them?" said Peter.

"Oh, puhlease!" said Lasker, rolling his eyes to the ceiling. "If you'd seen them, you wouldn't ask that!"

"So . . . ," I said with a slow shrug of my shoulders, "there was nothing."

Lasker shook his head, "No. I mean, well, no. They didn't stay by me very long. Except one stayed longer than the other."

"Really?" I said.

"Yeah. One of them went off—the bigger one, I think."

Peter and I exchanged glances. I think we both had the same idea: that one of the clay people had followed Hacheck out of the bar and murdered him, and the other stayed and watched me.

Peter looked at Lasker and said, "So there was nothing else? They had no reason to think you were interested in them"— Lasker started to protest again, but Peter corrected himself— "or that you were listening to them for some reason."

"Nope," Lasker replied with a single nod of his head, as if placing a period at the end of his sentence. There was a moment's silence, then he suddenly added, "I was really interested in the other guy, though."

I could feel my eyebrows coming together again, a sure sign that I was confused. "You mean the one who left? I thought you said—"

"No," said Lasker, cutting me off, "I mean the other guy."

"What other guy?" Peter asked.

"The beautiful one." Lasker's eyes took on a shine that I remembered from my youth: that shine you sometimes get when you're unattached and you see an attractive possibility.

"Who're you talking about?" I said.

"Oh, this guy—this guy that came up and talked to the foreign guy that stayed . . . the foreign guy that beat me up."

"Somebody came up and talked to the foreign guy? Somebody in the bar?"

Lasker rolled his eyes at me this time, in that special way that youth has of letting the elders know they're being thick.

"Of course somebody in the bar. This beautiful guy came up and talked to him while the other guy was away. I mean, I couldn't help but notice, he was gorgeous. I don't know what he saw in the foreign guy."

"Did you hear anything that they said?"

"Well, yeah," he said, then as if he thought it might sound as if he were simply eavesdropping, he added quickly, "I mean, not much because they were talking kind of low, but this guy really caught my attention . . . and I was . . . I wanted . . ."

"You wanted to catch his," said Peter kindly.

Lasker smiled at Peter. It was a nice smile, as if he was pleased to be understood.

"What was so beautiful about him?"

Lasker looked away from both of us, but his eyes were wide and he was smiling as he described this mysterious man. "He was tall and he had dark hair, a little curly or sort of wavy, and this beautiful skin, I mean clean, smooth, you know? And he had these really nice lips, and an expensive suit. And he was smooth."

"Smooth?" said Peter.

"Yeah, smooth, you know what I mean? He was just smooth."

Peter and I glanced at each other again. Apparently we had once more gotten the same idea at the same time: Lasker was describing the bogus Mr. Martin.

Lasker continued, "I tried to catch his attention, but all he was interested in was that little creep."

"What did he say?"

"The usual, I guess. I mean, it was a pickup, sure as shit."

"What did you hear?" Peter asked, pressing.

Lasker gave a noncommittal shrug and toyed with the hem of his robe. "Not much."

"Well," I said, getting a little impatient, "how do you know this guy was picking up the foreign guy, then?"

This seemed to make Lasker a bit defensive, as if he thought we were doubting his word. "I heard some of it. I heard a little."

"Like what?" said Peter.

"Well, like this guy says to the foreign creep something about the Harris."

"The Harris Hotel?"

"Yeah, something about the Harris . . . or wanting this little foreign punk to come see him at the Harris . . . or something like that. See? A pickup."

"Was there anything else?" asked Peter.

"Um . . . yeah, well, I think the good-looking guy gave him his phone number."

"He did?" I said, and I could feel my forehead creasing. I just knew that, like my mother, I was going to end up with lines on my face by the end of this business.

"Yeah. He wrote it on a napkin. I tried to see it, but I couldn't."

We fell silent for a minute. I was digesting this information and wondering what it meant, as I'm sure Peter was. Lasker continued to play with the hem of his robe.

"Did you see any of them leave?" Peter said at last.

"You bet I did," Lasker replied with a sly smile. "I watched the smooth one. He had a beautiful ass."

"Did he leave through the front door?" I asked.

Lasker looked at me as if I were nuts and said, "Yeah, through the front door. Where else would he go? And then the other foreign guy—the big one—came back. Then the two of them wandered away."

"Where did they go?"

Lasker rolled his eyes again, as if he thought we'd never learn. "I didn't watch *them*. Jesus, I keep telling you. . . ."

"You didn't see the foreign guys again?" asked Peter.

"Not till I went to the bathroom." Lasker looked at me and continued, "Then you went flying out of there and I went flying out of there, and the one guy—the guy that'd stayed by me at the bar—he kept after me, and when he caught up with me, he beat the shit out of me. And he kept saying I was following them, and I was following you, and asking me why, but he didn't give me any chance to answer, he just kept hitting me! I mean, look at me!"

He waved his hands over his body as if he'd worn see-through clothing for the express purpose of showing us his wounds. He paused for a moment, then said, "But I finally managed—I mean, I got away from him. I didn't even try to hit him or fight back, I just tried to get away from him, and I finally did. And I ran like shit. And he followed me for a little, but he stopped and went off in the other direction, I guess."

I thought about this for a minute. It at least jibed with what I knew of what had gone on, and it explained his panic when he'd seen me the next night. And it was easy to believe that he'd accidentally crossed these people since the exact same thing had happened to me. It was likely that the little clay person had noticed Lasker paying attention to their conversation and then assumed Lasker was coming to help me when he walked into the bathroom.

"One thing," said Peter, "after what happened to you at the bar Friday night, why one earth did you go back the next night? Weren't you afraid to?"

Lasker looked pained and turned his face away from us. After a few seconds he swallowed hard and said, "Where else would I go?"

There was an embarrassed silence. I would have liked to comfort him, but I felt that anything I said would sound empty. After a few moments I stood and Peter followed suit.

"Well . . . that's all we really needed to know," I said haltingly. "I really appreciate your talking to us. I'm . . . I'm sorry you got involved in this."

Lasker rose from the bed when he realized we were leaving. He actually looked disappointed.

"You're going?"

"I can't think of anything else to ask you . . . and, remember, you've got somebody coming over."

He glanced at a cheap electric alarm clock that sat on the floor by the bed, its lighted dial giving off almost as much light as the sickly floor lamp. His face was unreadable.

"Yeah, well, he's kind of late . . . and I guess . . . well, he's probably not coming now."

I looked at him, again not knowing what to say. All I could manage was "Oh."

He shrugged slightly and gave me a making-the-most-of-it smile and said, "I just met him last night. At Manmade. See? I'm trying a new place. I guess I can't expect a lot."

I smiled ruefully and said, "I guess not."

Out on the street I threw my arms around Peter and hugged him close to me. There were no people on the street, but I wouldn't have cared if there were. At that moment I was so goddamn glad I had him, I would have kissed his butt on national television if he'd wanted me to.

When I released him, we started down the street and he rubbed my back between the shoulder blades.

"I know what you mean," he said.

On the short drive back to the townhouse, we went over what we'd learned—or at least, what we thought we'd learned—so far.

"Well, that was revealing. . . ," Peter began. His tone implied that he was being ironic, but I wasn't quite sure whether Peter was referring to Lasker's outfit or what he'd said.

"Well, he might not have had hard facts . . ."

Peter turned his head toward me, his eyes narrowed and one eyebrow was raised.

"All right, all right," I said, laughing along with him, "his outfit was peculiar."

"It was only a peculiar way to entertain strangers. I see nothing wrong with it as a way to entertain suitors," Peter countered, his laugh replaced by a lascivious grin. "I think we can make a few suppositions, given what he saw and heard.

"For one," continued Peter, taking it upon himself to start the list, "it looks as though the big clay person—and I hope to God we learn their names soon, because I'm tired of referring to them as if they were something out of *Flash Gordon*. . . ."

"You didn't them see in the bar. That's exactly how they looked. Or moved."

"All right, all right," Peter replied with an irritation that I chalked up to the lateness of the hour, "so what I was going to say is it looks as if the big clay person is the one who killed Hacheck."

"Yeah . . . maybe. Unless he just lost track of him and was cruising the bar to find him."

Peter's face swiveled toward me again. "Cruising?"

"Sorry, it's the word that comes to mind. Anyway, he might have been looking for Hacheck."

"Yes. Well, Lasker also verified that this fake Martin actually came into the bar."

"I can't believe I missed him."

Peter leaned his elbow on the back of the seat and used his hand to prop up his head as he looked at me. It was done more for effect than anything else.

"You *weren't* cruising, remember?"

I feigned a nervous laugh, as if I'd been caught in an indiscretion, and said, "Oh, yeah, I forgot."

He paused for a moment, then said, "Did you think he was that good-looking?"

I glanced at him to see if he was serious, but he was presenting his poker face, so I had to wing it. "Yeah, but he doesn't have your character."

He broke into a smile. I was relieved.

"All right," I said, getting back to the matter at hand, "Lasker also verified that Martin left the bar by the front door, so he probably wasn't the one who killed Hacheck."

"Assuming that Hacheck left by the back door."

"Yeah. . . ." I felt for the first time that a little light was beginning to dawn. "And you know, it makes sense: say that Hacheck dashed out the back door and the big clay person followed him and killed him. That means they *knew* at that point that Hacheck didn't have what they were looking for, and that's why they came after me!"

Peter warmed to this. "That's why they were so *sure* that Hacheck had passed it to you!"

"That leaves me with one question. Why did the fake Martin come into the bar at all? Why did he talk to the little clay person?" Before he could correct me, I added, "I know that's two questions."

"Oh, I understand him doing that," said Peter. "I mean, in a crowded bar? You heard what Lasker said, nobody could really hear them. He only caught a little of it. Why not come up and confer with his confederates?"

"That's just it, he only conferred with one of them."

Peter sighed. "Who knows? Maybe one was enough."

"And that stuff about the Harris Hotel! What was that all about? Why would he need to tell the guy where he was staying? Why didn't the clay people already have his number?"

"I don't know! Maybe, if he's as cagey as you think he is, he just hadn't wanted them to know where he was staying."

"So why tell him then?" I pressed.

"Alex, I don't know. I'm tired. Look, this started on Friday night, it's now Monday night . . . excuse me, Tuesday morning, and we still don't have anything except questions."

"And two dead bodies."

"And two dead bodies," he repeated grudgingly.

There was a tense silence between us, the kind that tends to happen between loved ones when they discuss important matters in the car on the way home when they're overtired. I let it rest for a minute, then said, "You know we can't just let this go, don't you?"

He thought for a moment, and if his face was any indication, he looked like he'd like to argue the point, but in the end he just shook his head and said, "Yes, I know. But we can let it go for the night."

We had reached Fullerton, and I circled around the front of the house before parking the car because I wanted to see if everything looked all right. Of course, it was a wasted gesture, because everything did look all right from the outside, and after a split second's relief I involuntarily reminded myself that everything could be a mess inside. Like whited sepulchers, I thought irreverently, and once again was amazed at how much of the Bible a simple crisis will bring back to you.

As we walked through the back garden after putting the car away, I took Peter's hand and said, "Didn't we used to know someone who worked at the Harris?"

Peter turned to me, and even in the darkness I could see his face lighting up in a wide smile.

"Stevie!" he said with a laugh.

"Yeah. Stevie."

TWELVE

Mother and I were still finishing breakfast when Peter called Stevie. Peter had known Stevie a long time. I've never asked about the nature of their relationship before we met, because the mere thought of it conjures up visual images too disturbing to entertain. But I don't think they were ever physically close since Stevie is not Peter's type. I don't mean that Stevie is unattractive or anything, I just mean that he's the kind of person I can imagine having as a friend, but not as a partner. He's funny, and loud, and friendly, and you always have the feeling that despite the brashness he's caring and would stick by you if you were in trouble. But a little of him goes a long way. Next to Stevie, Peter and I seem positively suburban.

When Peter had completed the call, he came into the kitchen, sat at the table, and took a sip of his tea. He was wearing a dark gray suit that made him look like a million dollars in small bills that I'd like to peel away one at a time. With it he wore a crisp white shirt and a tie with large stripes, alternating maroon and gray.

"Well, that was very interesting," said Peter, setting his cup back on the table.

"What?"

"I think that's the first time I've ever heard Stevie Sullivan struck dumb!"

"And you wouldn't let us listen in."

"And I'll be damned if that James Martin character isn't registered at the Harris Hotel!" said Peter with a triumphant smile.

"You're kidding," I said, my jaw dropping. "You mean he actually registered as James Martin?"

Mother turned her face toward me, and her expression was one of utter amusement. "Alex, dear, James Martin is his alias. Why on earth wouldn't he register under it at the hotel?"

"Oh, yeah, right," I said, and I could feel my cheeks going red. Then I turned to Peter and asked, "So what knocked Stevie speechless?"

"What do you think? When I asked him if we could get a key to Martin's room."

"What did he say to that—when he was finished being struck dumb, I mean," said Mother, taking another bite of French toast.

"He said, 'You've got to be kidding.' What would you expect him to say?"

"But will he do it?"

"Of course he'll do it. You know Stevie! In all fairness to him, he really did hesitate and he demanded to know the facts, but, in the end, he said he'd do it." He turned to Mother and added, "Because he said he trusted *you*."

"Well, thank you very much, Stevie!" said Mother, saluting Stevie with her fork.

Peter turned to me and said, "He also said that if he ever found out that this was some sort of scam and we'd been out to rob the place all along, he'd give our address to a group of skinheads he's been sleeping with."

This is why I have just a little difficulty dealing with Stevie. Claiming to be sleeping with a bunch of skinheads is exactly the type of thing he would say just to be outrageous. The trouble is, it's exactly the type of thing he'd *do* just to be outrageous. It's hard telling. And I really hate to appear stupid, but I couldn't help it in this case. I had to ask: "Is he really sleeping with skinheads?"

"I asked him the same thing. He claims that he's really only sleeping with one. He also claims the one he's sleeping with decided he liked boys while in the process of beating one to death. I didn't pursue it."

We ate in silence for a few minutes, then Peter turned to Mother and said, "Jean, I know this is probably personal so you don't have to answer it, but what exactly happened between you and Frank after we left last night?"

"A rerun," she replied after a slight pause. "I do hate to hold moratoriums about relationships that are over, but I'm afraid that just what I feared at first has come true: Frank has seen this as a chance to rekindle our relationship."

Peter looked at her as if he thought she'd continue, but when she didn't he said, "Anything else?"

"Oh, yes, about the business at hand, Frank did say he was going to contact that Mr. Nelson, the man from the CIA who consulted with him, and find out if what's been going on with us has anything to do with their operation. So I was glad I didn't tell Frank about our little adventure last night. I figure if Mr. Nelson wants him to know about it, then he can tell him. Otherwise, I'd rather Frank didn't know that we were around when someone else got killed."

"I don't understand why we haven't heard from the CIA people ourselves. I can't believe they don't want to talk to us, even if it's just to tell us to keep our mouths shut," I said.

"Just another question among many," said Peter. "Perhaps the two of you will have some luck in getting some answers for yourselves."

Mother turned to him and asked, "So, when does Stevie get to work, and what are we supposed to do?"

Peter finished taking another sip or two of tea before answering her. He set his cup down again and said, "He's already there. He said he'd go ahead and program the key, so all you have to do is go to him and pick it up."

"I suppose there would be no sense in telling you that you couldn't go with me?" I said to Mother.

"Of course not! What would you do if you were caught? It'll be much better if I'm with you, because if someone does happen upon us, they'll be much more apt to believe we're in a room in which we don't belong by mistake if I'm there. Who would believe you'd take your mother with you to commit a burglary?"

I put my glass down with a thunk, narrowed my eyes at her, and said, "Anybody who knows us, Mother."

Peter wanted to go with us and once again threatened to call in sick in order to do so, but I told him that if we were caught, we'd look like some sort of gay gang with a British Ma Barker at the helm. So Peter kissed me good-bye and set off for work as usual, with a couple of minor differences. First, he scrutinized my face and didn't look any too happy with what he saw: dark circles under my eyes that signified that this business was getting to me. Second, instead of saying good-bye to him at the door, I accompanied him to the sidewalk and then, only half concealed by a large maple tree, watched him walk down the sidewalk toward the El until I could barely make him out. I don't know why, but I felt like I was watching my lifeline fade away.

My anxiety about Peter was a further sign that I was not taking this all as casually as it may have seemed. To be perfectly honest, I was shaken by the events of the previous night. I had, after all, seen somebody get shot through the head, which isn't exactly an everyday occurrence with me (though I'm told it is an everyday occurrence in this city, I'm not usually present). Granted, on Friday night I had met someone, namely Victor Hacheck, who was killed shortly after our encounter, but that didn't happen in front of me, and my life hadn't been in jeopardy that night. At least, I hadn't thought so.

But early that morning, when Peter and I finally got to bed after talking to Jerry Lasker, it really hit me that I'd seen a man killed. And it hit me hard. I didn't sleep a wink, and when I did (I realize that's a contradiction, but you know what I mean), I kept seeing the big clay person being shot through the head in the darkness. Only sometimes the top of his head would blow off like the lid of an overstuffed pressure cooker, and other times his whole head would just explode. I woke in a cold, shivering sweat several times, and Peter was good enough to hold me until I could get back to sleep. I'd like to think that Peter, Mother, and I had acted bravely (or foolishly, which often amounts to the same thing), but I was still human. This morning at breakfast I'd tried to keep a brave face on the whole thing, but I probably didn't fool Mother or Peter.

When I'd finished seeing Peter off to work, Mother appeared at the front door, closed and locked it, and joined me by the tree. She was wearing a light-tan peasant dress that flowed along with her graceful movements. It was cinched at the waist with a suede belt. She flagged down a cab, and we headed for the Harris Hotel.

The Harris is located at the south end of Michigan Avenue. I say the south end even though Michigan stretches almost the full length of the south side of Chicago. However, to die-hard north-siders, Michigan ends at Twelfth Street (Roosevelt Road), as if the opposite side of the street was an uncrossable chasm. The Harris is old: elegant-old, although not in the league with the Palmer House. It's the type of hotel where they keep the red plush carpeting as new as possible, the theory being that if the carpet looks good enough nobody will notice that the rest of the place is falling apart. For example, the gilding on the cherubs that grace the lobby's high cathedral ceiling has long since chipped away, and has not been restored under a management policy that believes, "If you can't stand close to it, it don't need to be fixed." They do, however, quickly vacuum up the occasional gold flecks that fall to the plush carpet.

The Harris is also one of those huge hotels that, in an effort to keep stray people from wandering around where they don't belong, has situated the front desk on the second floor, up an enormous, two-winged flight of stairs. Of course, the result of this setup is that everyone, including the guests of the hotel, end up wandering around the place trying to find the front desk. I'd only been here once before, but on that occasion I can tell you that the effect was like walking into the palace in *Cinderella*, ascending the staircase on which she'd lost her glass slipper, getting to the second floor, and finding that money changers had set up their booths there. Of course, it wasn't as bad as all that, but came close in terms of bustle. There were guests and bellboys and concierges and everything scurrying all over the place like well-dressed field mice.

The front desk was a long, mahogany counter that ran the entire length of the wall to the left of the staircase. As Mother and I reached the top of the stairs, we spotted Stevie Sullivan, busy giving the full front-desk treatment to a blue-haired woman who was much shorter than he was, and was tilting backwards, less from the height difference than from the sheer force of Stevie's personality.

Every man I've ever known named Steve has been gay. Of course, I should explain that I've really only known three men named Steve, and you have to remember the circles I run in. And this one was the only one to push it far enough to call himself Stevie. He came to an abrupt halt in his conversation with the blue-hair when he saw us at the top of the stairs. In fact, he looked so startled that you would have thought that a soap opera–inspired organ had crescendoed into a "ta-da" to announce our entrance. He quickly finished with her and slapped a bell. A rather good-looking bellboy appeared, took hold of the woman's battered luggage, and led the way toward the elevators with the old woman waddling behind him like a duckling. Stevie watched them go with an enraptured expression on his face that left no doubt in my mind which of the pair held his interest. It is a tribute to his powers of concentration that he could go from being startled when we appeared to watching the bellboy's ass, then immediately replacing his startled look when he turned back to us, as if there'd been no interruption at all.

As Mother and I approached the desk, I marveled once again at the way that some people can exude a really enticing sexuality without being particularly attractive. Stevie is one of those people. His eyes are large and wide, so they tend to look like they're bulging even when they're not. He always appears to be on the verge of delivering a leering aside in a particularly lurid sex farce. He was not exactly large, but not thin either, and looked equally at home in the uniform-red blazer he was wearing as he would have if he'd been costumed as one of the female characters in *Tom Jones*. He moved to one end of the desk, away from his co-workers, as we reached him.

"Hi, Stevie. You remember my mother?"

"Enchanté, madame!" he said, flourishing his hand to her as if she should kiss it.

Mother waited a beat before taking his hand, then twisted it sideways to shake it. The pause was enough to let him know to knock it off.

"Nice to see you again," she said simply, and a smile played about her lips.

"Yes, I haven't seen you since last year—the barbecue in your backyard last summer. Now, that would have been when I was dating . . ." He rested his crooked index finger against his chin and gazed toward the ceiling, then snapped his fingers and said, "Robert. Ah yes, Robert. Alas, that didn't last long."

As always, Stevie made me feel as if I was in a bad road company of *The Women*. Under the circumstances I thought it was highly irritating to be engaging in pleasantries, but I figured that Stevie, who was being more grandiose than normal (if you knew him, you'd know just how bad this was), was probably nervous as hell and trying to cover it up. After all, what we were asking him to do could lose him his job if anybody ever found out about it.

"Peter tells me you're dating someone new," I said.

Stevie pursed his lips and said, "Dating is hardly the word for it. But we're together whenever we can be."

I shook my head and smiled. "But a skinhead, Stevie?"

"A *recovering* skinhead, my darling Alex!" he said with a flourish. "It may be a little dangerous, because you never know when there'll be a relapse. But it's the best sex I've ever had."

"Oh . . . well . . . ," I said with a shrug.

The three of us fell silent. Mother and I glanced toward each other while Stevie's eyes continued to bug at us. Finally, his ample lips spread into a smile that almost touched his earlobes. He folded his hands on the desk and lowered his chin into them.

"Well," he said, his eyes rolling up to watch us from under his long, dark lashes, "I understand the two of you are engaging in a little espionage." He emphasized the last syllable of the word, which somehow made it sound as if he were referring to a woman's cleavage.

"Peter must have told you how important this is," said Mother, all business.

"Yesss," he said slowly, "important enough for me to lose my job over."

"Two people have died," said Mother.

"Millions have died, Mother Reynolds," Stevie replied, straightening himself back up. "I live on and I have to make a living."

Mother smiled. "Stevie, you know I hate it when you address me as if I were a nun."

"What Mother Rey—" I checked myself and began again, "I mean, what Mother means is that *our* lives are in danger. At least, we think they are."

"So Peter tells me. And that is the only reason, my darlings, that I'd risk anything of this nature. This may not be the greatest job in the world, but the pay is all right and the dental plan is fabulous."

"This is important, Stevie, important!" I said.

He glanced down the length of the front desk toward a tall, slender black woman who stood taking care of a middle-aged, ordinarily dressed couple. Stevie seemed to satisfy himself that we had not drawn her attention as he said to us through barely parted lips, "Sotto voce, please, sotto voce." Then he leaned in toward us and added in even quieter tones, "I know it's important. And frankly, no matter what the reason, I doubt if I'd do this for anybody other than Peter, firstly because we go so far back—" He glanced at me and flashed a wicked little smile. "Not as far back as that, Alex. . . ." I rolled my eyes and made a speed-it-up motion with my right hand.

"And secondly because I know that Peter is so damnably serious-minded. If this request had come from anyone else, I would have doubted their sanity or doubted their friendship. I can't do either one with Peter. He's the only person I've ever met whose veracity I am completely sure of."

Mother remained impassive, but I couldn't help raising my eyebrows at this.

He added hurriedly, "Oh, you're all right, and of course I've never had any doubts about your mother."

He looked at her and smiled broadly, a faint twinkle in his eye. But even that little bit of spark faded when he saw the look on my mother's face: clearly she was trying to convey to him that he was holding us up.

He blinked at us twice, said, "Well . . . ," half under his breath, then reached under the desk and pulled out a narrow plastic card of the type that currently serves as a room key in hotels.

"This," he said, showing us the key but not exactly in any hurry to hand it over, "has been programmed and should get you in the room."

"Thank you, Stevie," said Mother, reaching for the key. Stevie didn't extend his hand any further, and I noticed for the first time how pale he seemed to have become over the past couple of minutes. It occurred to me just how serious an act it was for him to be giving us the key. Stevie's and Mother's eyes met for a few seconds as she continued to hold out her hand. After a moment he seemed to mellow, reached over, and placed the plastic key in her palm. She closed her fingers around it.

"Room Eleven-twelve."

"Thank you," said Mother with feeling.

Mother and I started to turn and walk away, but Stevie stopped us when he said, "Wait!" with surprising firmness. As we turned back to the desk, he glanced back at the black woman, who was still busy with the ordinary couple. She was apparently as used to Stevie's antics as I was, and didn't bother to give him even the slightest glance. A look of pained relief came over Stevie's face as he turned back to us.

"What?" said Mother.

"I have to call."

"What?"

"Call! Don't you want me to call up there first to see if he's in his room?"

Mother and I glanced at each other, and I blushed in awe at our own stupidity. Both of us sighed, and Mother said to him, "Yes, please, would you do that?"

Stevie picked up a phone and dialed a four-digit number. He hummed an anxious little tune as he held the receiver to his ear and kept his eyes glued to my mother's right shoulder. After letting it ring at least a dozen times, he replaced the receiver and said, "No answer. That may only mean no answer, so be careful when you go up there. He may come wandering out of the shower, which I'd pay cash money to see, while you're doing whatever you're going to be doing."

"Thanks again," said Mother.

I added, "If you should see him coming in, call the room."

As we started to walk away, Stevie added to me, "And if you're caught, I expect you to use your many years of oral expertise to get rid of that damn key!"

I smiled back at him, and Mother and I headed for the elevators.

We managed to catch an elevator at the same time as the ordinary couple and the bellman who was escorting them to their rooms. The bellman pushed the button for the twelfth floor, and Mother pushed eleven. If the bellman had any doubts about our belonging in the hotel, he didn't show them. I felt decidedly conspicuous.

The ride was made excruciatingly long by the fact that the elevator was slow to begin with, and the wife of the ordinary couple spent the ride loudly blathering at her husband in the most charming of New York accents that they should have stopped before going up to their room to "buoy some waddah," which I believe translated to "buy some water." She went on at length to her long-suffering husband that she had to have "bahddled waddah," because she just couldn't drink "tap waddah." It was a relief to get off the elevator.

We stood looking down the hallway as the elevator doors slid shut behind us with an arthritic creak. A small, tarnished brass plaque on the wall pointed the way to the proper set of room numbers, and Mother and I went down the thankfully deserted hallway till we came to the end, where the door facing us had a lit EXIT sign suspended over it, so I figured it was the emergency stairs. The door directly to the right bore a small black plastic rectangle that said "1112."

Mother and I looked at each other, and she heaved a sigh and said "Here we go!" as she began to slip the plastic key into the slot above the doorknob. But I grabbed her wrist and said, "Wait!"

She furrowed her brow as she looked at me, and I explained, "We should knock first. If for some reason he's in there and just didn't answer the phone, we shouldn't just break in."

"What will we do if he answers?"

I hadn't considered that one. I thought for a minute and said, "Just . . . we can just tell him about last night."

Mother looked at me incredulously and said, "And how will we explain knowing where to find him?"

This took a little more thought. Then it hit me, and I said, "We'll just tell him we have our ways—and refuse to explain any more. Hell, that's the type of crap *he* pulled on us."

Mother grimaced as if she didn't think much of my idea, and truth to tell, neither did I. But I was counting on our not having to use it. I lifted up a fist and knocked lightly on the door with my knuckles. After waiting a few moments during which I could swear that not only had my breathing stopped, but my heart had stopped with it, as if it belonged to a fellow union that wouldn't cross the line.

Mother said impatiently, "He's not here," and slid the key the rest of the way into the slot. The lock clicked, and Mother opened it as quietly as if she feared he really *might* be there, and proceeded into the room, with me close behind her.

We stood by the door for a minute, listening for any possible sounds of movement, but there were none. Having decided that nobody was home, we relaxed a bit and looked around the room. For all the deteriorating elegance of the entrance and lobby to this hotel, the room was none too shabby. It was not exactly special, mind you, but it was a cut above the standard hotel room. The bed was made, so I noted with relief that the maid must have already been there, and we were less likely to be interrupted. The bedspread was not expensive, but it was clean, as was the whole room. If it weren't for the medium-sized suitcase that lay on a stand by the window, at first glance you would have thought the room was unoccupied. There was a twenty-inch television set on a tall stand by the six-drawered dresser, and a remote control was chained to the nightstand by the bed. All in all, it was a typical hotel room, though a little more expensive than most, and not the type of place I would expect to find a CIA agent staying. I guess I somehow had the idea that they would only stay in out-of-the-way, fleabag joints, where they would be less likely to attract notice. Then again, Martin looked a little too well put together to go unnoticed in a flophouse. I started to say, "Our tax dollars at work," when I realized once again that *this* Martin was not really with the CIA, but was an impostor.

When we had surveyed the room for a couple of minutes, I got this incredibly eerie feeling that one gets when invading someone else's domicile: like you're doing something very wrong and are in imminent danger of being discovered.

It dawned on me that we had no experience when it came to searching anyone's possessions, and apparently this thought struck Mother at the same time because she turned to me and said, "So, where do we start?"

"Well . . . ," I said, staying by the door and scanning the room, "all right, you take the desk, I'll take the dresser."

"Quite right," she replied, crossing to the desk which stood against the wall by the bed. She starting opening and closing drawers with the alacrity of a trained burglar.

I went directly to the dresser. I slid open the top left-hand drawer and found several pairs of black socks, rolled into balls and shoved on the left; there was nothing on the right. I moved the socks around to make sure there was nothing beneath them, then gently squeezed each ball to make sure that all that was inside was another sock. Satisfied on that account, I closed that one and opened the top right-hand drawer, and couldn't help letting out an "Oh, Jeez."

Mother turned from her rifling and said, "What is it? Did you find something?"

"Yes. The bogus Mr. Martin is a boxer man. I had him pegged for silk briefs."

"Alex, dear, *do* get on with it!" said Mother.

I should explain that before meeting up with Peter I'd had my share of lovers. I did, after all, live through at least part of the sexual revolution. Some of them I knew fairly well, and some of them, suffice it to say, not very well. But in each and every case my involvement with their underwear was on a completely voluntary basis on their part. I was surprised at how indecent I felt it was to rifle through a stranger's underwear when he wasn't present. I found nothing important. However, in a corner of the drawer, under two pairs of paisley shorts, I found a strip of condoms. I thought irreverently how comforting it was to know that, even in the middle of espionage, the bogus Mr. Martin was ready to play safely.

The rest of the drawers were empty except for one that held a bevy of identical white shirts. I closed the last drawer and turned to Mother, who had finished with the desk and was staring out the window.

"Find anything?" I asked.

"A sheaf of hotel letterhead and two cheap plastic pens with the name of the hotel on them. Oh, and there was a Bible in the bottom drawer that looks like it has never been opened—the Bible, not the drawer. You?"

"He practices safe sex." I sighed and went to her side.

"My, but there's a lovely view from here," she said, her gaze roaming out the window that looked out at Lake Michigan.

"Mother, we're here to search the room, not the shoreline."

"All right," she said, rising from the desk and sliding the chair back under it, "let's check the dressing room and bath and then get out of here."

"On that we both agree. Being in here gives me the willies."

Mother went into the bathroom and I could hear her rattling around in the medicine cabinet as I began my task. The dressing room amounted to a sort of anteroom to the bathroom, with sliding doors that covered a small closet. I slid open the doors to find several suits in varying shades of gray and blue hanging on the bar that stretched the scant length of the closet. Mother joined me as I started going through the pockets.

"Well, there's nothing much in the medicine cabinet, except a very large bottle of aspirin. I would say that our phony Mr. Martin is prone to headaches. What on earth are you doing?" This last was spoken as I pulled one of the trouser pockets inside out.

"I should think that's obvious. I'm going through his pockets."

She looked aghast as she said, "Alex, you can't go through a man's pockets!"

I stopped, looked at her in amazement, and said, "Mother, I just went through a man's underwear! And you just went through his medicine cabinet. This is a pretty odd moment to adopt feelings of delicacy!"

She hesitated, then clucked her tongue, and said, "I never thought we'd be brought to this," and started plunging her hands into the pockets of the suits at the opposite end from me. When we met in the middle, we still hadn't found anything. I reached up and felt around the two shelves over the clothing rack, but found nothing.

I slid the closet doors shut and the two of us stood there. Mother's expression seemed to match what I was feeling exactly:

a mixture of frustration and disappointment: disappointment at not having found anything, although we'd be the first to admit that we didn't know what we were looking for, and frustration because we were sure there had to be something here, if only we knew where to look.

Ready to concede a failure, Mother took the lead and said, "All right, darling, let's get out of here."

I nodded my agreement and I started to head for the door, when something suddenly occurred to me. I stopped Mother and said, "Wait a minute. You know, I just thought of something."

"What?"

"Where they always hide things in hotel rooms in the movies."

I crossed back to the dresser and dropped to my knees. I pulled out the top two drawers and looked under them. Nothing. I did the same with the middle two drawers, lowering my head further with the same result: nothing.

"What on earth!" said Mother.

I glanced up from the floor and said, "The bottom of the drawers, Mother. In all the old spy movies I've ever seen they hide important stuff in hotel rooms by taping it to the bottom of the drawers."

The bottom two drawers were too close to the floor for me to see under them, so I pulled them out and turned them over.

"So much for all the old spy movies you've seen," said Mother with an indulgent smile. It was when I turned the drawers over to slide them back into place that Mother said, "Wait a minute! Alex, look!"

I looked where she was pointing and saw that the dresser had a wooden bottom that rested on the floor. And in that wooden bottom was a manila envelope. I smiled at Mother, and fighting the urge to say "Aha!" reached in and pulled out the envelope.

"That could've been there for years," said Mother, though the excitement in her voice spoke volumes.

"This envelope is almost new," I replied.

We sat side by side on the foot of the bed, and I bent the metal bow-tie clasp and opened the envelope. Fortunately it hadn't been glued shut.

Mother peered over my shoulder as I flexed the envelope open and looked inside. There were several documents, the nature of which I really couldn't discern without removing them. I shifted a little away from Mother, upended the envelope, and allowed the contents to slide out on the bed between us. On top were four fax copies of handwritten letters. The handwriting was atrocious: small and cramped and barely legible, but it didn't really matter because the faxes were in a foreign language, so I wouldn't have been able to read it anyway. The one thing I could almost make out was the signature: each of the four letters seemed to be signed by Victor Hacheck. Unfortunately, we had no way of knowing to whom they'd been faxed.

I turned to Mother and said, "You speak more than one language. Care to take a stab at it?"

"Not Russian, dearest, and I'm assuming that's Russian," said Mother, who was pursing her lips as she perused the letters. After a minute or two she said, "I can't make heads or tails of this, but look here." She pointed to a paragraph in the center of the first letter. The paragraph in question broke momentarily from Russian to give a list of names which looked distinctly American: Larry Wyler, Joseph Smith, Andrew Peterson, Robert Dickson, and Matthew Corbin.

As I read the names, I could feel the furrows plowing across my forehead. I looked up from the sheet and said, "You know, Matthew Corbin sounds familiar."

"I don't know anybody by that name," said Mother.

"Neither do I. I don't know anybody . . . jeez, I don't know why that sounds so damn familiar."

Mother watched me for a moment, waiting to see if I'd call it to mind, but we were both disappointed on that score. I couldn't remember. She clicked open the bulky white shoulder bag she'd chosen for today's escapade and rummaged around in it for a moment, at last pulling out a small notebook which had a stublike pencil stuck within its spiral.

She held it out to me with a look of self-satisfaction, but I just looked back at her for a moment, then said, "You don't have any condoms in there, do you?"

She grimaced and handed the notebook to me, and I quickly wrote down the five names that appeared in the fax. I then shoved the pencil back into the spiral and handed them both to Mother, who dropped them back in her bag and clicked it shut.

"What have we here?" said Mother, putting the faxes aside.

Beneath the faxes was a small pile of pictures. Mother picked them up and started to look through them one by one, putting each on the bottom of the pile as she went, with me looking on. It was like looking at still frames from a movie in which I'd appeared without my knowledge: included in the bunch were pictures of me running from the bar and getting in the taxi. Seeing these photos made me distinctly uneasy.

"So he *did* follow you up the street," said Mother, her voice taking on that school teacher harshness it occasionally got when she suspected someone of a breach of etiquette.

"Not necessarily," I said, "those might have been taken by the clay person that followed me."

"I suppose . . . ," she said slowly.

"But look at these . . . ," I said as she continued going through the pictures.

The next couple of pictures were also candids—the subject apparently wasn't aware his picture was being taken—and were of the small clay person. The background was unfamiliar to me, but I was sure it wasn't Chicago and thought it would be safe to assume it was Russia.

"There's something written on the back," I said.

She flipped one of the pictures over, and written with a small-gauge felt pen was the name "Ivan Volkov." The next couple of pictures were similar but of the taller clay person, the one who'd been shot last night, and on the back was written "Leonid Fomin."

"There," said Mother, "we can stop calling them the clay people."

I shook my head, not at what she'd said but at something else that was nagging its way toward the front of my mind. "I don't understand. Why would this bogus Martin need pictures of these guys if they're working together?"

"Probably for identification. If they're his confederates and they're from Russia, he might have procured pictures of them somehow before they arrived in this country so he'd have some way of identifying them."

"I guess . . . ," I said doubtfully.

She turned to the next one, which was a picture of Volkov and Fomin in front of a dilapidated building from which hung a sign that said CHINA WEST. They appeared to be entering it.

"China West?" said Mother, "What's that?"

"An SRO."

Mother wrinkled her nose at the picture and said, "From the looks of it, I hardly think it's that popular."

"Not standing room only, Mother," I said measuredly. "A single room occupancy hotel. Something of a flophouse. I think it's just south of the Loop."

"Oh! D'you think they were staying there?"

"I don't know. They look like they're going into it."

"Why on earth does he have these pictures?" said Mother, furrowing her brow again.

"There's a couple of more here." I tapped the remaining photos with my index finger, and Mother had just started to pick them up when the phone rang.

The sound of the phone had about the same effect on me that I would expect if I had a panic attack in the middle of a cave, and the silence between the rings was louder than the phone itself.

"OH, JESUS!" I exclaimed, jumping up from the bed.

"What?" said Mother. "It's just the phone!"

"I told Stevie to ring up here if he saw Martin come in!"

"Oh, Lor'!" said Mother. She also leaped off the bed, gathered the envelope's contents into a little pile, tapped them on the dresser to get them even, and tapped her fingers on both sides to make sure they were neat. She then slipped them back into the envelope, which was made a bit more difficult because it was a moving target due to the fact that I was holding it and trembling. The phone continued to ring.

"Calm down!" she said sternly. "For heaven's sake, you were the one with all the ideas for explaining our presence here."

"That was our presence on the *outside* of the door, Mother, not the inside!" I said frantically as I pressed the clasp on the envelope back into place, then shoved the envelope into the bottom of the dresser. Mother slipped the right bottom dresser drawer into place easily while I tried vainly to shove the damn left drawer into place without first lining it up on its tracks. She finally slapped my hands away and did it herself, managing with very little effort. I almost took the time to be amazed at her calm.

We did a quick glance around the room to make sure everything was in place. I noticed that the chair wasn't pushed as far under the desk as it could go, and ran over to it to fix that while Mother smoothed out the bedspread, tapped it with her palms as if satisfied with her work and said, "There!"

I grabbed her wrist and in my panic could barely get the words out when I said, "You're not the goddamn maid, Mother! We've got to get out of here!"

Mother put an index finger to her lips and cocked her head a little. She went to the door, opened it as quietly as possible, and peeked around it down the hall. She motioned for me to come on. We slipped through the door, which slid shut.

Just as we heard the lock click behind us, we heard from the other end of the hallway the faint sound of the elevator bell ringing once to signify that an elevator was stopping at this floor on its way up.

"This way," said Mother, shoving open the door to the emergency stairs and pulling me in after her.

I had wanted to stay by the door to see if it really was the bogus Martin who got off the elevator, but Mother nixed that idea because there was no way we could have the door to the stairs open even a crack without his noticing. I whispered hurriedly that we could stay there and listen through the door, figuring that we could probably hear if somebody was going into his room, but Mother just looked at me and whispered back, "There really isn't any point."

We didn't run down the stairs for fear it would make noise and we'd be noticed, but my heart was racing enough to make up for our lack of speed. We proceeded quietly down two flights of stairs, then went out into the hallway and down to the elevators. I have to admit that when I heard the elevator bell ring twice and the down arrow lit up, my heart went from racing to standing still until the doors were fully open and we could see that it was empty. I realize that this was a foolish reaction on my part, because if that had been the bogus Martin returning to his room, there was no reason to believe that he would leave again right away. But I'm only human.

Once we'd reached the lobby, Mother waited by the staircase while I returned the room key to Stevie. He leaned over the desk and needlessly stroked my fingers as he pulled the key away. With those buggy eyes of his, it was impossible for him not to look as if he were leering.

"I see you got my message," he said.

"You mean that *was* Martin?"

"Oh, yes. I assume that there was no . . . problem?"

"No. We weren't seen."

"Hmm," he said, forming his lips into a little pucker and blinking at me. "Well, I'd *love* to frisk you to make sure you're not stashing anything, but I'm on duty." He glanced down at my crotch and added, "You don't look like you're packing anything more than you came in with!"

My own lips curled into something that felt like a cross between a smile and a warning. I thanked him again, and when I turned to walk away, I rolled my eyes so violently that I almost reeled backward and fell over.

Having noticed the momentary teeter as I approached her, Mother said, "What on earth was that?"

"Just a general reaction to Stevie, Mother. Never mind!"

We took a cab home, flush with our newfound success as burglars. Mother was exhilarated in a way that was becoming common to her, and I was definitely beginning to feel that she really *was* a thrill seeker. However, in this instance any thrill she might have experienced was tempered by the belief that our brief sortie to the hotel room had been a failure.

"We didn't find much!" she said, though from the way her face was glowing you would have thought we'd made off with the Hope diamond.

"At least we found the letters."

"Yes," said Mother with consideration, "I just wish we knew how the bogus Martin got hold of them. And that's my new wish for this little caper." She added this last with a coy smile to me.

"What?"

"Now that we've found Volkov and Fomin's names, so we no longer have to refer to them as the clay people, I wish to God we could find out this other man's real name, so we can stop calling him the bogus Martin. It's so damnably time consuming."

"Yes, Mother."

"Anyway, I wish we knew how he got hold of those faxes."

I gave this some thought, then said, "Well, you know, there's one thing we never thought of."

"What's that?"

"I guess since Victor Hacheck was killed, and we think—or thought—that this bogus Martin did it, I got to assuming that Hacheck and Martin were on opposite sides in whatever's going on."

"Um-hmm," said Mother, her expression clearly indicating that she had no idea where I was going with this.

"Well, isn't it just as likely that they were on the same side? I mean, we know that the bogus Martin and Fomin and Volkov were working together—the fact that he sent Fomin to kill me last night should put any doubts to rest—well, doesn't it follow that Hacheck was actually working with them, too?"

Mother continued to look at me for a moment, then a light

dawned. She nodded her head and said, "Ah, I see what you're driving at. A falling out amongst thieves."

"Exactly. Maybe that's why they were all so damn frantic to find out if he'd said anything to me. They wanted to know if he'd given away their game."

"Whatever their game is," said Mother, curling her lip as she considered.

"Maybe these names I copied from that one fax will lead somewhere. I just wish to hell I could remember where I've heard of Matthew Corbin."

I stopped and looked at her for a moment, not really wanting to say what I was thinking, but I took a deep breath and went ahead anyway. With two people dead, you really can't spare someone's feelings. "And you know, the fastest way to find out if these names are important would be to give them to Frank."

Mother gave me a stern look, not because she thought I'd done something wrong, but to convey that she was very serious about what she was about to say:

"Nothing doing, darling."

"But Mother . . ."

"Nothing doing. It's clear to me after last night that I can't rely on Frank without him wanting to start up again, and I just don't want that. We'll have to leave him out of this business unless it's absolutely necessary. And even then I'll have to think about it."

She was wrong. When it became absolutely necessary, she didn't have to think about it at all. I did.

It was a little after eleven A.M. when we arrived home. The phone was ringing as we walked in the door, and Mother went to the kitchen to put on a pot of tea while I got the phone. I said, "Hello?" and was greeted by an agitated voice that sounded faintly familiar to me.

"Is Peter there?"

"No," I said, "he's at work right now."

"No, he isn't."

"Excuse me," I said warily, beginning to remember to whom

this voice belonged, "may I ask who's calling?"

"Is that Alex?"

"Yes," I said, becoming impatient, "who is this?"

"It's Arthur Dingle."

"Oh, Mr. Dingle, I'm sorry."

Mother came into the room, apparently drawn by the tone of my voice. "Who is it?" she mouthed at me. I covered the mouthpiece while I whispered back, "Peter's boss."

I said into the phone, "Aren't you at the store?"

"Yes, I am, but Peter isn't."

"He isn't?" I said in disbelief, my lower intestines starting to turn over.

"No, and he was supposed to be here at ten."

"Mr. Dingle"—I could barely get words to come out of my mouth, still not wanting to believe what I was hearing—"he left for the store at . . . about twenty after nine!"

"Well, he never got here," said the store owner.

THIRTEEN

When I put down the receiver, I noticed for the first time that the red light on our answering machine was blinking. I pushed the "answer-play" button, and the tape rewound itself, then played the messages. The first was a call from Mr. Dingle asking where Peter was and why he wasn't at work. The next four calls, the caller had hung up without leaving a message.

"What is it?" said Mother. "What's going on?"

"It's Peter. He didn't make it to work this morning."

Mother paused for a moment, and the look on her face was of total disbelief. "He left here almost two hours ago, and it hardly takes him any time to get to Oak Street."

"I know that," I snapped. "Something's happened to him. Oh, God. Something's happened to him."

Mother shook her head resignedly and said, "Well, we've no choice now, we have to call the police and tell them everything."

"No!"

"Alex, we have no choice. If Peter's missing, we have to call the police!"

"NO! We can't risk it! This has to have something to do with this Russian business, though I don't know why they'd take Peter."

My brain seemed to be functioning at a highly accelerated rate, spewing a lot of information around in my head, but not properly processing anything.

As all those thoughts and ideas spun around wildly in my mind, there was one thought that was underlying all others: I didn't want to lose Peter. The past four years had been the best in my life. He'd come along when I wasn't looking for anyone and had really not even considered pairing up with anyone in particular. But then Peter entered the scene and changed all that. He didn't have to work his way into my heart—he just arrived with his luggage one day and set up shop as if a room had always been ready for him there. Although I readily admit how much I love him, I think that like everyone else I'd be hard pressed to admit how much I'd come to need him. But it's the truth. And life without him was something I hadn't considered since we'd met. I didn't want to consider it now.

"It'll be all right, Alex," said Mother kindly but firmly. She didn't want me giving way to panic.

"But why the fuck would they want him? What's the point? He's not the one who got us into this mess—I am. And we've already turned over the damn matchbook, they must know by now we don't still have it."

Mother thought for a moment, her face turned slightly aside from me as she considered the possibilities. I studied her face during the silence. She might be holding up, but the worry she was feeling was evident. Her eyes were set and tight as she stared at nothing, the corners of her mouth turned down slightly in the nearest she ever came to a frown.

"Perhaps . . . ," she said, turning toward me, "perhaps it's a way of keeping us out of it. Maybe they think if they hold Peter, they can keep us from interfering."

I was almost hysterical. "We haven't been interfering. We've been trying to give them what they want!"

Mother clucked her tongue. "We were interfering last night—and that man was killed."

"That wasn't our fault! The CIA asked me to meet him."

159

"And we were interfering this morning. Playing at being burglars! What idiots we've been! And now look what's happened. We never should have gotten involved in this to begin with!"

There was absolutely no note of recrimination in her tone when she said this, but her words stung anyway. And it must have registered on my face, because she inhaled sharply when she noticed my reaction and she crossed to me and put her hands on my shoulders.

"I didn't mean that the way it sounded, darling. None of this was your fault. All I meant was that once we accidentally got involved we should have told Frank everything and then stayed the hell out of it and let the professionals handle it."

"But we couldn't do that," I said, frustration almost choking my words. "Remember, I had that stupid matchbook without knowing it, and that's what they were after. We couldn't help being involved."

"You're right. I know it. I said the same to Frank." She shook her head as if she was dismissing all extraneous thought, then said, "Enough of that. There's no point going back over it now and wondering what we should have done. The question is, what are we going to do now?"

"I don't know," I said.

"I'm still in favor of calling the police. Alex, you must realize this has gone way beyond us."

I don't know how the conversation would have proceeded from there, but as it happened, we were interrupted by a phone call. I was so wary of answering the phone again I almost waited until the machine picked it up. But I remembered in time that whoever it was who'd been calling hadn't wanted to leave a message on the machine, and I had a feeling that whoever was trying to reach us was someone I needed to talk to.

Mother stood by watching in grim silence as I picked up the receiver and pressed it to my ear. I was so filled with trepidation that it was almost a full thirty seconds before I tentatively said, "Hello?"

"Mr. Reynolds, at last you've come home," said the Russian-accented voice.

I plucked up some courage and said, "What do you want, Mr. Volkov?"

There was a moment's silence during which I could sense the surprise of the caller. Surprise and anger.

"Ah, so you've discovered my name. It would be best for you if that was all you discovered."

"What do you want, Mr. Volkov?"

There was another brief silence, and I could just feel the bastard smiling into his end of the phone.

"I have something that belongs to you."

I swallowed hard and said, "What?"

"I believe you mean who. That's the proper word in this case, I think. I have taken your friend."

I swallowed hard and, trying to keep the emotion out of my voice, said once again, "What do you want, Mr. Volkov?"

"I want what Victor Hacheck gave you in that . . . bar."

I closed my eyes and gritted my teeth. "I don't have it. I gave it to the CIA."

"Mr. Reynolds, I assure you that your friend is very uncomfortable. I would suggest you stop lying to me and do as I ask."

"I don't—"

"I had a friend, too, you know, until last night. I had a friend. He seems to have gotten himself killed when meeting with you. I assure you that I will not hesitate to do the same to your friend. What is it that you say in your Bible? An eye for an eye . . . a friend for a friend?"

"You don't understand—"

"I do understand, Mr. Reynolds. It is almost noon. I will give you three hours to decide what you will do. I will call you back then. If you decide to be sensible, your . . . friend will be back with you by tonight. If you are not sensible, you will not see him again. I'm sure I need not tell you that if you involve the police *this time*"—he emphasized the last two words as if he knew we were directly responsible for the police having shown up the night before—"I will kill him anyway."

The line went dead.

The words reverberated in my head—"You will not see him again. . . ."

"What did he say?" Mother asked, waking me from my reverie.

I looked at her, and I was so tense now that I felt like my skin was tightening around my skull, like all the water had been sucked out of my body and my outer layer was stretching across my skeleton.

"Just a minute," I said. I ran up to my room and retrieved my pack of cigarettes, pulled an ashtray from the desk drawer where I kept it stashed just in case I felt the need, and brought both back downstairs.

Mother was absolutely and unequivocally against smoking, but in my absence she had gone to the kitchen and brought out a pack of matches.

"Here, darling," she said.

"I'm sorry."

"It's all right, it's all right. Now, what did he say?"

I pulled a cigarette from the pack, which was still almost full, lit it, drew in some smoke, and began to pace as I exhaled. "He has Peter, just as we thought. And he will give him back in exchange for 'what Victor Hacheck gave me in that bar.' "

"Oh, dear," said Mother, sinking into a chair. Her expression was almost completely blank, save for the way her eyebrows drew nearer to each other in the middle. After a moment she looked up and said, "Did you tell him we didn't have it?"

"Of course I did! You heard me! I don't know why the hell they don't believe me! He told me that I have until three o'clock to decide to give it to him. And if I don't, he'll kill Peter."

Mother watched me pace back and forth for a minute, then said as evenly as she could, "Alex, we have to call the police."

"We can't! He said—Volkov said not to. He said if we called the police, he would kill Peter no matter what."

"Well, what are we going to do?" she said, rising from her chair. "Even if we wanted to give it to them, we don't have the damned thing! What are we going to do?"

"I don't know! Jesus, I don't know." I took another drag on the cigarette and exhaled. It had the effect of holding back the tears that I was sure were going to break through soon, anyhow.

"I know I said I didn't want to do this, but we can call Frank again."

"No!"

"But be sensible! Frank is our friend, and he can be discreet . . . if we tell him—"

"NO!" I said, and this time it was almost a shout. I took a deep breath to calm myself down and continued, "Can he discreetly carry out a manhunt? For God's sake, there's nothing we can do!"

"Alex, think: we know this bogus Martin is involved, and we know where he's staying now. We can tell Frank that, and he can bring him in."

"Are you crazy? That would be doing exactly what Volkov said not to! They're in it together. Volkov will know if the police have questioned Martin . . . or whatever his goddamn name is."

Mother's expression hardened even more, and her eyes widened farther. "There is nothing else we can do. Don't you see? We have to tell the police. We don't have the matchbook, and we don't have anything else. All we have is the list of names we got from Martin's hotel room, and a good job that'll do us. We have barely three hours, and we don't even know where to start to identify them."

I stubbed the cigarette out into the ashtray, which I'd kept in my hand as I paced around. I drew another one from the pack and lit it. Mother said nothing.

A silence full of tension unlike anything I'd ever experienced with Mother had fallen between us. I continued to pace and smoke, and Mother stood in front of the couch, looking at the floor and clenching and unclenching her hands. I don't know how long we would have gone on like that had the doorbell not rung.

I went to the curtains, which we were now keeping closed all the time through some silent mutual consent. I peeked through a slit on the side and saw Frank standing on our doorstep. I wouldn't have thought it possible, but I tensed even more at the sight of him. Still holding the curtain I looked over to Mother and said, "It's Frank."

She looked up at me, and her expression was full of determination, but it was impossible to read exactly what she'd determined. I pointed my cigarette at her and said, "Not a word."

She continued to stare at me impassively as I went to the door and admitted Frank.

Frank could never really be considered a breath of fresh air, but at that particular moment he came into our house like a stale wind. Though he exuded his usual determination, he definitely appeared to have been cowed somewhat by whatever it was Mother had said to him when they'd had their talk. I had the feeling that this visit was some sort of unspoken test or challenge, as if he were bent on pressing his position in Mother's life. It was *just* the added attraction we needed now.

The worst part about it was that at this moment I wasn't sure of where Mother stood, not with Frank but with me. She usually honors my wishes as much as possible, but at the same time she's not one to give in when she feels very strongly about something. I knew that no matter how much I wanted to keep the police out of this, no matter how much I feared disobeying Volkov's edict, if Mother felt strongly that we should tell them, she would.

Frank said, "Hello Alex," to me in a noncommittal way, with a glance at my cigarette, the presence of which seemed to tell him something. He went to Mother and said, "I'm on my way to area headquarters, and I thought I'd stop by and tell you I got hold of Agent Nelson, the man I'm working with from the CIA, and he said some things that were kind of strange."

"What do you mean?" asked Mother, raising one eyebrow.

"He seemed to know all about you, and he wanted me to convey a message to you."

Mother and I glanced at one another nervously.

164

"What would that be?" said Mother as innocently as she knew how.

"He wanted me to tell you that in light of last night's events he wants you to 'stay out of it'—whatever that may mean."

Frank's expression was triumphant as he stared at her, as if he'd caught her out in some sort of lie. It was really the first time since they'd known each other that I could see a touch of what Peter disliked so much about him. I would have given anything to have wiped that look off his face.

"What?" said Mother after a beat.

"You heard me."

I could see it in his face. He knew. He knew a hell of a lot more than we thought he knew. And I was *really* tempted to blurt out what had happened to Peter and ask him for his help. But that thought was immediately negated by remembering how many times I'd been fooled since this whole thing began, and I didn't want that to happen again. Not with Peter's life at stake. Mother glanced over at me, and I could see that she, too, had noticed the tone of Frank's voice and had come to the same conclusion I had. Her eyes seemed to beseech me for permission to tell him what was happening, but as soon as Frank turned away from me, I glared at her and shook my head rapidly from side to side. From the look on her face, it was clear that she knew the extent of my anxiety on this point, so she kept still.

She simply looked at Frank and said, "Well, I'm glad you stopped by with that message," as if she were a hostess who was getting rid of a guest who had stayed a trifle too long.

Frank glared at her for a moment, then said, "Sure, yeah, all right."

As he crossed to the door and opened it, Mother said, "Frank, I really do appreciate it."

He glanced back at her over his shoulder, more for effect, I thought, than anything else. Then after this dramatic pause, he said, "By the way—you know, another Russian was killed last night."

Mother and I couldn't have looked guiltier if we'd pulled the trigger ourselves. I could see it on her face and I could feel it on mine.

Mother's mouth barely moved as she said, "We haven't seen the paper yet today."

Without another word, Frank passed through the door, closing it behind him.

It was a relief when our own private policeman was gone. I took another drag from the cigarette, blew out the smoke, and said, "Thank you."

Mother heaved the most disgusted sigh I'd ever heard from her and said, "I have never felt shabbier in my life."

"I have no room to feel shabby right now, it's all I can do to handle the panic. We have to figure out what we're going to do!"

We were silent for a minute, but both our minds were racing so quickly that if there'd been a third person in the room, he could have heard our brainwaves. I went back to pacing back and forth and smoking as if there was no tomorrow. Mother dropped into the chair from which she'd risen earlier and brushed at her skirt: it was a nervous gesture that I rarely saw her exhibit since she's not prone to nervousness.

At last she said, "Perhaps we could give him a decoy. You took a matchbook with you last night, didn't you?"

"Well, yes," I said, continuing my pacing, "but I had the CIA with me last night, too. And I never thought I'd actually have to give the thing to the guy. We can't give a decoy to Volkov, he must know what the real one looks like—and it doesn't look like any matchbook I've seen here. It was red and glossy. Hacheck must've brought it with him from Russia." I puffed a few more times on my cigarette, then turned to Mother and said, "There's only one thing we can do, as I see it: get the real matchbook back."

"But Frank just got through saying that the CIA doesn't want us involved anymore."

"What the hell do I care what the CIA wants? What've they ever done for me? We have to go and talk to Martin."

"What makes you think they'll give it back to us?"

I crushed the remainder of the cigarette out in the ashtray

and laid the ashtray on a table by the couch. "I don't know, there's something really strange about that whole matchbook thing. Both Volkov and Fomin claimed that I hadn't given it to the CIA, which is ridiculous, because I did. Unless . . ."

"Unless what?" said Mother.

"Unless the real Mr. Martin didn't turn it over to the field agents like he said he would."

Mother paled at this suggestion, as if the thought that an actual CIA agent might do something shady was more deplorable than she cared to think about. I almost found that funny. At last she said, "Oh, but that's ridiculous. He must have given it to them."

"There's only one way to find out."

"Well, what are you going to tell *him?*" said Mother, the frustration in her voice beginning to match mine. "I can't believe he'd just hand the thing over to you without explanation."

"Then I'll just have to tell him what's happened to Peter and hope he'll let us handle this our own way. We can't afford for the CIA to be involved anyway. Not if last night is any indication. We don't have any choice. We've got to get that matchbook back!"

FOURTEEN

The cab ride back downtown to the CIA recruitment office would have been silent, were it not for the fact we had one of those cabbies who delight in telling you their life stories. Given the strain we were under, I found his monologue exceptionally irritating. It seemed like hours before we arrived at the Federal Building.

We caught the elevator to the seventeenth floor. Thankful there weren't any passengers getting off before we did. That made me feel as if the gods were in our favor and we were being given a straight shot to the CIA.

We entered the outer office and were confronted by the stony glare of the secretary who'd been there on our previous visit. Her hair looked as if it hadn't moved a muscle since then, which added to the effect of her somehow having shellacked it into place. She was wearing a different dress—a knit in an unnaturally bright pink that no one over five years old should wear. Her eyes immediately fastened on us as we came through the door, and she scanned Mother and me as if she'd never seen us before, which didn't say much for the way she'd tried to memorize us the first time. I didn't feel in the mood to deal with her, so I marched through the office with Mother in tow.

"What—wait . . . ," the secretary said as we passed her desk, but Mother replied simply, "Don't bother to announce us," as I opened the door to the inner office and passed through.

The secretary was up like a shot and followed us to the door, barking, "You can't just go in there," to our backs. Then she grabbed hold of the doorknob with a white, spiderlike hand and said to the startled Mr. Martin, "I'm sorry, sir, they just barged on in."

Martin's dull blue eyes were wide with surprise, then his senatorial lip curled and he looked past us at his secretary and said, "That's all right, Lorraine."

Lorraine. It figured.

Mother and I both watched her as she narrowed her eyes at us as if she could squeeze poison darts from them, twisted the doorknob, said a quiet "Very well" to Martin, and exited, closing the door noisily behind her.

Martin turned to us, and his expression transformed from surprise to something approaching condescension.

"Well, my two amateur agents!" he said, pushing his chair back to expose his protruding stomach, which seemed to be really straining the capacity of his belt.

"Mr. Martin—" Mother started, but Martin shook his head at her, put his palms up to stop her, and smiled in a way that let us both know that he considered us just short of idiots.

"You got me into quite a bit of hot water, you know. I understand that business that the field boys set up last night went sour."

"Not through any of our doing," said Mother. She was on her high horse now. "And I told you when you came to our home with that ridiculous scheme that I thought it was too dangerous for us to be participating in!"

"That you did, but I can tell you that the boys were miffed at you for blowing it."

"I don't give a bloody damn what your 'boys' are miffed about! *My* boy could've been killed!"

"Yeah," I said ineffectually, "besides, we didn't blow it. That fake Martin guy didn't show up, but one of his buddies did."

"So he must've known it was a setup, somehow," said Mother. I could now understand the look on Martin's face. We were sounding more idiotic by the minute. I mean, how often does one's mother talk to the CIA about setups and henchmen?

"Now, Mother," I said, willing to take some of the heat off the CIA (especially since we now wanted their help), "to be perfectly fair, I told you at the time I thought that man who called himself Martin sounded like he thought it was a setup."

"Quite right," said Mother hotly. "All the more reason *they* shouldn't have involved *us*."

Martin smiled, the condescension in his expression growing. He looked like a congressman who was about to proposition a page. "Well, little lady, you really are a pistol!"

Both Mother and I gaped at the man, our expressions frozen in incredulity.

Martin gave her one of those looks that is meant to convey that the looker is tired of being made a fool of.

"You come here with some cock-and-bull story about being followed by foreign agents and phony government agents coming to your door, and like the big sap I am, I actually buy it! Then the field boys set up some sort of sting last night, and the person *you claim* has been impersonating me don't . . . doesn't show up. And some stranger ends up getting himself killed. I should have my head examined for listening to you in the first place, and here you are again! What? Did you think up some more stories?"

"What are you saying?" asked Mother, her jaw drooping with shock.

"You two are really something, you know that? You must think I'm a big fool, and I suppose I've given you every reason to believe that. But I'm not as big a fool as you think I am!"

"But—" I started to protest, but Martin cut me off. He leaned back in his chair with a loud creak and linked his fingers behind his head, once again revealing two identical underarm stains on this shirt. His face beamed some sort of triumph at us as he said, "Is this how you two get your jollies? Making up stories like this and getting everybody all worked up about 'em? I'll bet they love you down at the police station!"

The irony of that statement, given Mother's relationship with Frank, was lost on me at that particular moment since I was still immobilized with disbelief. It was a good thing that Mother took the lead because my mind and my mouth had gone blank at the same time. I had no idea what to say.

"Do you mean to tell me that you don't believe anything we've told you?"

"Why keep it up, lady?"

There was a second's pause, during which I'm sure Mother wondered, as I did, whether or not Martin was joking. But the expression on his pudgy face showed that he was deadly serious.

"But what about last night? That man did come—not the one we were expecting, but his friend, and he tried to kill my son . . . *would* have killed him if one of your men hadn't shot him first!"

Martin was not to be swayed. "I may not work the field like the other boys, and I may just be the low-class head of personnel, but I recognize horse pucky when I step in it."

"But why—"

"So your boy had the bad luck to have somebody try to hold him up. What the hell d'you expect in some out-of-the-way place like that in the middle of the night?"

"*We* didn't choose the place!" said Mother indignantly.

"So what?" said Martin, with an annoying amount of pride in his voice at having worked the whole thing out—and I couldn't help thinking that this wasn't his own idea, that the "field boys" had come up with this scenario and delivered it to him. "So what if some holdup man had the bad luck to try it on with somebody that was being covered by the CIA?"

"A hold-up man!" I exclaimed.

"But he was one of the men who attacked Alex in the bar . . . he said to him—"

"Please, lady, spare me any more of the stories, all right? I'm not in the mood for any more . . . fairy tales." When he said this last part, he lowered his head slightly and stared up at me from under his eyebrows. I was really angry with myself, because I could feel my face reddening with anger at this cheap shot, and I would have given my right arm to avoid having this big oaf thinking he'd gotten to me. Besides, we still hadn't gotten to the point of our visit, and it was an important point, though I already felt we were lost.

"So, if you don't mind me saying so, you've taken up enough of my time. You think you could tell me why you came here today?" said Martin. A tiny bit of saliva darted into the corner of his mouth.

"We've come about the matchbook," I said.

Martin stared at me in disbelief. It was a look that shouldn't have surprised me, given everything he'd just said: but the look on his face was mixed with uncertainty, and that did surprise me. He licked away the bit of saliva, then suddenly slapped his palms against the top of his desk and laughed derisively. "Don't that beat all! After that bunch of crap yesterday you've come to me about that crappin' matchbook! That really does beat all!"

I took a deep breath to quell my anger and said, "Mr. Martin, this is a serious matter."

He laughed again and said, "I'm just sure it is."

"We need the matchbook back!"

He stopped laughing for a fraction of a second, then laughed even more loudly. It sounded false and mocking. I would've given anything to have slapped him hard with the back of my hand, but I couldn't afford any such gesture at the moment.

He made a show of calming himself down, smoothing the greasy hair back off his forehead, and said, "So you want the matchbook back! Why? It have sentimental value or something?"

"Mr. Martin," said Mother, her tone trying desperately to convey that this was very serious, "Peter . . . Alex's friend . . . has been—"

He cut her off. "I told you, I don't want to hear any more stories."

"Has been kidnapped," Mother continued, closing her eyes for a brief moment to draw the strength to maintain her composure, "by one of the foreign agents. The partner of the one who was shot last night. They want what Victor Hacheck gave to my son, the matchbook, but we gave it to you. We have to get it back. We have to give it to them."

Martin had replaced his fingers behind his head, and with an expression of utmost smugness had watched Mother as she'd spoken. I could've killed him. He looked as if he were humoring a precocious child.

"Why, that's real exciting, ma'am."

Mother looked shocked. "Mr. Martin—"

"But if these bad guys want that matchbook back, they're outta luck."

"What do you mean?" I said, and my voice sounded so choked I barely recognized it as my own.

Martin leaned forward in a sudden, angry movement and slapped his fists down on the desktop. "Because I passed it on to the field boys. I passed it on because I believed that story you told me. Why the hell do you think I'm in such hot water?"

Mother's forehead creased heavily. She shook her head and turned her palms up questioningly, as if she would have liked to ask him why, but couldn't get the word out.

He noticed her discomfiture but didn't wait for the question before he said, "Because there was nothing in it!"

"What?" we said in unison.

"There was nothing in it. Nothing in it at all! It was just an ordinary matchbook."

"That's impossible," I said hotly.

"We . . . they went over it with a fine-tooth comb. Didn't find nothing!"

"But there has to be something!" said Mother.

He simply shook his head at her. "And believe me, nobody's

too happy about it. As for getting it back, I'm sure whatever was left when the boys got through with it has been pitched by now."

Out came the soiled handkerchief that we had yet to see on this visit. He mopped his forehead with it and shoved it unceremoniously into his back pocket. Then he smoothed back his hair again and turned his watery eyes from Mother to me and back again. His expression became more serious.

"Look, you've wasted enough of our time. Why don't you run on home now?"

I was about to open my mouth to protest, but Mother stood up suddenly and said, "Well, I guess we'll get no more help here."

"That's right!" Martin replied, his bushy eyebrows arching over his dull eyes.

"Come along, Alex," said Mother.

I looked at her as if I thought we should try further, especially with Peter's life at stake, but I realized that she was probably right: we were just wasting our time there. I rose from my chair but Martin remained in his, not bothering with even the most perfunctory politeness. Mother opened the door, and I almost collided with her when she stopped suddenly and turned back to Martin.

"Oh," she said, "I almost forgot." She started to rummage in her purse and said to me, "Maybe he can help us with our list."

"Huh?" was my ineffectual reply.

Mother pulled the little notebook out of her purse, and flipped through the pages trying to find her place. "Mr. Martin, I wonder if you could tell us if you've ever heard of . . ." She turned three more pages before she found the one with the list, then stopped, tapped the list with her index finger, and said:

". . . Matthew Corbin?"

The effect was as if she had hit him under the chin with a two-by-four. Martin had been playing at looking through documents on his desk to make us feel even more insignificant while we exited. When Mother said the name, Martin's head snapped back with enough force to propel his chair back about half a foot. His eyes were wide and glazed. He took barely thirty seconds to think before he shook his head angrily and said, "No, I've never heard of anybody like that. Now I'm busy."

"Hmm . . . or Larry Wyler? Or Joseph Smith? Andrew Peterson? Robert Dickson?"

"Mrs. Reynolds," said Martin, making a great show of reaching the end of his patience but looking a little too pale at this point to carry it off, "I said I'm busy. If ya don't mind?"

Mother smiled. "Not at all."

"You think he was telling the truth? I mean about there being nothing in the matchbook? Maybe there really was something and they just don't want to admit it."

"I hope not. I'd like to think the CIA would do something to help us get Peter back, if the matchbook still existed."

"And if they didn't think we were crackpots."

"Yes," said Mother slowly.

"What are we going to do now? The matchbook was the only thing we had to trade, and it doesn't even exist anymore!"

Mother's face grew grave with thought, and I was sure at that point that this case was going to further line her face. She said, "The only thing we have to go on is this list of names."

"Why did you ask him about Corbin?"

"I don't know . . . I supposed that maybe the real agents had told him something about what they were working on, and maybe he'd heard the name."

"What about that?" I said, my own face wrinkling. "What about the way Martin reacted when you mentioned those names?"

"That was quite odd," said Mother. Then her lips, which had been pursed, relaxed into a smile. "You know, it's a good thing for Mr. Martin that he's only in personnel. He certainly wouldn't have made a very good agent."

"No, he didn't do very well hiding that he'd heard of them. That means Corbin must have something to do with this CIA business."

"But darling, *you've* heard of Matthew Corbin, too."

I sighed heavily, once again feeling as if we were simply running around in circles. We pondered our current problem in silence for a couple of minutes as we stood waiting for the streetlight to change. When it did and we started across the street, I said, "So how do we go about identifying the names on that list?"

"Well. . . ," said Mother slowly, "there's always the library. We can check out the current *Who's Who* and whatnot."

"For God's sake, we have less than three hours now!"

"I don't know what else to do. You know, the library will also have the newspaper indexes so if they've done something noteworthy recently they'll probably—"

"Oh, my God!" I said loudly, coming to a stop in the middle of the street. It's a credit to Chicago that none of our fellow pedestrians even turned their heads, except for the couple that barked something at me about getting out of their way.

"Alex, what is it?"

I turned to her slowly, my mouth hanging open both in surprise and stupidity.

"Kidnapping! I just remembered where I saw Matthew Corbin's name!"

There it was in glorious black and white: "American Businessman Returned." Mother had thankfully not yet thrown out the Sunday paper, so it was still in a brown paper bag beside the kitchen garbage can waiting, as Mother put it, for one of her darling boys to take it to the alley. I retrieved it, spread it on the kitchen table, and paged through it quickly, trying to find the article I had scanned briefly on Saturday. And there it was.

The article was about an American businessman, Matthew Corbin, who had been abducted in Moscow and held for ransom. After eleven days and nights, the company for which Corbin worked had paid the ransom through an unknown source, and Corbin had been returned. Unfortunately, Corbin could apparently offer no information whatsoever about his abductors. He had been attacked from behind, then blindfolded. The only thing he had to say was that his abductors had not harmed him (except during the initial attack when he was taken), but that he hadn't eaten well while in captivity.

"That's all very interesting," said Mother, "but what does it tell us?"

"A lot of things. One is that the man who called himself Martin must have some connection to this. Why else would we find Corbin's name on a fax in his room? He must have something to do with this kidnapping. And I'll bet if we *did* go through the newspaper indexes at the library, we'd find that these other four men were also kidnap victims."

"Maybe," said Mother doubtfully, "but that doesn't explain what Victor Hacheck, and Volkov and Fomin, as well as this bogus Martin fellow are doing here. All that kidnapping is going on in Russia."

"Not all of it," I said pointedly.

Mother shook her head ruefully. "You're right about that. But that still leaves us with the question, what are they doing here? I would think that if you have money, Russia isn't that bad a place to be . . . sort of like New York."

"So?"

"So . . . if they are involved in some sort of kidnapping ring, and they're at all successful at it, as these people are"—she tapped the newspaper article—"then you'd think they'd be doing all right in Russia."

"Mother, I'm really missing something here."

She sighed and said, "What I'm trying to say is, if they're kidnapping Americans for money and they're getting away with it, then you'd think they'd be safe as long as they were in Russia. But you know they don't take kindly to kidnapping here in America . . ."

I rolled my eyes at this, because Mother's penchant for the natural understatement of the British has a habit of rearing its head at the oddest moments.

". . . no, honestly, Alex. You would think America would be the last place they'd want to be."

I thought about that for a moment, then suddenly the gates

in my brain blew open, the flood poured through, and for the first time in days I thought I had some inkling as to what the hell was going on around here.

"Unless . . ."

"I do hate it when you do that, darling. Unless what?"

"Unless something went wrong. Oh, my God, we've got to get Peter away from these people right away."

That is when it happened.

I reached into my shirt pocket for my pack of Marlboro Lights and drew a cigarette out of the pack. As I did, I heard a soft, muted rattle in the pack. I looked into the opening and shook the pack, which was now about two-thirds full, and thought I saw something move. I glanced at Mother, then turned the pack over and let the object slide out onto the newspaper. It was a small gray cylinder, no wider than a cigarette but about half its length. I had no idea what it was, but I knew exactly how it'd gotten there. The moment I saw it I realized what Hacheck had done: when I'd handed him the pack, which at that time was only shy two or three cigarettes, he slipped this thing into it, shoving it back and down between the tightly packed cigarettes. It hadn't worked its way free until I'd smoked a few more (actually, several more in the past couple of hours).

"That bastard!" I said. "He set me up!"

"What do you mean?" said Mother, looking at the little gray tube that lay in the palm of my hand.

"I mean he set me up! That matchbook was a blind! It's this thing that they're after!"

"I thought they were after the matchbook."

"That's just it! Don't you see? They don't *know* what they're after. Even the phony Martin told us that. They don't know what Hacheck was carrying, they just knew that he was going to pass it to somebody here! That motherfucker slipped that goddamn matchbook into my pocket as a blind!"

Mother said halfheartedly, "Alex, please, your language."

I ignored this. I found my language perfectly valid for the occasion. "Think about it, Mother. He *let* them see him put that damn matchbook in my pocket, when he'd already slipped this into my cigarette pack."

"How?"

"I gave him the damn pack to take out a cigarette."

"Well, I still don't see—"

"Mother, this way it didn't matter what happened to me as long as those foreign guys thought they were after the matchbook. It didn't even matter if they killed me—they probably wouldn't have bothered with my cigarettes!"

Mother's eyes were riveted to the little tube as I rolled it between my thumb and forefinger. She was obviously putting this all together in her head, and when she was finished, without moving her head she swiveled her eyes in my direction and said, "That son of a bitch!"

"Yeah, that son of a bitch!" I echoed, and closed my fist around the tube and took out a cigarette.

"Now we know what they were after," said Mother as I lit up, "but we don't know what it is."

I smiled at her, my eyes narrowing, "I don't know what it is to *them*, but I know what it is to me: a claim ticket, to redeem Peter!"

Mother looked at me in a way that made me fear that rough weather was ahead. Her eyelids drooped to about half-mast, and she sucked in the right side of her lips.

"What?" I said, trying to mask my apprehension with irritation.

"Well. . . ," she said as she folded her arms across her chest, "if these really are the same people who kidnapped that man in Russia . . . they're professionals."

She stopped, and I prodded her on with a simple "Yes?"

"It's comforting to know that . . . if we can go by the story in the paper . . . that if we do what they want, they'll release Peter."

"Yes?"

She took the little tube from me, held it between two fingers, and shook it. "Whatever this is, it must put the kidnappers in jeopardy. Why else would they go to so much trouble to retrieve it?"

I was afraid I knew where she was going with this, but I really didn't want to understand her. I just answered her with "So?"

Mother could always read me like a book. She laid her hand on my arm and kept her voice even but firm. "Alex, these are very bad people. We know they kidnapped Peter, we think they kidnapped that man in Russia, and they probably kidnapped all the people on that list and put them and their families through what we're going through now."

"So?" I said, pulling my arm away from her. "I don't care about all those people! I just want to get Peter back safely. That's the only thing that's important to me."

"I know that, darling, and it's the most important thing to me, too. But there's something else that's important: these people need to be stopped."

"Not at the expense of Peter."

Mother smiled and rolled the tube between her fingers.

"Well, darling, if we're clever, maybe we can do both!"

I raised an eyebrow at her, and she turned her glistening blue eyes at me and said those fateful words, "I've got an idea."

Oh, Lord, I thought, once again I'm Ethel Mertz.

FIFTEEN

Actually, Mother's idea wasn't all that bad, if you set aside the difficulties, the most obvious being there was no way in hell it could work. We were taking a few chances. Well, we were taking a hell of a lot of chances, but only a few of them are worth mentioning. The first and most important to me is that we were assuming that Volkov really *was* staying in the China West Hotel. Mother's whole plan hinged on the assumption that that's what the picture we'd found in the bogus Martin's room meant. So that was the first and most important variable. If he wasn't really staying there, then the plan was a failure to begin with. Second, we were assuming that the China West was also where Volkov was holding Peter. This would be a logical assumption since it wasn't the type of place where one's victim-holding was likely to be interrupted by pesky maid service. And the neighbors weren't likely to complain about the occasional cry of torment. The third chance we were taking was more of a dim hope than anything else: that when Volkov left the building, he'd leave Peter alone. This one worried me because I didn't think he'd be foolish enough to leave a hostage unattended, and because if he would, it seemed most likely that Peter had been . . . disabled somehow.

And adding to my anxiety on that point was the fact that we didn't know where the bogus Martin was at the moment, though Mother had an idea about that, too.

All of this went through my mind as I waited by the pay phone for Mother's call. I had strategically parked the car about half a block down from the China West so as not to be too obvious, but to have as good a view of the front door as possible. As soon as the car was situated, I hotfooted it to a pay phone by a corner of the building. I called Mother and gave her the number of the phone, hung up, and stood there waiting for her to call back. Her plan was this: she would take the call from Volkov, tell him we'd come to our senses and would return the object to him, and tell him to meet me at the seal pool at the Lincoln Park Zoo. We thought that was a good spot for two reasons: he knew where it was, since he'd followed us there; and it was about ten miles from the hotel. She would immediately call me at the pay phone and tell me if he'd taken the bait.

It was not a particularly hot day—in fact, for Chicago it was down right pleasant, only about seventy degrees—but I could feel sweat dripping from my armpits and rolling down my sides as I waited for her call. And I kept looking at Peter's watch, which I was now cherishing as if it were a lock of his hair.

At exactly 3:03, the phone rang, disturbing a silence that was as eerie as those sudden blips they have in the movies just before a blast goes off. I snatched the receiver up, pressed it to my ear, and heard my mother's anxious voice:

"He's coming."

"All right," I said, and was about to hang up when I heard her call my name through the receiver. I put it back to my ear, and she said, "Listen—I called Stevie at the Harris and had him ring Martin's room. There was no answer. We don't know where he is, so you be extra careful."

I swallowed hard and said, "Okay," and hung up. I was really anxious to get back to the car, which is where I intended to watch for Volkov.

It was about five minutes before he came out of the flophouse and headed east toward the El. I popped open the door of the Civic and climbed out, feeling more than ever like a G-man in more ways than one. In my right pocket were a few twenty dollar bills Mother had given me just in case I needed to "grease someone's palm" as she put it, and in my left pocket was the gun. As I'd left the house, Mother had called after me, "Don't forget your gun!" as calmly as if she'd been saying, "Don't forget your hat!"

The China West Hotel is one of those places that probably looked like a flophouse the day it opened, and has gone downhill from there. The stairs are crumbling, the gargoyles that festoon the doorway are chipped and broken, and a good old Chicago brick will sometimes pop off the building out of the blue as if the years of clinging to this hotel have finally taken their toll and the bricks are committing suicide. During the summer it's not surprising to find the clientele trying to beat the heat of this unair-conditioned building by pulling their mattresses onto the fire escape that snakes up the back of the building and sleeping there. The additional lumps go unnoticed.

I walked into the lobby, and my nostrils were assailed with the sweet smell of decay. You could almost feel the dust mites running underfoot. I don't know what color the carpet had been, but it was brown now, and the walls were covered with dingy wallpaper that had water stains strategically placed to immediately catch the eye. A loose-carpeted staircase went up just to the left of the front desk.

A man sat behind the waist-high desk. He appeared to be short though he was propped up on a stool, and he was bald except for a dark band of hair that ran around the back of his head from ear to ear. The lack of hair on his head was made up for by the thick coat of fur on his arms and chest, the hair of which sprouted from the neck of his stained T-shirt like a moldy bouquet. He was the type of person I just knew had to have huge tufts of fur on his back. From the corner of his mouth was the last half of a cheap cigar that looked so damp it might have been previously swallowed and rejected. He was thumbing through an old copy of *Playboy* whose pictures were covered with so many greasy fingerprints I wondered if the subjects were having chills wherever they were. I had to believe that having a naked picture of myself pawed by this person would be like having somebody walk over my grave.

I approached the desk, and the man's face hardened, though he didn't look up at me. I cleared my throat, and he said, "Yeah?" sending a little stream of brown spittle down his chin from the cigar. I felt my stomach clench.

"I was wondering if you could tell me . . . my cousin is staying here, and I'd like his room number."

He rolled his eyes up to mine though his head didn't move. He said, "Your cousin's stayin' here?"

"Uh, yes. He's visiting from Russia."

The cigar slid a fraction of an inch up his cheek. I realized after a moment that this was what passed for a smile with this guy. He said, "You let him stay here?"

There was an unexpected note of irony in his voice. I swallowed and replied, "Well, yes . . . our family doesn't . . . really get along."

"Uh-huh," he said, and let out a little bark of a laugh that widened the little brown stream.

"Can you tell me what room he's in?"

"What's 'is name?"

"Volkov."

The cigar inched a little farther up, then the man said, "We don't have no Volkov here."

I don't know why I'd expected the clay people to have used their own names, but it hadn't really occurred to me that they wouldn't. I said the first thing that came to mind. "Well . . . um . . . usually when he comes to this country, he Americanizes his name."

"Look, bud. . . ," he started, looking as if I was taking him too far away from the women he was slathering over, but I cut him off by pulling a couple of the twenties from my pocket. His eyes went down to the money. He really looked as if he would have loved to tell me to go fuck myself. But money's money. A little bit of spittle dripped from his chin, landing with a soft splat on the left nipple of the woman in the picture over which his moon face hovered.

"So," he said with feigned disinterest, "what's his American name?"

"I don't know which one he's using this trip," I said, sliding one of the twenties over to him. His face turned down toward it, but I could just sense the interest dripping from him—as well as other things too disgusting to mention. It crossed my mind that further greasing his palm would be overkill.

"Then how'm I supposed to know who he is?"

I leaned in toward him conspiratorially, keeping far enough away that nothing could jump from him to me, and said, "He was staying here with a friend. They're both Russian. One tall, one short." I went on to describe Volkov to him, all the time holding the second twenty under my right hand on the counter.

When I finished the description, he said, "Room twenty-nine, second floor." And without another word, he slid the money under his magazine.

I glanced down at him as I went up the stairs. Without moving the rest of his body, he crumpled the bills and shoved them in his pants pocket. Just as I'd thought, there was a dark growth of fur peeking out from the back of his T-shirt. I shuddered.

The hallway on the second floor was as filthy as the lobby. Every other ceiling light was out. I thought I saw a mouse scurrying away from me down the hallway, but only because I caught some sort of movement on the floor out of the corner of my eye. I was trying not to look down. The hallway was deserted, and the door to the fire escape at the end of the hall was open in a failed attempt to admit some fresh air. Seeing the outdoors from this place was like getting a glimpse of Heaven from the pits of Hell.

I found the door to twenty-nine. The numbers had long since fallen away, but had left their shadows on the door. I pulled the gun from my pocket, feeling more and more as if I were in a really fey version of *Miami Vice* and knocked on the door.

I waited. There was no sound but a faint scurrying further

down the hallway, but it didn't sound human. I pressed my ear to the door, hoping that if Peter was in there alone, he would try to make some sort of noise. After knocking again and waiting, I decided that the room was either unoccupied, or nobody had been left to guard Peter.

I pulled out my wallet, extracted my Visa card, and slipped it in between the door and the jamb at the doorknob, which had the only lock visible. Being a basically honest person, I'd never known how to do this sort of thing until one day when I had accidentally locked myself out of the house while Peter was at work and Mother was in Japan. A friendly neighbor had noticed my plight and shown me how easy it was to break in with a credit card. He had slid the door open in this fashion, and I had thanked him with a great deal of relief. I then refused to leave the house until we had deadbolts put on every exterior door.

I heard the lock unlatch, and slipped the card back in my pocket and aimed my gun at the door. I turned the doorknob and kicked the door open.

There was one bed in the room. On it was Peter. They had stripped him, spread his arms over his head, and tied each wrist to the corresponding bedpost. They had spread his legs and tied his feet likewise to the foot of the bed. He was gagged.

I moved cautiously into the room and said quietly, "Is anyone here?" And Peter shook his head, and his eyes implored me for his release.

I shut the door, pocketed the gun, looked down at him, and said, "You know, I've had fantasies about you like this."

The closest approximation I can come to his reply is: "Nmmph nmmmph," which he said as he strained to raise his head to look at me. A quick glance (which is all that was required, given his natural state) showed that he was virtually unbruised, but when I went to remove his gag, I noticed a bloody spot on the left side of his head.

I pulled the gag away, and Peter said, "Christ, untie me! I feel like things are crawling all over me!"

"You'll be all right. You can go home and take a shower," I replied as I untied first his ankles, then his wrists.

"I'm going to have to be parboiled before I forget this. And I may need a hot colonic."

"Please, you're turning me on," I intoned.

"How in the hell did you find me?"

"It's too long a story, but you'll be proud of us. Suffice it to say that Mother and I are getting better at this spy business. How did they get hold of you?"

Once untied, he drew himself up into a sitting-fetal position. He alternately rubbed his wrists and his ankles, as if he couldn't tell which hurt more.

"I don't know. Somewhere along the way to the El everything went black. Oh, Christ!" He raised his hand to the left side of his head. "That hurts. My head's splitting."

"You don't remember anything?"

"I remember everything going black, and I remember waking up here with that fucking Russian leering down at me."

"Was anybody else here?"

He shook his head, and almost immediately realized that moving it was a mistake. He winced. "No. No. Not that I saw. But there might have been before I came to." He had stilled himself so that his head wouldn't throb, and carefully went back to rubbing his wrists. His expression became very serious. "How long have they had me?"

I rolled my eyes. "Less than one day, Camille. Now let's get out of here. Where'd they put your clothes?"

"How they hell should I know?" he said loudly, then immediately paid the price: his hand went back to the knot on his head. He added more quietly, "I only recently became aware that they were missing."

We quickly made a circuit of the room, but his suit was nowhere to be found. And with the acuteness that one often develops with one's spouse, I could feel his anger building up. And if I read him right, he was more angry about losing the suit than he was about having been kidnapped. We went through the dresser drawers, and found nothing but a cockroach so big I was sure they were charging him rent.

"You know, I'm really beginning to feel very undressed," said Peter.

There was a closet that was about two feet by two feet, and on the floor of it was a beat-up old duffel bag. I unzipped it and dumped the contents on the bed. There were several pairs of soiled underwear, a couple of crumpled shirts, and one pair of pants with an extremely busy pattern of tiny yellow and white checks. I picked the pants up, unrolled them, and held them up.

"Not your style, but they'll have to do."

Peter reached out for them as if they were diseased, his eyes narrowing and his lips going so thin they almost disappeared.

"They're plaid."

This managed to find the end of my patience. "I don't give a fuck what they are, it's all that's here! Put them on and let's get out of here! It'll be a while before the Russian gets back, but we don't know where the hell Martin is."

Peter grimaced as he pulled on the pants. "The real one or the fake one?"

"The fake one. We had Stevie call his room, but there was no answer. Which means he could be anywhere."

Peter pulled the clasp together at the waist of the pants, which dropped to the floor when he let them go. Volkov had at least four extra inches around the middle, apparently. Peter yanked the pants back up and held them to his waist. In addition to the waist problem was the fact that though not particularly tall, Peter had about six inches on the Russian (I'm talking about height here). In this getup he looked like he was wearing a fat man's pedal pushers. And still he looked sexy. Go figure.

"This isn't going to work," he said disgustedly.

"The car's only about half a block down, you'll be fine," I said as I crossed to the door. "Put on a shirt."

He looked at me out of the corners of his eyes for a second, then curled his nose and said, "This'll be enough, thank you."

I shrugged and said, "All right," then as quietly as I could, opened the door. I peeked both ways down the hallway, saw that the coast was clear, then motioned to Peter to follow me. I wasn't about to go back through the lobby, so I led the way to the open fire escape at the end of the hall and down the stairs to the alley. The fortunate part about going this way was that we could walk down the alley, which was deserted except for a couple of winos going through garbage cans, to the end of the block, which put us right about where the car was parked. The unfortunate part of it was that like most alleys, it was covered with slime. And Peter was barefoot. When we reached the end of the alley, he said, "A shower, a hot colonic, and a tetanus shot," through gritted teeth.

But in a matter of minutes we were in the car and on the way home, and I was filling him in on how we'd figured out where they had him: only I have to admit, I made Mother and me sound . . . just a little surer of ourselves than we had been. I didn't see why I should upset Peter with boring details about how many holes there'd been in our reasoning. He listened with as much attention as he could, occasionally brushing the pants legs with his hands as if he truly felt dirty and couldn't help himself. The only thing that really caught his attention was when I told him that we'd found what the CIA and Russian agents were looking for.

I got Peter home in record time, and I have to give Mother credit for her restraint. Despite the obvious anxiety in her eyes over Peter's condition and everything, a little bit of a smile played about her lips when she saw what he was wearing. But she didn't laugh. And Peter was fortunately so preoccupied with wanting to take a bath or shower or both that he didn't notice. I saw him safely ensconced in a lilac-scented bubble bath, and he immediately pulled his loofah down from the rubber shelf that hung from the shower, lathered it up with eucalyptus soap, and began to scrub himself so hard I thought he'd take off the top layer of his skin.

I found Mother waiting for me at the bottom of the stairs with her arms folded. "Now what?" she asked.

SIXTEEN

I stood at the base of the Sears Tower, one of the world's tallest buildings. It is actually a series of towers of varying heights that bolster one mammoth tower. I looked up at the side of the building where I was waiting—the only side that is a sheer expanse from the ground to the top—and found the sight fairly nauseating. I didn't see how anyone could work here. But for my little errand, Sears Tower served a purpose: it was almost four-thirty, and since there's about a zillion people working in this building, at rush hour it was the busiest place I knew of. And I wanted to be in the middle of a really big crowd when I met Agent Nelson and gave him this goddamn tube, because at this point I didn't trust anyone.

That was our plan: we'd called Frank and asked him to relay to Nelson, the CIA agent he'd been working with, that we'd found what he was looking for and that I'd hand it over to him at four-thirty at the northwest corner of Sears Tower. Frank would not be coming here with him because he had an errand of his own to run.

The crowds had started to pour out of the building, and it was all I could do to stand there without being pushed one way or another down the street along with the flow. I glanced at Peter's watch. It was four twenty-five, and even though he wasn't late, I was feeling awfully antsy. I looked down one street, then the other, tapping my foot when I wasn't shifting from one to the other. It was really stupid to be looking for him like that, because I didn't know what he looked like, but Frank had explained to me that Nelson *did* know what I looked like. I wanted to ask Frank how, but stopped myself because I knew whatever the explanation was, either I wouldn't believe it, or it would just make me feel more paranoid. This really was one of those rare times when I thought ignorance was bliss.

Four minutes and a least a dozen more glances at the watch had gone by when I saw him. Not Nelson. With a shock that almost immobilized me, then a sinking sense of panic, I saw him: the bogus Mr. Martin. With his appearance at this inopportune moment, I no longer thought he looked swarthy, he looked like the devil himself. My partially paralyzed mind couldn't grasp how he'd found me, but he had. And after the momentary pause in all my bodily functions, I bolted. I fled from the corner and ran for the Wacker Drive entrance of Sears Tower, but the last thing I saw before I fled was that he'd noticed my flight and was in pursuit.

I pushed my way through the forceful crush of businessmen and -women that spewed forth from the revolving doors of the tower. In the lobby there was a further mass of people pressing one another closer and closer to the doors. I had a sudden, horrific sense of having been catapulted into Fritz Lang's *Metropolis*.

Though Sears Tower is one of Chicago's most famous buildings, I'd never bothered to come inside it before, and was completely perplexed. I didn't know which way to turn, and the ever-increasing horde of people didn't make deciding any easier. In front of me there was a huge wall with hallways going east on both the left and right sides. I glanced back over my shoulder and saw a Red Sea of people parting just slightly as the bogus Martin pushed his way into the building. I knew I couldn't stay where I was because it was like swimming upstream and I was in imminent danger of having the crowd sweep me right back into the arms of my pursuer.

I headed to the hallway on my right.

About twenty feet along, there was an elevator hallway on the left. I turned into this just as one of the elevators dinged and people poured out in a way reminiscent of the stateroom scene in *A Night at the Opera*. As I stepped into the elevator, I glanced back and saw the bogus Martin rounding the corner just in time to see me. Fortunately, the elevator doors closed before he or anyone else could join me (though I doubt if anyone else was going up at this time of day).

To my dismay, there were only two buttons on this elevator: "66" and "Lobby."

"What the fuck?" I said to nobody. But I realized at the same time I had to press "66" for fear the elevator doors would simply open again if I didn't press something. I hit the button, and the elevator sped skyward with a silence that was perfectly ominous. In a matter of seconds the doors slid open on the 66th floor and I was greeted by yet another throng, so packed in the hallway that they almost fell into the elevator. And they didn't look any too happy to find someone already in there.

Pushing my way out into the hallway seemed to start the flow of people into the elevator, almost as if I'd broken some invisible barrier that released them. As I pressed on down the hallway, my brain kept trying to figure out what the hell to do next. And I couldn't think of anything that seemed sensible. The only reason I'd gotten out of the elevator at all was that I honestly thought that if I just went back down, I'd find the bogus Martin waiting for me. At the same time, since the building had several banks of elevators, he might be just as likely to try to find me by following in the direction he knew I'd gone as he was to try covering all the elevators, which would have been an impossible task. I thought movement was better than any other option.

As I got out of the elevator hallway, I heard at least three other elevators signal their arrival, and I felt sure that the bogus Martin would be on one of them. The only problem was, without taking those elevators, the only way to go was up: there didn't appear to be anything on this floor other than a set of escalators that took you to 67. So up I went.

A glance back down when I reached 67 showed that I'd been right: he'd followed me up, and was heading for the escalators. I was sure he'd seen me, because I was the only one going up, which made me awfully conspicuous. Fortunately, there was another bank of elevators just around the corner from the escalator, and one was ready when I got there. I jumped on and pressed the top button. This was the local for floors 67 through 102. I tried to reason it out, and, though I was still having brain trouble, it came something like this: I'd go to the top floor, find the stairs, and start down. The bogus Martin would be hampered by the fact that there were thirty-five floors from which to choose, and he'd have no way of knowing which floor I'd gotten out on. I hoped he would realize that finding me was a lost cause, and give up. In the meantime, I would just start down the stairs, which I thought would at least make me feel that I was on my way out of this mess. When I got tired or felt enough time had passed, I could exit onto one of the floors and take an elevator the rest of the way down. I tried to put aside any thought that he might simply go down and wait for me in the lobby. I pressed the button marked "102."

This elevator traveled up with the alacrity of the express elevator, since nobody stopped it on its way. It whispered to a halt, and the doors slid open at the the 102nd floor. There was a bevy of people waiting for the elevator up here, but all were so anxious to get out of the building and go home that very few gave me any sort of notice. And when out of the corner of my eye I noticed that a couple of people seemed to be looking my way, I adopted the famous Chicagoan "I know exactly where I'm going so leave me alone" look. I glanced at my watch and headed down the hallway exactly as if I knew where I was going. I hung a right at the end of the elevator hallway and headed down a hall that was lined with identical generic offices. The door to one of the offices was open, and through the office window I could see that the late-afternoon sky was very clear. I also got an idea of exactly how high in the air I was—just the view through the window made me light-headed. Near the end of this hall was the door I'd been hoping for: a rather undistinguished door with the usual red-and-yellow exit sign.

In the distance behind me I could once again hear the ding of the arriving elevators. I gripped the doorknob of the exit, twisted it, and went through. As the door clanked behind me, I immediately became aware of the vacant whoosh of machine noise coming from overhead. Just knowing there were 102 flights of stairs beneath my feet made me feel as if I were about to slide down a gaping black hole into the belly of a beast. I grabbed hold of the handrail and steadied myself. "I'm not afraid of heights!" I said aloud, as if hearing the words would make me believe them. Actually, I'm *not* afraid of heights. But there's heights, and there's heights. I had already decided that Sears Tower was taller than any building ever needed to be.

I could just barely make out the sound of an occasional door opening and closing, and the sound of footsteps descending the staircase somewhere in the distance (I assumed they were descending because they seemed to get softer), then another door would open and close, and they'd stop.

I stood there for quite some time, listening and grasping the handrail, and after a while I sank down to the stairs and sat, without letting go. I wasn't immobilized with fear, but more overwhelmed with the size and scope of this damn building, and the staircase that yawned below me like endless entrails. I had to keep fighting a sort of weird falling sensation, the kind you sometimes have in dreams. When I next looked at Peter's watch, it was about twenty after five. Any movement I'd heard above the din of the overhead machines had apparently ceased.

Then I heard it. A door opened and closed, only this time it was closer than those I'd heard earlier. There was a pause, and then I heard the footsteps. They moved slowly (furtively, my mind said). I waited to hear another door open and close, but instead the footsteps just continued. They were not receding into the distance, but coming nearer.

I stood up quickly, my mind racing. On the one hand, if it was someone who worked in the building, they might realize I didn't belong there, but at this point I thought I'd be safer if they called security and got the police. On the other hand, if I waited long enough to see who it was, and if it was the bogus Martin, by the time I saw him it would be too late for me to get away. While trying to decide what to do, I heard another door open and close a little farther down. I peered down in between the railings to see if I could see anything, and I did: there was a hand some floors down sliding slowly up the railing. It was unreal, as if someone had taken the scene from *The Lodger,* where the hand quickly slides down a winding banister, and was playing it backward in slow motion. The hand was moving so deliberately that I have to admit it struck fear into my already panic-stricken heart. I decided that absence was the better part of valor.

But going back out onto the 102nd floor was too risky since I'd be trapped while I waited for an elevator. Then again, since it was the last floor with public access, the bogus Martin might assume that I had been forced to go that way.

I crouched down and untied my shoes, then slipped them off. I headed up the stairs as quickly and quietly as I could. Even with the progressively louder machinery noise, I was sure that whoever was below would be able to hear my stockinged feet as I climbed the stairs. I realized as I passed the 105th and 106th floors that the machine noise was only part of what I was hearing. The other part was, I think, the fluctuating internal pressure of this part of the building as it was buffeted by the high winds that would be a natural occurrence at this altitude. As I went higher, I could feel the pressure closing in on me as if I were in a submarine that was about to burst. I wondered irrelevantly if this was a phenomenon limited to extremes in atmospheric conditions, like those found at great heights or great depths.

I passed 107 and 108. There were doors at each landing, but they were locked.

The noise was almost deafening now. I paused for a moment, gripping the handrail tightly. After I'd caught my breath (or what little air there was up there), I peeked back between the railings. I had been banking on the idea that whoever it was coming up behind wouldn't think I was stupid enough to go up past the 102nd floor, where I would be trapped. Unfortunately, he *did* think I was stupid enough. The hand continued its gliding ascent up the railing, only its speed had increased, if I wasn't mistaken.

I took a couple of deep, panting breaths and went on upward, for some reason feeling dizzier as I went, as if in this closed, windowless space my body could somehow sense the great height it had attained. I finally reached the 110th floor.

There was a flight of six stairs (I counted them), with a handrail painted bright red, leading to a heavy metal door. I gulped hard because I thought I could guess where that led. My ears popped. I realized if this door was locked, I was really lost.

I decided to take one last look between the railings of the endless staircase, and when I did saw that my pursuer was still on the trail. I now had accepted that whoever it was *was* my pursuer, because I couldn't imagine what anybody else would be doing up here at this time.

I took a deep breath and went up the six steps. The door was locked.

Of course, I hadn't brought the damn gun, because I hadn't thought I'd need it. I shook the doorknob, and was surprised to find that though the door was locked, the knob was quite loose. I shook it, twisted it, shook it some more, and pulled as hard as I could on it. Despite my panic I thought I heard, very faintly amidst the general din, a metallic clank on the other side of the door, and realized that the doorknob on the other side had fallen off.

I twisted the doorknob again. It was now very loose. I thought it likely that if I twisted a little more and pulled it, the doorknob on my side would pull out. Instead, something totally unexpected happened: the door popped open. I went through it onto the roof, closing the door behind me.

In my determination to get that door open, I had forgotten that I didn't want to be there. I was immediately blown sideways by the winds that howled mercilessly across the roof like waves crashing over the decks of ships. I'm sure I would have gone right over the edge of the roof, had it not been for something that I'm really not very proud to report: I swooned.

I also learned at that moment that "swoon" is one of those words that sounds exactly like what it describes. I had swung my eyes around the perimeter of the roof as the winds crashed against me, and seen how high up I was, then my head reeled and I went down, flat on my face. The swoon was caused by that feeling that you sometimes get when you are at a dizzying height: not that you're going to be blown off it (though that was highly probable under the circumstances), but that some irresistible urge is going to compel you to throw yourself off it. For the first time in my life, I came close to vomiting from pure fear.

I would have lain there, digging my fingers into the surface of the roof, were it not for the fact that before going through the door I had tried to pull the doorknob free so I could take it with me, making it harder for the bogus Martin to follow me, but it wouldn't budge, and I didn't have time to wait.

There was very little cover on the roof. There are two huge antennae poking up into the clouds, their lights blinking steadily because this goddamn building is so goddamn tall they have to warn approaching planes of their presence, and there was a variety of large metal boxlike things jutting up from the floor as if they'd sprouted there. I didn't know what their purpose was, but I thought they'd serve my purpose. I crawled toward the nearest one on my hands and knees, afraid to stand erect for fear I'd get blown off the building, and then I rolled over on my butt, bracing my back against the box.

The city spread out before my eyes—the altitude so high and the view so clear I felt like I could see the curve of the earth. I felt the breath going out of me and my head going light again, so I closed my eyes and shook my head quickly. My stomach sank and I felt as if the roof were shifting beneath me. When I opened my eyes again, I noticed something that almost made me doubt what little sense I had left: there were two enormous hooks standing ominously on the very edge of the roof, with a complicated series of ropes and machinery around them. I was trying to figure out what they were there for, when I heard another noise.

Above the roar of the wind I heard the metal door fly open, banging against the wall. I knew at that point that if my heart didn't stop before the day was out, I would live forever. I turned myself around slowly so as not to make any noise (as if anyone could have heard me), raised my head up carefully, and looked over the top of the metal box behind which I'd taken refuge. Standing in the doorway, his tailored suit flapping around him violently in the wind, was the bogus Mr. Martin. I dropped down and rebraced my back against the box.

"Reynolds!" he yelled. It sounded like a voice calling from a storm. "Reynolds! You're out here! You must be!"

Of course he received no answer but the howling of the wind.

"Reynolds! I'm not who you think I am!"

And I don't think you are who you think I think you are, were the words my mind silently spun out as reply.

"Alex!" he yelled, as if my first name would get more of a response. "Alex! I'm Agent Nelson. Agent Nelson of the CIA. Commander Frank O'Neil set up this meeting between you and me so that you could turn over the information you found."

Oh God, I thought, in a mental panic unlike anything I'd ever known: I can't believe anybody. All these people who know something or other about each other, or are able to ferret out information that they can use against people, or to bamboozle people, the way this very man had when he'd first come to our house. People who told you they were one thing, and turned out to be another. People who were plausible liars. People like Victor Hacheck, who hadn't given a second thought to endangering the life of a total stranger. Oh, God, I thought, I'll never again know what to believe. I was suddenly overwhelmed by a feeling of loneliness that was totally outside my experience. And with it came that same unnerving sense of being compelled to throw myself off the building. I made a mental note that I would never challenge heights again . . . if I lived.

"Alex! Please listen to me! I am Agent Nelson, and I've been working with your mother's friend, Frank O'Neil. I know I told you that I was James Martin, and you know that that was a lie, but I had my reasons. If you'll come out and come down with me, I'll explain it to you. But I need for you to turn over the object that Victor Hacheck gave to you. The welfare of a lot of people in Russia—Americans in Russia—depends on my getting it."

Apparently he turned his head this way and that to look around the roof from where he was standing by the doorway, and so his voice came and went on the breeze, which gave it a strange, disembodied effect. In my giddiness, I thought this entirely appropriate, because I didn't know who this man was. I didn't know if he'd ever give me his real name.

There were a hundred questions I wanted to call out to him, that I thought wanted explaining before I would reveal myself. The trouble was that if I called out, I would reveal myself—and I couldn't do that.

"Alex! You have to believe me! What Victor Hacheck gave you is the culmination of several months of work, and without it all that work will be wasted and many, many people will be in danger. The worst part about it is, somebody from the inside is in on it!"

From inside what, my mind asked?

"Somebody inside the CIA is working with them. Alex, I *need* the information Hacheck gave you. Look"—his tone became much more rueful, at least as much as was possible in this wind— "I know what you and your family have gone through these past few days. I know you don't have any reason to believe me. And what I'm asking you to do is to go beyond that and take a chance. Take a chance that I'm telling you the truth. Come down with me, and Commander O'Neil and I will explain the whole situation, I promise you. I ask you to believe me."

My head sort of rolled involuntarily on my shoulders, as if the swirly mess in my mind was working its way out. I had one thing to say for his argument: taking a chance that he was telling me the truth now, that he was actually Agent Nelson, was probably no more risky than any of the other chances we'd taken lately. And there was the fact that he had come to the bottom of Sears Tower at the appointed time, which would indicate that he *had* talked to Frank. But could I even trust Frank? On the other hand, I told myself, Mother had not been able to locate the bogus Martin when we set her plan for rescuing Peter into action. But it was just as likely that this man had followed me to Sears Tower. But then how did he know about Frank? I tried to remember the look on his face when I saw him, to see if it could give me a clue as to whether he had been surprised or shocked or looked as if he were simply coming to meet me. But my mind spun, and I couldn't grasp the picture.

"Alex, please!"

I was torn between the idea that if he didn't come out onto the roof looking for me, I could just sit rooted to this spot forever and he would go away, and the idea that I might as well give up and take a chance on trusting him because there was no other way out of this anyway. I opted for the latter, but I wanted to have a look at him first. So I turned around again, slowly, and inched my head up over the top of the box. There he stood, slightly outside the door to the roof. He had his arms wrapped around his middle, and both his suit and his usually well-groomed hair flapped madly in the breeze. But other than that he looked serious. I can't explain it better than that.

Suddenly, before I raised myself up, his head snapped forward just slightly, and he looked completely startled. Then his legs wobbled and he started to fall. Behind him, in the shadow of the doorway, was a hand holding the barrel of a gun, the handgrip of which had just been used to knock him cold. Once he'd hit the ground, I saw the person who belonged to the hand and the gun: it was the real James Martin.

A thought flitted across my mind on the breeze and didn't

stay: the second door's slam. The second door I'd heard open and close in the stairwell. It had never occurred to me that someone might be pursuing my pursuer.

The whole thing came clear to me now, as I suppose it does to people on airplanes who know they're about to crash, or people stuck in a car caught on the railroad tracks just before impact with an onrushing train. It came to me in the form of questions: why would an ordinary personnel director carry a gun, even if he worked for the CIA? And what the fuck would he be doing up here? And how had he found us? The real Martin wasn't supposed to be in on this. How had this pencil-pushing personnel person known about this meeting? And the answers to a few questions started to come to me, like why the big clay person, Fomin, had met me under the overpass, and why Martin had reacted in such a peculiar way when Mother had asked him about Matthew Corbin and the other men on the list. Way in the back of my mind there was a small, nagging doubt that there might be plausible explanations for these things, but I have to give myself credit in one respect: by this time, my ability to give the benefit of the doubt was gone. I knew.

Unlike the bogus Martin—or Agent Nelson as I supposed I was going to have to believe he was, now that he'd been rendered useless—the real Mr. Martin begin to search the roof immediately, but his search was pretty slow going since every direction he turned, he seemed to be walking against the wind. For someone who was obviously out of shape, he was doing his damnedest to hold his own. I knew it would be only a matter of minutes before he discovered my hiding place, unless I was able to keep moving around out of his sight. But this seemed impossible. There was too much space between the big metal whatever-the-fuck-they-weres, and I knew he would see me if I tried to shift to another one—that sort of thing only works in the movies.

I inched my way over to the side of the building, in between the giant hooks. Huge, thick ropes were coiled around them and hanging off the building, the remaining rope coiled beneath it and through a mass of some unidentifiable machinery. I decided there was nothing for it but to look over the side of the building to see what it was.

With my eyes closed, I slowly pushed my head over the low wall that rimmed the edge of the roof, then opened them just barely enough to see, in hopes that I could blur out the drop below. Through the slits I could see it: a window washer's scaffolding, hanging about six feet down from the top of the one side of the building that was a sheer drop to the ground. I closed my eyes and said a brief, silent prayer, because I knew in a flash what I had to do. The only hope I had here was that even if he searched behind every possible hiding place on this roof, he wouldn't think I would go over the side.

And that's exactly what I did: I grabbed one of the ropes hanging from the giant hooks so tightly that I might have flattened the thing in my hand, took hold of the edge of the wall with my other hand, and hoisted myself over the side, lowering myself onto the platform of the scaffold.

I lay on my back, letting that sickening, rushing, falling feeling wash over me as the scaffold was buffeted against the side of the tower by the howling wind. Though the scaffold had high, sturdy sides, I still felt I couldn't stand on it. I looked straight up at the sky, at the two antennae shooting up from the top of the tower, their red lights slightly dimmed as they were engulfed by a passing cloud. I closed my eyes and prayed again.

I felt as if I had been lying there forever, though I'm sure that my sense of time had taken a nosedive off the side of the building. It could have been seconds, but it felt like hours. I didn't look at the watch, because I felt that any extraneous movement would send me hurtling down the 110 stories to the pavement below. I've often heard that when someone falls or jumps off a building, they die from heart failure before they hit: though it has never escaped me that there's no empirical evidence for this. I wasn't ready to have this point proven to me.

When I felt I had stayed there long enough, when I could take it no longer (somehow these two feelings magically coincided with each other), I started to devise how I was going to get back up onto the roof. It really would have been a simple task, had it not been so far down to the ground, because it wasn't that far back up: it just required me to grab the ledge and pull up as I kicked my legs over the wall. But somewhere in there would be a moment, no matter how brief, when my feet wouldn't be touching anything. That bothered me. I had just gotten myself up on my knees, and was bolstering myself to get up the rest of the way, when he came.

Martin's head, shoulders, and right arm, the hand at the end of which gripped a gun, suddenly loomed over me. I recoiled slightly, but my brain was quick enough to realize that I had nowhere to go. It finally occurred to me as his pasty, paunchy face hung there above me who it was he reminded me of: Sydney Greenstreet in every movie he ever made. He no longer looked like the backslapping, good ol' boy he'd appeared to be in his office. Now he looked like a demented senator. It irrelevantly crossed my mind that that was redundant.

"Give it to me," he barked, all the good-natured pseudo-Southernness gone out of his voice. "Give it to me!" His right hand was turning white from the tension with which he was holding the gun. I chose not to answer, because I couldn't think of anything to say.

"You fucking faggot, you've been in my way ever since Hacheck got here, but it's gonna end now!"

"How . . . how . . . ," I started to say, but no more words would come out.

"I followed you, you idiot! I been following you since you left my office . . . since you asked me about Matthew Corbin. Then I knew you knew too much. I knew you were on to it. I knew we had to get rid of you right away. I been following you." With a little flick of his head over his shoulder, he added, "I suppose that's the guy that Washington sent out here."

I gulped and said, "I suppose he is."

"Then he'll die after you!"

"Wait! Wait!" I said, frantically trying to think of a way to stall him. "Please! I've got to know something. Why did you set me up the other night? Why did you send me to the overpass and send Fomin after me? I mean, you knew where I lived! Why didn't you just kill me and my family there?"

He smiled in a way that made my skin crawl. That smile said that he thought he was really clever.

"Because we weren't after you! I didn't know who the feds had sent here, and I had to flush him out." His mouth twisted. "Just the way you tried to flush me out with that fucking fake matchbook! That's why I had you set up a meeting with that fed. Fomin was supposed to take care of both of you, but your friend over there"—he gestured with the gun back toward where Agent Nelson had fallen—"didn't fall for it and didn't show up."

"Then who shot Fomin?" I asked.

"Not me," he replied with a broad, satisfied smile that made my blood run cold. "I was at home with my wife." He pushed the gun nearer to me. "All the time . . . at first . . . I thought you just got mixed up in this by accident. . . ."

"We *did!*"

He shook his head as if to signify I shouldn't even bother. "First you meet Hacheck in that bar, then you come up with the names of all the people we've . . . they've kidnapped, then you meet a fed here. You sure led us on a chase, you sure have! But it's over now. You know that! You must have Hacheck's evidence on you, otherwise you wouldn't have been meetin' that fed. Give it to me!"

"Mr. Martin . . . this was all a mistake. Don't you understand that? Everything we told you in your office was true! I was just in the wrong place at the wrong time. I wasn't *meeting* Hacheck. And we really did think it was the matchbook you were looking for."

I half wondered why he didn't just shoot me and get it over with, but it crossed my mind that there was an outside possibility that if anything remained of my remains after a 110-story splat on the pavement, that someone might find the tube.

"That don't matter to me anymore," he said, and he pushed the hair back off his forehead. Sweat poured off his brow, but he made no attempt to mop it up as he had in his office. "Once I get that damn evidence and get rid of you, I'll be home free."

This one really required a weighing of my options. I held tightly to the rope and stared up into his eyes, which looked wilder to me by the minute. Finally, I took a deep breath and said, "No, you won't."

For the first time, he looked uncertain. "What do you mean?"

"If you've been following me since we left your office, then you know that I found Peter and rescued him."

"So what?" he barked, his voice reflecting that he was not happy with his subordinate.

"In order to do that, my mother diverted *your* friend Volkov to the Lincoln Park Zoo. The seal pool, to be exact, where he followed us a couple of days ago."

"Yeah? So what?"

"So when I was sure that Peter was safe, we called Police Commander Frank O'Neil and sent him to the zoo to pick up your accomplice. And I can pretty much count on him doing it, one way or the other. He's a damn good cop!"

"So?" he demanded, less sure and more angry. "So what's that mean to me?"

"Do you think Volkov will stay silent when he's in custody? He'll probably tell everything he knows!"

"So what? Nobody's gonna believe some fucking Russian over me!"

"With the CIA after you? And if you kill me?"

God, that logic came out of nowhere, but it made sense to me. The only thing was, even with making sense I wasn't sure it would make any difference to Martin. A startled look came over his face. Then his brow furrowed. Then something so unexpected happened that I had nothing for it but to act instinctively: he lunged at me, yelling, "You fucking bastard!"

He didn't shoot, he just grabbed at me, and his action threw him off balance. Without thinking, I reached up and caught hold of his shirt and yanked on him. A choked croak came out of his throat. With his being off balance, and the angle at which I'd pulled him, and the ever-howling wind, he seemed almost to glide over my head. He went sailing off the building, over me, over the scaffolding, and fell screaming down the concrete canyon to the street below. Out of my sight. Out of my hearing.

I slid down to a sitting position, my back against the part of the scaffold that abutted the tower. I closed my eyes. In my mind there was a blissful silence. The irregular rhythm of the scaffold as it knocked against the tower was almost reassuring. After a few minutes I climbed back onto the roof.

I found Agent Nelson where he'd fallen, though he was rousing. He'd turned over on his back and was holding his forehead, as if the impact of the gun butt against the back of his head was rebounding against the front. When he saw me coming, he pulled himself up into a semisitting position. I offered him my hand and said, "Come on, Nelson, let's go home."

I pulled him up and he swayed uneasily for a moment. I put his right arm over my shoulder to support him.

"I'll help you," I said.

"Ooooo," he said, putting a hand to the back of his head where he'd been hit. As we approached the door, he said, "Reynolds . . . the next time somebody's chasing you, go down, not up! Everybody makes the same damn mistake. If you go up, you're trapped. Go down! For God's sake, go down!"

"You have no idea how many men have said that to me," I said as we started down the stairs.

SEVENTEEN

There's a lot I don't understand," said Peter with only the barest twinge of petulance. He didn't like not being in the know, especially when his privates had been exposed to a Russian.

It was late that evening. The five of us sat around our living room holding a postmortem on the affair. Agent Nelson, who had informed us that his first name was Lawrence, was seated on the couch with Mother: an arrangement that Frank, who sat nearby on a straight-backed chair, was none too happy with. Nelson held a Scotch on the rocks in one hand, and Mother was holding her usual, civilized cup of tea. Peter and I were sitting near each other on chairs facing the couch, and each of us had a snifter of brandy. Our fingers interlaced from time to time, which did not escape the notice of Nelson. Frank wasn't drinking.

James Martin's dive from the top of Sears Tower had made a big splash on the evening news. However, the media only identified him as an unidentified man. I shudder to think of how they identified what remained of him as a man. Agent Nelson had shared with Frank the identity of the body, but Frank didn't relay it to anyone else. I knew that the general public would never know.

Frank and his fellow officers had dutifully gone to the seal pool at the Lincoln Park Zoo and picked up Volkov, who was now in custody, but was not inclined to talk about anything. He had, according to Frank, reverted to a highly imperfect understanding of the English language, responding to questions with a blank stare, signifying that he was but a poor foreigner who didn't understand what was happening to him. Frank was not happy that we'd deceived him for so long (and that Nelson had also deceived him, since it turned out that Nelson had not been very communicative about our involvement in CIA business), but he was very happy to be part of the denouement.

"What don't you understand?" said Nelson.

"Well, for one thing," said Peter, leaning forward, "what started this whole thing to begin with?"

"Oh, Mother answered that one!" I chimed in.

"I did?" she said.

"Yes. Actually something you said made it really clear to me. You remember when we found that article in the paper about Matthew Corbin's kidnapping? You said something like 'If they're kidnapping people for money and getting away with it, they'd be doing all right in Russia—you'd think America is the last place they'd want to be.' Remember?"

"Yes. . . ."

"Well, that's when it hit me: what if one of them *wanted* to be in America?"

Nelson smiled. "You really *did* get it then."

Mother looked from him to me. "What? I don't understand."

"Correct me if I'm wrong," I said to Nelson, then turned to Mother, "but even though they were getting away with a lot of money in Russia, there's a difference between the good life in Russia and the good life in America."

Nelson was nodding his head.

I continued, "I suspect that Victor Hacheck wanted to come to America, and was willing to sell out his buddies to get here."

"Is that true?" said Mother to Nelson. Frank shifted in his seat.

"Your son's hit the nail on the head. Victor Hacheck contacted us and told us he would turn over information about a kidnapping ring in Russia—an organized group grabbing Americans and holding them for ransom—if we would give him asylum in America. Kidnapping is a growth industry in Russia, you know. He was to turn the information over to us on his arrival here."

"Wait a minute," said Frank, and I got the sense that he was anxious to split some hairs here. "The CIA has an office in Russia, doesn't it?"

"Um-hmm."

"Then why did you let Hacheck come here? Why didn't you make him turn it in to them there before you'd give him transport?"

"That was where he had us. Like most criminals, he didn't trust anyone, let alone us. He didn't trust us to carry through with our promise of sanctuary. He insisted on dealing with our Washington headquarters directly. He said he wouldn't turn it over to us until he was on American soil."

"Sounds pretty smart."

"Not really," Nelson replied with a hint of disdain in his voice. "After all, we could always have sent him right back if he couldn't deliver. I'm afraid that he wasn't really very bright, but like a lot of people of his sort, he was crafty."

"And what exactly was *it?*" Mother asked. "I've never seen anything like that little tube."

"We provided him with the necessary equipment to take . . . special photographs . . . of abductions and transactions. That was the proof we wanted. That's what he was carrying. Film."

"How did James Martin fit into all of this?" asked Peter.

Nelson looked at me and smiled again, and said, "Do you want to try that one?"

I smiled back and said, "Well . . . something came to me in a flash when he conked you on the head and I realized *he* was the culprit."

"Will you stop talking like a B movie?" said Peter with a laugh.

"Sorry, I mean when I realized he was involved." I looked at Nelson. "Did it have something to do with background checks?"

"Background checks?" said Mother, her forehead wrinkling over her amused eyes.

"He's right again, Mrs. Reynolds. We don't know yet how the Russian end of this ring first got hold of Martin, and we may never know since both Martin and Hacheck are dead, and we can't expect the ones who are still alive to do much talking. I suspect that it was through . . . someone in our Russian office, though I hate to admit it. That would also help explain why Hacheck was so insistent on not dealing with our Russian office. Hopefully the film he took will shed some light on that. Anyway, part of Martin's job was doing background checks on potential CIA recruits, which gave him fairly unlimited access, through us, to a lot of personal information on a lot of people—including Americans working in Russia—including information on their assets and the assets of their companies."

"Oh, good Lord!" said Mother, setting down her tea. "So he would come up with the most likely candidates for kidnapping, and they would snatch them and then give Martin a cut of whatever ransom they got?"

"Um-hmm," said Nelson, "like I said, we don't have all the links yet, but now that we *know* Martin was involved, we should be able to find the proof. After all, he had to be doing something with the money."

"And his friends—other members of the kidnapping ring—followed Hacheck?" said Peter.

"Yes," said Nelson, his tone a bit more disdainful, "and that's an example of why I think Hacheck wasn't any too smart. For one thing, his friends must have somehow caught on to the fact that Hacheck was about to duck out, and they contacted Martin, then followed Hacheck here."

"How do you know that?"

"For the simple reason that once Hacheck contacted us, we started keeping a very watchful eye on him, and . . . monitoring his correspondence." He was a little hesitant when he said that last bit, as if he was embarrassed to admit the CIA was reading someone's mail (as if that's the worst thing they could ever be accused of).

"And?" I prodded.

"And two days before he was to leave for Washington, he received a letter and a ticket to Chicago on Aeroflot."

"On what?" said Frank.

"A Russian International Airlines flight that comes direct from Russia to O'Hare. The letter said it was too dangerous for him to come to Washington, so we would meet him in Chicago."

"Why didn't you just tell him it was a fake?" said Peter.

I shook my head. "I think I can answer that one, too: they wanted to trap the American contact in the kidnapping ring here, isn't that right?"

"Exactly. We knew one of our people was involved, but didn't know who. This was a way to confirm it. That's why instead of stopping Hacheck from coming here, I came too."

"That isn't the story you told us when you first came to us," I said.

Nelson shrugged. "I told you what was most expedient."

I wasn't sure I liked his answer.

Forever willing to give the benefit of the doubt, Mother said, "Isn't it possible that Hacheck just had an attack of conscience about being part of a kidnapping ring and wanted to put an end to it?"

"Oh, please, Mother!" I said, rolling my eyes.

"What?"

"Well, in the first place, he could have done that without leaving Russia. And in the second place, he thought nothing of endangering *my* life when he realized he was in trouble."

"I'm afraid that's true," said Nelson, nodding in agreement. "You could never accuse Victor Hacheck of altruism."

"I have another question. What about the shooting of Fomin?" said Peter. "The other night under the overpass. Who shot him?"

Nelson smiled at me, and I returned the favor. "You did,

didn't you," I said more as a statement than a question.

"How did you figure that out?" He actually looked surprised.

"Because while we were hanging there on the tower, Martin denied having done it. He sneered when he said it, but I believed him anyway. It's just as I thought: you knew the whole thing was a setup when I called you, you decided that it would be a good time to get the goods on one or more members of this gang, so you went there and waited. Martin sent Fomin to flush you out and kill both you and me—that's why he insisted I go there, even though I didn't really need to. And you shot Fomin when he was about to kill me."

"I plead guilty," said Nelson, his smile growing rather self-satisfied.

"I guess you saved my life. I suppose I should be grateful."

"Aren't you?"

"Why did you fire the second shot? The one that just missed me?"

For the first time in our acquaintance, Nelson laughed. "To get you out of there! You're possibly the only person I know who'd hang around somewhere that shots are being fired!"

I nodded ruefully. I wasn't about to admit to him that I'd been afraid to move. We all just sort of grinned stupidly at one another and acted as if it were a lark that this man had shot at me, and endangered my life by using me to get to other people.

I sighed and said, "There's two things you can clear up for me, if you will."

"Um-hmm?"

"One of the reasons we suspected you was because you were seen talking to Volkov at the bar, so we thought you knew him. What were you doing?"

"As you may have noticed from Victor Hacheck, there is no honor among thieves. When Volkov was left alone at the bar, I simply took the opportunity to approach him about the possibility of turning informant . . . for an unspecified price."

"I see." I nodded thoughtfully. "That only leaves one thing that I really don't understand."

"What's that?"

"Why in the hell did you call yourself James Martin when you came here? Why didn't you just tell us your real name, or if anything, use a different name from one of the suspects?"

Nelson's beautiful olive skin actually reddened. "That is the one area where you proved too clever for me."

"How?" said Mother, her face beaming.

"I used Martin's name on the outside possibility that you would call the office here to find out if we really had an agent by that name. It never even occurred to me that you'd go down to his office and confront him. I'll probably be demoted for that one!"

We talked a little while longer, then Agent Nelson said it was time for him to leave. He'd be going back to Washington as soon as possible. Frank looked elated at the news.

Mother clucked her tongue and said, "That's a shame, we'd like to have you to dinner!"

Frank did not look elated at that one.

As for me, I couldn't help feeling a tinge of melancholy at this news. Like I said before, I'm not a thrill seeker, but the past few days had certainly been a change of pace. Peter and I, our arms around each other's waists, saw Nelson to the door. Mother went with us, and Frank sort of lingered behind in the living room, as if he was disinclined to leave until he was sure Nelson was gone.

At the door, Nelson turned to me and said, "You know, I realize the three of you have been tossed around in the middle of this business, but I think you were pretty damned clever to put as much of this together as you did with the little information you had, and you certainly showed a lot of bravery. Especially you, Alex."

I could feel my face turning red. I shuffled a little and said, "Thank you."

"You know, we might be able to find, occasionally, a use for someone of your . . . ilk. Maybe we could call on you from time to time, if there's a need?"

I winced a little at his use of the word "ilk," because I had a feeling that he didn't mean it in the nicest way. But I couldn't stop my heart from racing at the thought of this newfound career.

"We'd be glad to help," I said happily. "Just think of us as your little government gays!"

"Are you out of your bloody mind?" said Mother, folding her arms across her chest. "After all the danger they put us in you would even *think* of working with them?"

I just smiled.